TEN LITTLE MYSTERIES

New mysteries inspired by the
Golden Age of Detective Fiction

GOLDEN AGE
MYSTERIES LTD

First published in 2025 by Golden Age Mysteries Limited

ISBN: 978-1-0369-2636-6

Cover design by Devilish Creative

Contents

Introduction

How to define 'the Golden Age of Detective Fiction'? It's a useful label, and a slippery one. Immediately, it summons certain ideas: a 'whodunnit' puzzle, an amateur detective, a setting in the 1920s or 1930s, English country houses, characters with stiff upper lips. While some great examples of the genre have all these things, others have fewer or none.

For example, one of the greatest Golden Age detective novels, Agatha Christie's *And Then There Were None*, has no detective! Few people would deny its place, at least within the canon of the Golden Age.

Several sets of 'rules' for detective fiction were produced between the First World War (1916-1918) and the Second (1939-1945), a period of time in which 'detectivist' Dorothy L Sayers once claimed, 'half the world is setting riddles for the other half to solve.' One of the best-known sets of rules is the 'Decalogue', a so-called 'Ten Commandments' for writing by Ronald Knox, a Catholic priest and crime writer. Knox published the Decalogue in 1928. These are tongue-in-cheek, not actual prescriptive rules. At their heart is a sense of fair play in the contract between writer and reader, but they are also snobbish – they poke fun writers who took short cuts, and mock the clichés of the genre.

The rules (paraphrased) are:

1. *The criminal must appear early in the story.* It was common in 1928 as it is now for readers to despair at writers who introduce the murderer towards the end of the action, making the gameplay aspect seem unfair.

2. *Nothing supernatural can appear in the story.* It is a cheap trick to blame the unexplained on the paranormal. A ratiocinative genre requires everything to be explained in logical, worldly terms.
3. *No more than one secret passage or room.* Carolyn Wells (1864-1942) was infamous for including floorplans and maps in her novels, omitting to mention passages between them which made impossible crimes possible.
4. *No secret, undetectable, or unknowable poisons are allowed.* Like Rule 2, a poison unknown to science is a cheap shot, not in the spirit of Golden Age detection, because it denies the reader the chance to work out the truth.
5. *No 'Chinaman' must figure in the story.* This is a reference to the racist 'Yellow Peril' stereotype pervading magazine and thriller culture in the 1920s. Taken as a general point, it refers to the use of lazy stereotypes and sensationalism.
6. *The detective must solve the case, not be helped by accident or intuition.* The easiest rule to break while preserving fair play, Rule 6 is based on the idea that the mystery novel is a game and competition – the detective cannot have an advantage over the reader.
7. *The detective cannot be the criminal.* Otherwise, players of the game are not evenly matched because the detective is withholding knowledge.
8. *The detective must 'declare any clues'.* Again, this is straightforward fair-play. It also reflects a difference between Golden Age fiction and the earlier Sherlock Holmes school. Holmes can declare that he identified the owner of a hat because of initials sewn into the brim, of which Watson and the reader learn only after the deduction ('The Blue Carbuncle', 1892) but a Golden Age reader would expect to see those initials.

9. *The detective's sidekick should be slightly stupider than the average reader, and should not conceal their thoughts.* Again, this is about fair play and there is a clear reference here to a rather famous novel of 1926.
10. *No twins unless the reader is 'duly prepared'.* The use of an identical twin to establish an alibi or how someone could be in two places at once was then, as now, a cliché. It is also lazy. Unless it's done well.

Critic Howard Haycraft summarised the rules as: '(1) The detective story must play fair. (2) The detective story must be readable.' Of course, most writers broke most if not all of these rules, at times, but the best ones kept the spirit. So, too, do the writers in this neo-Golden Age volume.

This book contains ten original mysteries, from an international assortment of skilled authors, each inspired by and indebted to the Golden Age of Detective fiction. The influences of Christie, John Dickson Carr, Margery Allingham, and their peers are clear to see, and so are the those of the films and legacies this genre inspired.

'Deal in Death' by J.S. Savage takes us to a local pub in 1926, where a card game provides a cover for secrets. Gameplay was a hallmark of the Golden Age, with the fundamental premise of a puzzle – a battle of wits between reader and detective – animating much of its appeal during a complex geopolitical age. Thematically, bridge and other gambling games form a cornerstone of the genre, most famously in Agatha Christie's *Cards on the Table* (1936), where four people sit down to play a few rubbers. A fifth sits and watches and, by the end of the evening one of the four has murdered him. Savage takes us far beyond the game, though, into a world of smuggling, a shipwreck, and emotional ghosts, and brings us a new case for his detective, Inspector Graves.

Anya Page's 'A Gathering at the Grange' gives us an atmospheric portrait of a tragedy-laden country house in the First World War. Page was inspired by looking into the war's influence on Golden Age mysteries with the writing group Wolsey Writers, and 'meandering down research rabbit holes'. Like Dorothy L. Sayers' shell-shocked Lord Peter Wimsey, Page's characters play out the consequences of war while facing their own complex issues in a tightly-woven mystery.

Moving to the 1930s in Arthur Bernard's 'Ding Dong Dell', we encounter the marvellous medium-cum-sleuth Miriam Lazarus, Spiritualism and mysticism were extremely fashionable in the interwar period and in part popularised by Sherlock Holmes creator Arthur Conan Doyle, a true believer. Many Golden Age writers incorporated it into their plots, always 'playing fair' (there had to be a rational explanation!). For example, John Dickson Carr's *The Plague Court Murders* (1934, written as Carter Dickson), concerns the murder of a spiritualist who is apparently killed by the ghost of a seventeenth-century executioner. Bernard was inspired particularly by Christie's *The Sittaford Mystery* (1931) and *Dumb Witness* (1937) and the film *Mrs Pym of Scotland Yard* (1939), noting: 'In these stories the supernatural element turns out to be illusory, but what if the sleuth had a *genuine* gift? ... The story remains a true whodunnit, but with the solution confirmed by magic.'

J.C. Bernthal's 'The Body in the Bathtub' takes us to a country house in the 1920s, with a locked room. In recent years, 'locked room' seems to have become a catch-all term for 'closed circle of suspects' but in the Golden Age it meant what it said: this subgenre of murder mysteries referred to seemingly impossible crimes where the body is found in a sealed room to which apparently no one had access. Carr was the master of this format, and *The Hollow Man* (1935) is his most famous example.

'Midnight Blue Sonata' by Jorge Molina taps into two golden ages at once: those of detective fiction and of cinema. As Molina says, '[b]oth have an air of glamour, style, and other-worldly escapism that I feel really lacks in modern entertainment'. But it isn't an old-fashioned story: the detective-sidekick pairing in 'Midnight Blue Sonata' brings the subtext among the smoke and glitter of the movies. Molina also engages with one of the key tropes of Golden Age mysteries – but to say which would be to spoil it.

Claire Tyler's twisty 'Murder on the Honeymoon' offers a picturesque setting for an apparent suicide that is not what it seems. While the jury is out over how 'escapist' crime fiction really is, there is an inevitable, intimate connection between holidays and interwar detective novels, particularly those set in vacation locales. As crime writer Martin Edwards has claimed, Golden Age authors 'found that stories with holiday settings helped to create a sense of distance and unreality'. Tyler's choice of detective, and the touching conclusion, show that this 'unreality' can enable Golden Age nuance at its best.

'Vaulting Ambition', a contemporary detective story from David Hill, takes us into the sporting world, with Golden Age influences including a closed community, a seemingly impossible crime, and a killer twist. Hill's victim receives threatening text messages, which calls to mind the poison pen letter, a trope commonly linked to the Golden Age. It is significant that nearly all the great detective writers of the time relied, to a greater or lesser degree, to such a literary device in their stories, including Christie (*The Moving Finger*, 1942), Carr (*Night at the Mocking Window*, 1950), Sayers (*Gaudy Night*, 1935), J. J. Connington's (*For Murder Will Speak*, 1938), Edmund Crispin (*The Long Divorce*, 1951), and Elizabeth Ferrars (*The Stop that Wouldn't Clock*, 1952). The device shows uniquely how close to the surface tensions simmer beneath our clean plotting and social facades.

M.E. Reynard's 'The Cookery Show Conundrum' provides a definitively twenty-first century backdrop for a classically-inspired mystery: a reality television show. With its closed community of suspects in a unique setting, it follows a tradition established by the Golden Age greats. Food and cookery have always been there in Golden Age mysteries – what was poisoned in Sayers' *Strong Poison* (1930)? Would Rex Stout's Nero Wolfe solve anything without a good meal or a fine beer? Cookery is an intensely personal and an intensely social thing – and when it mixes with family tensions it can be a recipe for murder.

'Tapestry', Nic Whittam's multigenerational mystery, is an excellent example of exploring big themes via a tightly plotted puzzle. Whittam started with a piece of art: a cross-stitch that got her thinking about the artist, 'the person who'd had the patience to complete the piece.' The intrepid sleuth, determined not to let sleeping murder lie, is a hallmark of the Golden Age, and, like 'Tapestry', some key works of the period, like Christie's *Five Little Pigs* (1944), hide the truth in conflicting testimonies.

We close with something different. Jonathan Ruffle, best known for creating BBC Radio 4's *Tommies*, presents a screenplay, for a truly unique project, 'The Bureau of Impossible Crimes'. Transporting us into an alternative reality, where T.E. Lawrence has faked his death to join a mysterious government bureau, Ruffle brings us 'The Case of the Vanishing Spitfire', which could change the course of the upcoming war. Disappearance lies at the core of Golden Age detective fiction. From people (Ethel Lina White's *The Wheel Spins*, 1936) to weapons (G.K. Chesterton's 'The Oracle of the Dog', 1926) to rooms (Carr's 'The Crime in Nobody's Room', 1940) or even buildings (Ellery Queen's 'The Lamp of God', 1935), anything or anyone can suddenly vanish into thin air. When this occurs, it generally happens under circumstances that seem, at a first look, utterly impossible. But, even in an alternative reality, we know we'll get an explanation.

Each of these ten little mysteries is supremely creative, inventive, and engaging. Did the authors adhere doggedly to Knox's ten commandments? No – nor should they have. Like the pioneers of the Golden Age, these ten authors show that the genre and its legacy have never just meant one thing.

Moving, comic, and always mysterious, these tales are sure to keep you guessing – and reading.

Deal in Death
by J.S. Savage

It's ten years to the day since my dear uncle departed this world. I would be lying if I said he had little influence over me, for I became a policeman just as he was. His first case was the fruitless search for Jack the Ripper, his career becoming more successful thereafter. He worked the streets of London and caught some of the most notorious criminals from the early part of this century before retiring due to ill-health to the town of Deal where I was the local Police Inspector. My career was a somewhat different and less thrilling experience. Deal is a small fishing village on the east coast of England, and though smuggling had once been rife, it dried up after the Napoleonic Wars. By the time I retired four years ago, when the war against Hitler ended, crime itself was virtually unheard of in the area.

You may be wondering why I am telling you this, and why the story must be told today. Well, among my uncle's possessions which were bequeathed to me, was an envelope with strict instructions that it must remain unopened until ten years had elapsed. I have just opened this, and to my surprise the envelope contains a wax-sealed letter addressed to me from Inspector Graves. If you are oblivious to this man and his achievements, I would be surprised, for Inspector Graves was the most celebrated and respected Scotland Yard detective of his day. He was renowned by name and sight throughout the country and frequently appeared in the newspapers having solved the most baffling and famous of cases. He worked with my Uncle Terence on many occasions, and I never heard anyone be spoken of with more warmth or admiration by that good man whose words held such weight with me.

I had the pleasure of meeting Graves when he came to stay shortly after my uncle's forced retirement. My pulse is quickened now as I hold his unopened letter in my hand, for the contents must surely relate to that visit and the unsolved murder case that simultaneously occurred.

The year was 1926. After suffering a mild stroke, my uncle was recuperating with me while we sought more permanent accommodation for him. I lived then, as I do now, on Middle Street, that ancient vein which runs through Deal, separating the shops from the sea. The street itself possesses an asymmetric beauty; the tightly packed houses are all different shapes and sizes, a collective of individual endeavours built with bricks which were the crumbs of empire. Though the smell of salt is thick in the air and the squawking of the gulls is incessant, the sea breeze is neither heard nor felt, fended off by the ill-matched houses.

Inspector Graves, keen not to add to my burdens, chose to stay at the local inn, The King's Head, which sits staring at the sea. I protested this decision with as much vehemence as I could muster, though in truth having Uncle Terence staying with me was an unexpected occurrence and I feared I could not provide the famed detective with the comfort I would wish to, had he also elected to sample my hospitality.

And so, it was on a cold and stormy Monday evening in February that, with an umbrella in one hand and Uncle Terence leaning on the other, we walked the short distance to the King's Head. Graves had kindly offered to come to us, but Uncle Terence, feeling able, insisted on different surroundings for the evening and the lively atmosphere of a pub, despite the hostile weather.

Graves was talking with the landlord, Colin Whittaker, when we entered, but he saw us immediately and politely broke off his conversation to greet us. He had acquired a table next to the fire and three pints of amber ale. The bar itself is large and forms a square in the centre of the room. Around all four sides, patrons can stand and drink or sit along one of the walls as we were doing. The rough stone walls are covered with the paintings and bric-a-brac found in almost all old taverns. Copper pots hang from the ceiling beams and dusty, old ale bottles line the bowing shelves.

Comfortably seated, I could assess Graves properly. I had seen his photograph in the newspapers many times, though I now saw that the modern invention had failed to capture the bulk of the man and the intelligence which lay behind his blue eyes. He wrung our hands warmly and after introducing himself to me, he enquired as to my uncle's health.

'Don't worry about me Graves, worry about yourself! There'll be twice as many villains for you to catch now that I'm not around to do it for you!' ribbed my uncle.

As the jokes and reminiscences continued, the inn began to fill with rain-soaked wretches seeking shelter and sustenance. I took the few steps to the bar to replenish our tankards. Rose Whittaker was talking with her father.

'Rose, mind the bar while I get more cheese from the storeroom.'

'There's none left, father. I'll get more tomorrow.'

'Can't be! I got a delivery on Saturday! Those swine must be short-changing us like the butcher with the mutton last week!' Colin left the bar to begin his search.

'He never listens,' Rose said, turning to me. 'He'll be back in a minute, ranting and raving about how there's no cheese left, despite me telling him there's none. Anyway, you're in early, Police Inspector.'

'How so?' I replied, confused by her meaning.

'Your card club doesn't usually begin until nine.'

'Ah!' The young lady's meaning was now clear to me. Due to my uncle's illness and the arrival of Graves I had forgotten that on Monday nights I played in a weekly card game in a back room of the pub. 'It quite slipped my mind. Thanks for reminding me, Rose.' The young woman gave a faint smile, and I was ashamed to think that she could be quite pretty if she only tried. Her dark hair was tangled in knots and covered half her face which was devoid of any colour, artificial or otherwise. Her clothing was frumpy and did not flatter the slim figure that I knew she possessed; she looked like an old wretch. Then I remembered that life had not been easy for Rose, that she was suffering personal turmoil, and my shame was doubled.

When I returned to the table, Graves and Uncle Terence were talking in whispers. Not wishing to appear rude, Graves drew me in.

'I was just asking your uncle about the girl you were talking with at the bar. She seems terribly down about something.'

'I may be able to explain,' I said, deliberately keeping my voice low. 'You see she has a younger brother, Tim. He went missing a few weeks ago and still hasn't turned up, they are very close.'

'Strange,' mused Graves. 'I was talking to Colin before you came in. Presumably he's the boy's father? He didn't mention the missing child to me even though my occupation came up in our conversation.'

'Yes, well, Colin is of the opinion that the boy will turn up any day. He's run off before a few times; a bit of a troubled lad. There's no mother, she died giving birth to Tim. Rose takes on the maternal duty. Rose also has a young daughter of her own, Mabel. Still, Tim's been gone longer this time than any other. I've had all the neighbouring constabularies scouring for him but no sign yet.'

'How old is the boy?' asked my uncle. 'Thirteen, eh? Probably ran off to join the Navy. I've seen it happen many times. Young lads with their heads full of adventure and no thought to how their actions will affect those they leave behind.' Uncle Terence nodded in the direction of Rose who was now wiping a table nearby. She was half-turned from us and her hair concealed most of her face, but I had the distinct impression she was trying to listen to our conversation. Perhaps it was the slow movements of her hands or the fact she was cleaning the same corner of the table repeatedly whilst neglecting the rest, as though she was not concentrating on what she was doing.

'You said she has a daughter? How old is she?' asked Graves.

'Mabel must be seven or eight. The little girl's father was killed in the last days of the war, Rose and he were childhood sweethearts. He died before they could be married and before Rose found out she was expecting. She wasn't entitled to a widow's pension and had to rely on her father's goodwill to avoid destitution. Mabel will be upstairs playing with her dolls, I imagine.'

Our thoughts and words were then disturbed by the door opening and a cold gust from the sea slicing through the warmth of the room. Roger Frobisher, one of the players of my card game entered and proceeded through to the back room. I took this opportunity to explain my forgetfulness and my weekly commitment. My companions accepted my imminent departure with good humour and without reproach to myself.

'Who do you play with?' asked Graves.

'Colin Whittaker, and Roger Frobisher, the town councillor who just entered. Edwin Hooper, a local fisherman, and Jack Sessions, a local historian.'

'An interesting mix.'

'Yes. Edwin also has the unofficial title of "Pier master" bestowed upon him. Deal has no harbour; the pier dominates the seascape and Edwin occupies the hut on the end of it. His family have been fishermen as well as the churchwardens of Deal since time immemorial. He's a very devout man.'

'I wouldn't have thought a card game would appeal much to a man like that?' continued Graves.

'No, now that you mention it, he wasn't too fond of the idea when Colin first suggested a weekly game, but Colin also expressed a wish that a portion of the takings from the Sunday meat raffle be given to the church. Perhaps Edwin was swayed by this generosity. Anyway, we don't play cards for money so Satan can't be too pleased.'

'And Mr. Frobisher? He looked a reasonably straight-backed fellow.'

'Ha! Yes,' I replied. 'To be honest, I think he only comes for the social aspect; he's a widower who lives with his mother and not much of a card player. His work as a councillor keeps him very busy and I believe this is the one chance he gets to unwind. He's a pleasant enough chap, although somewhat morose at times. Can't be blamed, I suppose.'

'You said the last number of your game was an historian? Jack, was it?'

'Aha! Speak of the devil and he doth appear!' shrilled a voice over my shoulder. I turned to see the chubby face of Jack Sessions beaming a smile at us.

'Jack, I was just explaining our little game to my companions. I didn't see you come in.'

'I entered through the backdoor, through the courtyard. Good lord!' cried the man, his face glowing with pleasure. 'Is that? . . . Are you the famous London detective? Inspector Graves?'

'Pleased to meet you, Mr. Sessions,' replied Graves, who offered his hand.

Jack seated himself on the stool next to me, his eyes transfixed on my new friend.

'Tell me Inspector, are you here on a case?' The historian's voice bubbled with excitement.

'I'm sorry to disappoint you Mr. Sessions, Deal is out of my jurisdiction. I am here to visit my old friend Terence and to drink to his health.' Graves raised his tankard and crashed it against mine, the metal ringing like shields clashing in battle.

'Well, if you have questions about the local area during your stay or if you are interested in the history, I am more than happy to take you on a tour. Whether it is Deal Castle, or information about when Deal was home to the naval fleet or the history of the shipwrecks on Goodwin Sands, I think you'll find my knowledge to be unsurpassed. I can even do an armchair tour sitting here! That picture hanging above the log basket, that is the castle. It was built by Henry the Eighth when he feared invasion by the catholic countries of Europe. There, beneath the hanging pewter mugs is a painting by the famed artist D. Cox depicting the Spanish galleon *Cordoza* sinking after running aground. They say she went down with ten tons of gold and one hundred souls. Of course, she is just one of thousands that the sandbanks have claimed over the centuries. I could take you out on my boat to have a look, the Sands are only six miles out. Or if you prefer, we could go to Walmer, or Whitstable? That picture shows the *Golden Lyre* sinki—'

'I say, Jack, isn't it time we played our card game? You go on ahead and I'll join you in just a minute.'

'Oh, righto! Ha! Lovely meeting you, Inspector! I'll pop in and see you during our interval!'

'Sorry about that,' I said when Jack was safely out of earshot. 'He would talk all night if you let him—'

Graves, cut me off with a wave and a smile. 'Don't apologise my good man. I find all sorts of people interesting and when someone has such passion for a topic their enthusiasm can lift the soul. Besides, I was very interested in castles as a child: moats and arrows and sieges and the like. I may take him up on his offer; I'd like to soak up the history of the place.'

The last card player entered then. Edwin Hooper wore a worker's cap, shirt and charcoal-grey trousers beneath a long overcoat. He touched his cap when he saw me but didn't stop with us, instead proceeding directly to the backroom. I got my uncle and Graves more drinks before leaving the bar by the back door. I walked past the lavatories and Colin's private office; then straight past the storeroom and coal shed and into the courtyard. Our playing room was a little stone outhouse with a stove inside to fight off the cold. After a few moments' wait, Colin joined us with the deck of cards in his hand.

This was the third game the five of us had held since Colin's son went missing, and though Tim's name was never mentioned, the air seemed heavy with his absence. I was sure each of us was thinking of

Tim, when to break the awkward silence Jack asked Edwin how the plans were coming on with regards to fixing the church hall roof. You could always rely on Jack to say something, anything, in fact, at any time!

'I'm afraid it's going to cost more than we anticipated. It's such an old building, you see.'

'It certainly is,' replied Jack, who then went on to recount at length the history of St Andrew's church. We then talked pleasantly about village life and troubles as one would expect; Edwin kindly enquired about my uncle's health and Roger spoke of his mother's decline towards senility. Colin, however, didn't join in the conversation, in fact, he seemed oblivious that there were four men around him cursing the cousins, Time and Age. He stared at the cards with unseeing eyes and dealt them mechanically. His play was sloppy where usually he was one of the sharper players at the table. At the time I surmised he was thinking about Tim. The burden of a missing child must be great to bear, even for a man like Colin, who had frequently seemed emotionlessly bull-headed. He was always pleasant to his customers, but a man cannot hide his true self all the time, and the people of Deal were under no illusions that the landlord could be a severe man. It was rumoured that Tim had felt the force of his father's stony fist a few times and naturally it was assumed this was the reason the boy had fled.

You, dear reader, will undoubtedly have noticed that I have been describing Colin Whittaker in the past tense. Alas, the man did not live to congratulate a victor of our game.

About twenty minutes after we sat down to play, Colin said he had a bottle of brandy in his office and suggested we take a ten-minute break while he fetched it. Although this was highly irregular, none of us objected; a pinch of brandy would be most welcome on this cold, wet night. The party rose, each man to do as he wished for the short break.

Uncle Terence and Inspector Graves were laughing like schoolboys when I rejoined them at their table.

'How's the game going? Are you winning?' asked, Graves.

'It's rather odd; Colin doesn't seem to be altogether himself. He is making mistakes in his play and is very distracted.'

After a few minutes, Jack Sessions scuttled over to us, coming in from the rear entrance, and I remembered his promise to Graves that he would sit with us, but instead of the jovial expression I was expecting, I found myself looking at an ashen, almost terrified face.

'Police Inspector,' he said to me, the formal title used fermenting apprehension in my gut. 'I think you had better come. Quick!'

Not wishing to draw the other patrons' attention to our table by asking Jack to elaborate further, I stood up to follow the man. Graves rose at the same time, experience and warning tugging at his sleeve.

We left my uncle and followed Jack to Colin's office without a word being spoken. The door was ajar, through the crack I could see a man's horizontal leg. I pushed the door and saw Colin lying in front of his desk, facing us. On the left-side of the man's head, near his temple was a deep wound, blood was running down his face like tears; a shallow crimson puddle was forming on the wooden floor. A cream-coloured ammonite lay on the desk. I could see a small circle of blood, still wet, on the prehistoric fossil. I closed the door.

'He's dead,' said Graves, whose fingers were on the man's neck.

'He must've been killed in the last five minutes, just after we stopped playing,' I said, looking at my pocket watch.

The room held a chair, a desk, and a lamp. There was no other furniture.

I watched Graves rise from the dead man and look around the small office. The walls were wood-panelled, Graves inspected each one in turn. As I watched the great detective, I thought he must be looking for blood spatter; if a streak was found on the wall it may tell us if the killer was waiting there to attack Colin as he came in, or if the intruder entered when Colin was already in the room. If, for example the killer entered and struck, then the blood could not spray in the opposite direction from which the fossil was aimed.

'Do you know if a painting ever hung here?' asked Graves, looking at the wall behind the desk. Surprised by the question, I replied that I did not know, never having been in the office before.

'I think, perhaps, someone should tell Rose,' said Jack, bringing my attention to the wider ramifications of the body on the floor as well as the historian's presence which I had forgotten.

'Yes, we will, Jack, but first we must inspect the crime scene. It appears no doubt to be murder. Jack, can I trust you to go to the bar, have a stiff drink and not breathe a word of this to anyone until Inspector Graves and I come to you? It's a small room and won't take us long to look for evidence.'

The poor man nodded, his hands still shaking. 'Not a word,' I reminded him as I gently nudged him through the doorway.

'A nasty business,' said Graves once we were alone. He stooped to look closely at the ammonite. 'Looks to be a heavy old thing. You wouldn't have to swing too hard to cause much damage.'

'Hopefully the fingerprint boys will have some luck with it.'

'Hmmph. Tell me, what are your first impressions?' asked Graves.

'Well, an unplanned murder with an improvised weapon. A crime of passion perhaps. Colin was struck down in a fit of anger. So, it is likely he knew his murderer. Of course, if the assailant knew the ammonite was here it could have been planned, although killing a man when the bar is full of customers and the local Police Inspector is on hand is bold. Either way, it looks to be a very personal killing.'

'What else?'

'The killer was right-handed, the wound being on the left side. Unless, of course, he was struck from behind. Did you see any blood on the walls?'

'No, the fossil appears to have dented his head, most of the blood not seeping out until he had hit the floor.'

'So, we don't know if the killer was in the room waiting for Colin, or which is their dominant hand. I would, however, be inclined to think the killer was indeed right-handed,' I continued. 'Look at the position of the body, he is lying in front of his desk with his head on the left-side of the door as you enter. He is facing the door. If the killer was in the room, then I can't imagine Colin turning his back to them, and besides, there is nowhere to hide, so why would he be facing the door if the killer was left-handed.'

'I agree, although I can think of two points to counter your well-thought-out deductions,' Graves replied. 'Firstly, Colin could have had his back to the door when he was struck and his body twisted as he fell, although I admit this is unlikely.'

'And the second point?'

'The killer could have been hiding behind the door. Colin enters with his back to the assailant, he turns around and is struck, that would explain how the killer could have been in the room and how the body lies as it does, but in this scenario the killer would indeed be right-handed.'

'I suppose we had better proceed with examining the room further; I don't want to leave Jack on his own for too long. I believe he can stay quiet for a while but not indefinitely, he likes to talk to anyone who will listen, and he's had quite a shock. Let's look around.'

The desk was not locked, it contained two drawers, the contents of which were not revelatory. Some pencils, stamps and an order book detailing ale deliveries were in the top drawer. In the bottom was a snuff-box, an Allen key, a broken clock, and a book of raffle tickets. The sought-after brandy bottle stood on the desk next to a writing pad. Further inspection of the office proffered no clues to the identity of the murderer. It was a plain room which appeared to be infrequently used.

Next, we had the difficult task of informing Rose of her father's demise. I decided to use the backroom where we played cards to conduct all interviews and Graves kindly offered to find Rose while I got rid of my fellow players. In my most official voice, I told them to wait in the bar and offered no further information.

Rose entered, accompanied by Graves. She had straightened her hair and tied it under her chin so that most of her colourless face was still obscured. Her collar was turned up against the wind and the rain. Graves poured some coal on the stove, the little room becoming darker as he did so.

'Miss Whittaker, I'm afraid I have some bad news, this will come as a shock to you.'

'Oh no. It's Tim, isn't it?'

'No, Miss, it's not your brother. It's your father: he's dead. Murdered.' Rose stared back at me, uncomprehendingly.

'Father? Surely there is some mistake?'

I explained the circumstances as gently as I could, and the poor girl listened with her head bowed. When asked, she said that her father had no enemies that she knew of, and she could think of no one likely to commit such a crime. She said that the last time she had seen her father was at nine o'clock when he left the bar to play cards. Her father kept the ammonite on his desk as a paperweight, she said.

'Did your father keep any money in his office? In the desk drawers perhaps?' I asked.

'No, Inspector. All the cash is kept in his bedroom, in his safe.'

'You are sure there is no other safe? A hidden one, perhaps, in the office wall behind his desk?' asked Graves.

'I'm certain of it.'

'Thank you,' said Graves.

Not wishing to distress Rose further, I ended the interview. She left us with tears welling in her eyes and the unenviable task of informing her daughter that they were now alone.

'I took the liberty of informing your uncle about what's happened when I went to fetch the girl. I hope you don't mind. He's ringing through to the coroner to get the body collected and is standing guard by the office door.'

'Thank you, Inspector Graves. I appreciate your help in this.'

'The bar had emptied quite a bit, there were only four or five customers still there when the murder must have occurred. No one in the bar could have left to go to Colin's office without me seeing them.'

'And Rose?'

'She was in and out the back exit to the storeroom and to check on Mabel all night. I couldn't swear to her being in the bar or not.'

When a policeman speaks in confidence and asks that information not be shared, he does so not in the expectation that these instructions will be followed, but in the hope that the escape of information is delayed long enough that he can instigate preparations to hedge against any repercussions. Jack Sessions, however, was true to his word, and had not told anyone of his gruesome discovery. My fellow card players seemed shocked and upset when I entered the bar and conveyed the news of the landlord's demise. I seated them at the table next to Uncle Terence, in the hope that any confessional utterances or collusion might be overheard.

The few customers who Graves confirmed were in the bar at the time of the murder had their details taken and were let go. Then we summoned Jack to the backroom to get his account of the matter.

'What was your relationship with the deceased? Were you friends?' I asked.

'I wouldn't say friends. He could be a bit gruff, but we have been acquainted with one another our whole lives. Deal is a small place, as you know.'

'How did you come to play in his card game?' asked Graves, who had taken a pipe from his pocket and was drawing softly upon it.

'A few months ago, I was having a pint in The Ship tavern; I had just been researching the history of St. Andrew's church. It was raining, and Colin came in for a drink and some shelter. He asked if he could sit with me. We spoke about history, he seemed very interested, he said he'd like to ask me more about Deal's history and would I join his weekly card game, we could chat more then. Well, it seemed it would be rude to decline, especially after he showed so much interest in *my* hobby, so I thought it fair that I should participate in his.'

'I see. Can you think of any reason why someone would wish to hurt him?'

Jack looked from me to Graves and back. I watched his Adam's apple rise and fall and his cherubic face glow red.

'Jack . . . if you know something, you need to tell us . . .' I let my words hang, not wishing to push too hard.

'Well, there is one thing, but I wouldn't want you thinking I was eavesdropping or dishonest in any way!'

'I know you well enough to know you have a fine character,' I said as reassuringly as I could.

'Well—it's—the thing is, I heard something. When Colin decided to break off the game to fetch the brandy, I thought I would nip to the lavatory and then come and see your good self, Inspector Graves. But as I was walking past Colin's office towards the toilet, I heard him talking to someone . . . I don't know who. Honestly, I don't.'

'What did they say?'

'I didn't hear all of it, there were gaps where I couldn't make out what was said and I couldn't distinguish between the two voices, but I heard the words: *'The authorities may be on to us* - ______________________ *Liar! Don't lie!* __________________ *I'll get the sack! The money is hidden in the hall, in the place* ________________________ *take the boy to see whether* __________________ *illicit information* ________________ *the ship* _____________ *back to Scotland* ____________ *Roger* ____________' I'm sorry, Inspectors; that's all I heard. I was worried one of them would open the door and see me, so I hurried to the lavatory, when I came out a few minutes later the office door was ajar. Through the gap I saw a leg lying flat on the floor. I thought maybe Colin had fainted. I pushed the door and, well, you know what I found. Then I came and got you.'

Next, we elected to interview Edwin. The callouses on the fisherman's hands looked like barnacles stuck to a salt-sprayed keel. He appeared as grave as an undertaker, his face sallow and gaunt. He removed his cap and twisted it in his hands when he sat.

'Here, have some brandy,' I offered. 'You don't look too well, Edwin.'

'Such a shock Inspector, and those poor girls, it must be terrible for them.'

'Indeed, it must. Tell me, where did you go when we broke off play?'

'Nowhere really, I went to the coal shed to refill the bucket.' Edwin pointed at the brimming pail next to Graves's leg.

'Did you see anyone on the way there or back? Anyone going into or leaving Mr. Whittaker's office?'

'No, I went there and came back here without seeing anyone.'

Despite the sickly look of the man, he answered my questions calmly, his only movement his twisting hands.

'Can you please tell us how you came to know Colin?' Edwin shifted in his seat and was silent for a few minutes until he cleared his throat loudly.

'I—ahem—I was approached by him. You may not be aware Inspector but my fishing business, my family fishing business, I should say, has undergone a radical change in recent months. I'm afraid my brother Sam who I jointly ran the business with, decided to break off our partnership after a disagreement. Sam and I have always been very different people, opposites in fact, though I have always believed that blood is thicker than water and that any difference between us would not affect the family business. I was wrong.'

'I'm sorry Edwin, but I need to ask, what was the cause of the disagreement?'

'I had been using some of the money from the business to pay for repairs to the church hall. Sam does not share my faith and so did not agree with the use of the money. He became quite angry.'

'I see, and how does Mr. Whittaker come into this?' I asked, glancing at Graves who puffed noiselessly at his pipe.

'Colin found out about the dissolution of the business and offered to buy one of my boats. We had eight you see. When we split, Sam and I took four each and split the crew, but without the income from the other four boats I was in financial difficulty. The church you see . . . well, the sale of one boat cleared my debt and I can get by with three..'

'And once the sale was agreed, he offered you a seat at his card game as a gesture of friendship?' asked Graves.

'Something like that, yes. I'm not much of a player but I felt I couldn't say no. I know business is business, but he gave me a very fair price for the boat, and I was in a tight spot, so I was grateful.'

Roger Frobisher was the last to be interviewed. I was glad, for it had been a long night and the disparity between the winter air and heat from the stove was cultivating a confused drowsiness deep within me, no doubt stoked by the unexpected and violent drama I found myself at the centre of.

'Roger, can you tell me about your movements during the break in the card game? When Colin went to fetch the brandy?'

'I went through the courtyard and out into the alley to enjoy a cigarette.'

'Why not just smoke in the courtyard or in here?' I asked, perplexed.

'Because it was raining and there is an overhang in the alley which provides shelter. As to your second point, you will have noticed that I never smoke in here. It is a small space, and the smoke lingers, it would be inconsiderate to my fellow players.' Roger looked at Graves who took a long drag on his pipe and slowly exhaled the grey-green smoke in Roger's direction.

'I see,' I said. 'You didn't go to Colin's office during the break?'

'I most assuredly did not, Police Inspector!'

'Tell me, Mr. Frobisher,' interrupted Graves. 'Why would Colin Whittaker say your name in his office if he wasn't talking to you?'

'Presumably he would be talking *about* me, though I can't imagine why or to whom.'

'How did you make Colin's acquaintance?'

'Professionally. I am the local councillor. Colin wanted permission to build an extension here to add more rooms. He wanted to expand the bar into a more formal hotel.'

'That sounds quite bold, I thought tourism here is quite modest,' said Graves.

'It is. However, we often have naval ships stop here when they come down to do exercises from Scotland. Colin thought if there were more rooms for them then they might stay. Sailors on shore leave tend to spend a lot, he said.'

'I see,' I said, shivering despite the stove. 'And was the application approved?'

'It was, though that had no bearing on my playing cards. I play because I enjoy it. There are no dodgy deals or envelopes passed beneath the table if that's what you're thinking.'

'That's not what I am thinking at all,' I said, though of course that is precisely what I had been thinking.

Our interviews concluded, I let our suspects escape to their respective homes. Rose had retired to the living quarters above the bar to see to Mabel. She had left a set of all the keys with Uncle Terence, who we found snoozing in his chair by the dying embers of the fire.

The coroner and a constable had arrived and removed Colin's body while we were conducting our interviews. No fingerprints had been found on the murder weapon or door handle.

Graves accompanied us home through the wind and rain. Once Uncle Terence was safely in bed, Graves and I sat in my little living room, and enjoyed a whisky in front of the newly lit fire. Jets of blue flame spurted from the crackling logs, gas held within the wood for decades released and ignited by the expansive and destructive heat.

'Not one of them has a solid alibi,' I said, frustrated. 'Not a single one! We don't even have a witness to corroborate what Jack said he overheard! He could be making the whole thing up. He could have killed Colin and then come running to us to say he found him.'

'He could, but why? That is the question. Why? They all had the means; the ammonite was lying there ready to be used. They all had the opportunity, but why kill him?'

'Perhaps one of them owed him money. Edwin seems most likely. He admitted to being hard up, though I don't think he is a man to hold a grudge. You heard what he said about the falling out with his brother? Sam is friendly with Colin. I've seen them together a few times. If Edwin was bitter, he wouldn't continue playing in the card game.'

'His devotion seems genuine,' said Graves. 'Though I've known priests to murder before. Nothing can be ruled out.'

'And Roger?' I asked. 'What did you make of him?'

'He was right in what he said. Just because his name was spoken in the office doesn't mean he was in the room. He seemed very sure of himself I thought. He had an air of superiority that I detest.'

'I say, what was the idea with the picture hanging on the wall? I thought you were looking for blood.'

'Hmm?' Graves was staring deep into the flames, my question bringing his senses back to life. 'Oh, there is a hole in one of the wood panels, as if a nail had been removed. I thought it odd that's all, I would expect a picture to hang higher.'

I saw Graves off from my doorstep. The wind had again picked up, rendering his umbrella practically useless. Of course, I offered a bed for the night, but he declined stating that when you got to his age you became impervious to bad weather. I watched him as he strode down the street, past the dark, glistening houses, until he was lost to me, engulfed in storm and shadow.

I awoke to the sound of seagulls arguing over breakfast rights. From my bedroom window I could see faint, ghostly light on the horizon. The storm had passed through the night, the sky was cloudless yet still dark.

I prepared a fire for Uncle Terence and left to meet Graves. Rose, despite her grief had cooked him bacon and eggs. They were sitting alone in the bar, Graves eating and Rose sipping tea, her hands clasped tightly around the mug.

'Would you like something to eat, Inspector? I made plenty,' she said to me when I entered.

'Thank you, Rose. I'm famished. I thought Inspector Graves was the only guest staying?'

'Oh, he is, but I always make a feast.'

'I suppose it keeps her mind off things,' I said to Graves when Rose went to get me a plate. 'It's good to keep busy during times of grief.'

'We'll have to keep an eye on her,' Graves said in a low voice. 'She burnt her hand in the cooking oil this morning—distracted no doubt. I heard her yelp and found her in the kitchen running her hand under cold water. Her forearm had red marks on it too.'

'You mean cut marks? Self-harm?'

Graves stopped himself from replying, Rose having interrupted us by bringing in a steaming plate of bacon, toast, and eggs.

'Rose, do you know if your father lent money to anyone?' I asked.

'Oh no, father would never do that. He was very thrifty. I have to fiddle the figures just to get good quality meat and bread. He would never waste a penny if he could help it and certainly wouldn't lend money to anyone.'

'And yet, he bought a fishing boat. Did he like to sail? Or was he planning on catching his own fish to serve here?'

'Father bought a boat?! That's news to me inspector!'

Our stomachs full, Graves and I walked along the beach to the pier, the shingle crunching beneath our feet like fresh snow. The air was cold and briny, a strong breeze blew in from the boiling sea. From the shore we could see two trawlers returning, their decks filled with mountains of fish. Edwin had already returned. He saw us approach and opened the door of his hut to us. The inside consisted of fishing nets, buoys, poles, scuba equipment, oars, and all manner of seafaring paraphernalia. The room itself smelt so strongly of fish that I wondered how the stench did not cling to the man himself. A solitary desk was the only piece of furniture that would belong in an ordinary office.

'How can I help you gentlemen?' he asked.

'We have only one question,' I said. 'The trawler you sold to Colin. Did your brother Sam attempt to buy it from you first?'

'No, he did not. His pride would never allow for him to talk to me, let alone pay me money.'

We left Edwin to his work. Graves and I walked through the archaic warren of streets and houses that form the oldest part of Deal on our way to St. Andrew's Church.

'You think Sam Hooper paid Colin to buy the boat, thereby securing it from Edwin?' asked Graves.

'Well, it would make sense. Sam gets a fishing boat, his pride intact, and besides, what use could Colin Whittaker have for it?'

Following the unwritten laws known the world over, we stopped talking when we entered the church. The vast space was filled with silence, the only movement was the flickering of candle flames caused by the draft we had let in. Our intent was not to pray but to make our way to the church hall at the rear. A search showed the decrepit roof, though there was no sign anywhere of hidden money or indeed of Tim.

By mid-afternoon our exertions, although fruitless, had led to a rumbling in our bellies. Graves, eager to sample what the sea had to offer, was soon eating plaice and chips soaked in vinegar (my own penchant being haddock) and was staring out across the swollen grey expanse. We were sitting on a bench, usually frequented by the old and bereaved when Jack Sessions appeared at our side.

'Good afternoon, inspectors! Making the most of the break in the rain, I see! I say Inspector Graves, I was just going to the castle, perhaps you'd like to join me? It's closed to the public in the winter, but I am fortunate enough to possess a set of keys, given my position in the Deal Historical Society.'

'I would be delighted, Jack. You can do without me for a few hours, can't you?' Graves said, addressing me.

'Absolutely, where shall I meet you later?'

'The King's Head. Six o'clock,' replied Graves.

'The King said what?' chortled Jack. Our faces must have shown confusion for Jack explained his little joke and we laughed politely, though I felt for Graves: a few hours in the historian's company may seem interminable if this poor joke was just a taster of what was to come.

In truth, I was glad to be alone for a while. Having such a great detective by your side can make you question your own competence, and I was sorry to say that the case was not progressing as I would've liked. Roger Frobisher on the face of it appeared to me to be the prime suspect, his name having been heard spoken in a heated conversation moments before Colin was killed. However, he had no motive as far as I could tell and there was no evidence that he had ever been in Colin's office. The words overheard (if Jack could be believed) did not present me with any tangible clues, rather they confused my thinking further. Who was lying? And who were the authorities *'on'* to, and with regards to what? As the senior authority in the area, I found these words both baffling and disheartening for I could not fathom what they could relate to.

I spent my afternoon going over old ground. I visited all the suspects again, bar Jack, and asked variations on the same questions hoping to find a discrepancy in someone's story. I was disappointed; everyone gave the same answers of denial and ignorance. I visited Sam Hooper in the hope that he could ignite the case or my intellect but again I was out of luck. He claimed that he had no dealings with Colin other than a friendly 'hello' when their paths crossed. He also claimed he was alone on a boat at the time of the murder, though I couldn't really suspect him; if just one of Edwin or Roger were telling the truth regarding their alibis, they would have seen anyone enter the courtyard.

Graves was quiet and pensive when I met him that evening. He smoked his pipe and stared into the fire, barely touching his tankard. He stayed on for a few more days assisting me in my fruitless investigation until he was required to return to London. I never saw him again. When Uncle Terence died ten years ago, Graves was abroad, working on a case. He missed the funeral as a result.

And so, life sailed slowly by in Deal. With no new leads my investigation was dead in the water. The details of the murder and subsequent enquiries were filed away into a dusty storeroom, the drama spoken of more infrequently by the locals and police alike as time passed.

With Colin dead, Rose sold the pub and took Mabel away to Yorkshire to live, leaving a forwarding address should Tim ever show up. He never did.

Roger died a few years ago. He retired shortly after Colin's murder to care for his terminally ill mother. He never visited the King's Head again to my knowledge and became somewhat of a recluse in his later years.

Edwin, I am sorry to say, died at sea nearly fifteen years ago. A storm swelled unexpectedly. Edwin, alone, was lost with his trawler. I sometimes imagine him in his last moments, staring at the huge waves, certain of his impending doom, yet calm, his composure held tightly together by his unshakable faith. I hope his last thoughts were not of regret for a past crime, a crime which has haunted and mocked my sleep for years.

Jack can still be seen roving around Deal with a map in his hand and a smile on his face. He moves slower these days, but his enthusiasm for local history is as strong as ever.

There was one last interesting development, though not entirely connected with the case. A few months after the murder, when life had resumed some form of normality, I received an anonymous tip-off in the form of a letter. The result of this was the arrest of Sam Hooper for smuggling. He was caught red-handed thanks to the information I received and later sentenced to ten years. He died in prison from tuberculosis.

These fraught memories lead me to today and the letter from Inspector Graves which I now hold. I shall pour myself a large brandy to fortify myself against its contents . . .

My friend, I hope you can forgive me. I know only too well the despair and anguish an unsolved case can cause a policeman and I am ashamed to say that I could have prevented you these terrible emotions had I chosen to do so. It is my sincere hope that when you read my reasons for keeping certain discoveries from you, an element of understanding and forgiveness will prevail.

My first confession must be that it was I who informed you about Sam Hooper's criminal activity. After the murder of Colin Whittaker, I had Sam followed until my suspicions were confirmed, but you'll want to know what led me to him . . .

The possibility of a smuggling operation first entered my mind when Jack Sessions spoke a few careless words. You remember the joke he made about The King's Head when we were eating fish and chips? It made me think, what if the words Jack heard on the night of the murder held a different meaning than what Jack assumed. You remember what Jack said he heard?

'The authorities may be on to us________________ Liar! Don't lie!________________ I'll get the sack! The money is hidden in the hall, in the place________________ take the boy to see whether________________ illicit

> *information ________________the ship_____________back to Scotland________________Roger____________’*

When I considered the words, the double meaning of some became clear to me, even ‘Roger’, that radio command for the affirmative. Then I remembered the hole I found in the wall panelling and the Allen key in the drawer, and I wondered if Colin had a radio hidden and maybe he was talking to Sam who you mentioned Colin was friendly with. I can confirm if you insert the Allen key, it will open the panel to reveal a radio set. And so, I started to piece things together. Now allow me to fill in the gaps with what I think Jack actually heard. Of course, I will be wrong in the precise wording, but the gist will be correct.

> *‘The authorities may be on to us. They know about the Golden Lyre! Don’t lie low! We need to move fast! I’ll get the sack, the money is hidden in the haul, in the plaice. You put the gold in the buoy and take the buoy to sea (weather permitting). If Inspector Graves tries to elicit information from Jack about the shipwreck he may go back to Scotland Yard and get a dive team. Roger, over and out.’*

You see, Colin knew I was from Scotland Yard and was no doubt intrigued and paranoid about why I should be in Deal and in his pub. He would have heard Jack mention the Golden Lyre to me and may have thought I asked about it whereas Jack spoke of it without any prompting from us. You remember Jack saying it sunk with gold onboard? Well, there isn’t ten tons of it down there anymore! By starting a weekly card game, Colin could have the local Police Inspector, the local councillor, and the Pier master, (in essence the people who posed the greatest threat of rumbling him) in one place and under his watchful eye while Sam dived to the wreck to bring up the gold. I’m afraid they may have made Jack an unwitting accomplice, he undoubtedly told Colin all he needed to know about the treasure-laden wrecks with Colin feigning interest in local history. They then kept the gold hidden in a buoy on the boat before selling it for cash. If the gold was discovered, they could claim ignorance, and cast blame onto Edwin who owned the boat before he sold it to Colin.

But what, you will be wondering, does this have to do with the murder? Well, nothing. Colin Whittaker was killed by Rose. She saw him go into his office, then as he was about to leave it, she went in and struck him with the ammonite. Herein lies the real tragedy of the story; Rose killed her father to protect her brother and daughter. We know Tim suffered at the hands of his father and you remember I told you I saw marks on Rose's arm when she burnt herself? Do you remember how Rose would tie her hair to hide her face? Well, Rose suffered physical abuse as much as Tim, and she feared for Mabel who was so young and whom she loved so much. Why would her cruel father treat Mabel any differently than Tim or herself, she thought? I think, in some unconscious way she intended to be caught for her crime. That's why she killed Colin when she did—when I was there. The goodness in her knew that justice would have to be served and it probably would have been had Jack's testimony not confused the whole affair. I confronted her with the truth which she did not deny. She held out her hands to be taken away, but if I had acquiesced and led her to the gallows, would I also not have been condemning that innocent child whose well-being was the reason Rose had stained her soul with blood?

I took the coward's way out, my friend. I defaulted to a technicality: Deal was not in my jurisdiction. I did not hinder your pursuit of the culprit, but I did not help it either.

When I visited Deal Castle with Jack I found evidence of habitation—food wrappings, crumbs of bread and cheese. Tim was staying there, Rose brought him food when she had time to slip away from the King's Head. I gave her the idea of selling the pub and making a fresh start. The address in Yorkshire which Rose provided to you belongs to my sister-in-law, who was to warn me if ever you wrote to it.

I must tell you that Rose, Tim and Mabel sailed together to Australia to start a new life in April 1926. Rose writes to me often; I am happy to say they have prospered and are living good, peaceful lives.

Now you know the truth, my friend, and the burden of responsibility is inherited by you. The passage of time does not diminish the magnitude of the deed committed in the eyes of the law. Mabel will be grown up now, you can still prosecute Rose if you wish using this letter as evidence. The decision is yours. But ask yourself, why do we do what we do?

When I am summoned to the Old Bailey to give evidence in court, I pause on the steps and look at the statue of Lady Justice holding scales in one hand and a sword in the other. I say a silent prayer as I look at the words inscribed beneath.

'Defend the children of the poor and punish the wrongdoer'

Your friend,

Graves

The fire crackles before me as I sit staring at the letter in my hand. The hungry flames shall be fed.

A Gathering at the Grange
by Anya Page

Saturday 21 January 1950

DEATHS: On Sunday 14 inst. Peacefully in her sleep, Evelyn P_, aged 63. Widow of Percival P_, long-time resident of this town. *The Burlington Daily Times*, Burlington, North Carolina, USA.

I will never forget my last visit to the Grange. It was in early '18. I had finally been passed fit and was on my way back to re-join the 5ths in France. As I was leaving my club, I was hailed by a thin stooped man slowly mounting the steps.

'You don't remember me?' he asked. 'It's Tristan,' he continued. 'Lionel's brother. Lionel P_. I was a few years behind you at school.'

But for his voice, I would hardly have recognised him, he was so altered. Tristan could only have been about twenty-five years of age, yet he had the drawn, haggard looks of a much older man. I don't suppose that I was looking any better, but when you are away, you imagine time stands still back at home. No-one gets any older and everything stays the same.

'So good to see you.' he said. 'We hadn't any news for so long, we wondered if . . . ' he broke off. 'Damned shame about Lionel.'

His brother, my oldest friend, had been killed at Cambrai. I had no adequate words to empathise with his loss. Lionel was by no means the first of my friends to die. Tristan indicated to his walking stick.

'Copped a blighty back in November. There's still a chunk of shell left in there.' He rubbed his leg as he spoke, 'Been at home recuperating. You wouldn't recognise the old place. Father handed it over to the War Office. We've got beds in the ballroom and the place is overrun with VADs. You should look us up. Father would be delighted to see you.'

I had spent carefree school holidays at the Grange. Sunlit summers of tennis and swimming and tea on the lawn. Now those days seemed to belong to another man, from another time. I had a few days before I needed to report for duty and no fixed plans. It was perhaps not wise, to revisit the past, but at that moment it offered more than the future. And I was greatly indebted to Lionel and Tristan's father, who was the only paternal figure I encountered during my childhood. Thus it was twenty-four hours later I found myself back at the Grange.

The Grange was of such proportions that, despite having ceded a significant number of its rooms to the Red Cross hospital, the family quarters did not appear to be in any way reduced in comfort or convenience. When I joined the party gathered in the drawing room just before seven in the evening, my host was pouring drinks. Now in his sixties, Arthur P_ was still a handsome man. Tall, with a noble air that somehow encouraged others to fall in with his generous way of looking at the world.

'Welcome, my boy, welcome!' He shook my hand, his grip still as firm as that of a much younger man. 'What will you have?' As he poured my whisky, I looked around the room.

'I'm afraid we've not got much company for you; we live very quietly these days.'

I assured him that a few days peace and tranquillity in the countryside was most welcome. There were six people in the drawing room. Eustace Overbury was the family lawyer, visiting after an absence of several months. He was a solid, sensible man of around fifty. He was listening to an elderly gentleman with military bearing and a luxuriant growth of whiskers.

'Infernal cheek! Turned out they were selling the game back to my batman. And it ended up on the table at the mess!' he exclaimed and guffawed at his own anecdote.

Did Arthur have a problem with poaching on the estate? Yes, there had been a few more cases recently, but he didn't begrudge a man with a family to feed. I had encountered many men like Major Hobson. Veteran of the South African wars, brought out of retirement to support the war effort. He turned his attention to me. Where had I seen action? When was I going back? Good, good, ready for a final push. I had no inclination for a military pep talk so I made my excuses and went to join Tristan. He greeted me cheerfully. Arthur's beloved wife had birthed four sons in quick succession before dying of influenza in the seventh year of their marriage. Perhaps as a result of the early death of their mother the bond between Arthur and his sons had always appeared to me as an enviably close and loving one. Tristan was the youngest of the sons. In looks he favoured his father and Lionel, being tall and blond and of athletic build. The middle two sons, Percival and Mortimer, must have inherited their dark hair and more compact stature from their mother. The names of all four sons were entirely the gift of their mother, further testament to Arthur's devotion to his romantic wife.

Mortimer P_ was leaning over the back of a chaise by the fire, talking intimately with a brittle looking young woman.

'Good to see you again.' His smile did not quite reach his eyes. He glanced at my uniform. 'Failed the medical, but someone had to stay and help Father run the business.'

The last was said rather too glibly. I suspected that it was something he often had need to explain. Arthur P_ was a wealthy man and the war had made him wealthier still. His textile factories clad thousands of men in khaki, including all but one of his sons. I recalled that even as a child

Mortimer was able to wriggle out of anything unpleasant. The brittle woman was introduced as Evelyn.

'Evelyn's a nurse,' Mortimer explained. 'We're lucky to have her with us. She is quite the favourite with our patients.'

'I'm grateful to be able to be of some use.'

Tristan had mentioned the VADs, but I was surprised to find one of them in the family party. In my experience, the sisters scrupulously guarded the time of their nurses both on and off duty. Evelyn patted the chaise next to her indicating that I was to join her. Mortimer frowned and moved away slightly. Close up, she looked a little faded. She talked animatedly, her eyes travelling between Mortimer and myself as if gauging the effect of her attention.

'I understand you're quite one of the family,' she began.

I acknowledged Arthur's many past kindnesses to me and that I had spent a great deal of my childhood at the Grange.

'Your visit is such a tonic for Arthur. It's been a terrible business,' she said confidingly, 'first my dear Percival and then Lionel's death.'

I raised an eyebrow in enquiry at her proprietorial tone, but she continued.

'You must look in on Percival while you're here. It will cheer him up. I do my best of course.' Evelyn looked down, modestly. And then her expression hardened.

I sensed the woman enter the room, even before I saw her. She was exceptionally beautiful. In the last letter that I had received from Lionel he had written that his father had recently and surprisingly remarried after many years as a widower. He had however omitted to tell me who his father had married. I felt at once hot and cold and unable to breathe. I wished I was already on the train to France. She had the type of looks that made every other woman in the room appear a poor second. She crossed the room to stand next to Arthur, tilting her head up towards him as she spoke. She was wearing a simple, yet elegant dress. Her hair was swept up and pearl earrings glowed in her ears.

Evelyn was still talking, but I found myself straining to hear the conversation between Arthur and his new wife. Tristan noticed my disorientation.

'I forgot you've not met our new stepmother,' he said, *sotto voce*. 'Father married her at the end of last year. The whole business was transacted very suddenly. He went off to inspect the factories and came back with Constance. All very mysterious. She's a good sort, though.'

Evelyn sniffed. Constance P_ had of course had the advantage of being forewarned of my arrival. She greeted me composedly with a charming smile although her hand shook slightly and I detected a wary look in her eyes. She apologised for having kept everyone waiting. A small drama in the kitchen where Cook was missing one of the pies she had baked yesterday.

'Is she sure it's missing? She's not the most reliable . . . ' Mortimer began.

'I swear she can't see beyond the end of her nose,' commented Evelyn, 'there was a piece of bone in the broth yesterday.'

'Winifred has been with us for years,' said Arthur firmly. 'She may be a little old and slower. But that is all the more reason to look after her.'

'As you can see, our father is still championing his charitable causes,' drawled Mortimer with an unpleasant smile at Constance. 'And where is the indispensable Clarissa this evening?' he continued.

'She'll be buried in her old books and have forgotten the time again!' laughed Evelyn, with a toss of her head. 'Another one of dear Arthur's waifs and strays.' She smiled at me as she spoke as if it were an old joke that we shared. 'He calls her his assistant, but he doesn't really need one. Mortimer sees to everything now. I suppose it makes her feel useful.'

Just then, the drawing door opened and a small dark haired young woman sidled in.

'There you are,' said Mortimer quite impatiently, given that the clock on the wall above the fireplace was only showing a few minutes after seven.

'I'm so sorry,' she said. 'I lost track of time.'

'Don't scold the girl,' admonished Tristan. 'You're not late, Clarissa. Constance has only just joined us too.'

The girl merely nodded when introduced and stayed standing by the door, half in shadow.

'Shall we go in?' Constance asked. She swept gracefully from the room, leaving a faint, familiar trace of tuberose.

Percival did not join us for dinner, but no-one commented so I assumed his absence was not unusual. Mercifully, the Major busied himself with his food, sparing us his views on the Nivelle offensive and the French management of the war. Mortimer was full of talk about business opportunities, trying to persuade his father that the best and most lucrative of these were to be had in America. This was clearly an old conversation and I got the impression that Arthur was immovable in his opinion. Constance and Evelyn spoke of a fundraiser for the Red Cross hospital. Tristan and Eustace Overbury engaged in an enthusiastic discussion about the relative merits of lavender or ceanothus for attracting bees. Tristan had grand plans for the regeneration of the gardens. Clarissa rarely spoke and I suspected this was due to her position in the hierarchy of the household rather than a lack of conversation. She was not strictly beautiful but had an intelligent face and watchful eyes. I fear I did not earn my keep as a conversationalist that evening.

I had become accustomed to bad dreams. The faces of the men I had lost visited me nightly. But that night my rest was disturbed by visions of a woman. She was laughing at me. Cold, mocking. I woke sweating. I lay in a tangle of sheets watching the light creep along the top of the curtains, disorientated by the silence and the absence of pre-dawn activity. Eventually, needing to be active, I dressed and headed downstairs, passing through the familiar corridors to the kitchen and out of the back door. The grounds were dreary in the half-light. The rose garden had given way to vegetables. The borders of the flower beds were straggly and unloved. I followed a set of tracks across the damp grass towards the tennis courts. There was no-one around.

I carried on past the pavilion, across virgin grass down towards the lake, towards the bench, where I sat a while. I had not been there long when I heard someone moving behind me. The low morning sun was burning through the cloud and dazzled my eyes as I turned and saw a man walking towards me. His silhouette was familiar. His face was strangely smooth and unmoving as he greeted me.

'You weren't at dinner last night.' I commented, trivially.

'I prefer to eat alone.' He gestured to the mask which covered half his face. 'The surgeons did their best but slurping through a straw is best done in private.'

'I can't imagine,' I began.

'I'm sure you've seen worse. I should be grateful I suppose. To be alive. I didn't plan on coming back. I got as far as the railway station after I was discharged from the hospital in Boulogne. I could almost see home. But then I lost my nerve. It seemed appropriate, somehow, to stay closer to the war. Father came looking for me. Found me floundering in laudanum and brandy. Insisted I come back with him. Got me the best doctors. You know how he is, always trying to put things right.'

'It's very good,' I said, meaning the painted likeness.

'It's not so bad here,' he remarked. 'Now that the old place is full of other relics.'

'Arthur seems well.' I commented. 'He hasn't really changed at all.'

'Apart from saddling himself with a wife young enough to be his daughter you mean!'

'It does seem a little out of character.'

'Not really,' said Percival. 'You know Arthur. He can't resist a big chivalrous gesture. He hasn't said much, but she will turn out to be the orphan goddaughter of an old friend who once saved his life or similar. And she'll have got herself into some sort of trouble, money, an unsuitable man or some such thing. He might be old but he can't have failed to notice how exceptionally beautiful she is!'

So, that was how it was. We sat in silence.

'I met Evelyn,' I offered.

'That was a mistake,' Percival said. 'I met her in the summer of '14. I'd only known her a few months when I joined up. When I realised how badly messed up I was I wrote calling it off. But she seems determined that nothing has changed. A terrible coincidence, her being a nurse here.'

'She seems dedicated.' I observed.

'Father encourages her,' he said. 'I can't see why she stays. It's certainly not for love and not for pity.'

'It's good to see you again,' he said. 'I'll be on my way, my morning constitutional.' I think he smiled behind his new tin face as he walked away.

Suddenly hungry for breakfast I headed back to the house. As I was retracing my steps towards the tennis courts I saw a slight figure in a dark dress flitting away from the pavilion and hurrying towards the house. I headed along the side of the house towards the kitchen and the back door, hoping to enter as unobtrusively as I had left earlier. As I was passing the study I heard Arthur say heatedly,

'You're asking too much. I can't help.'

In all the years I had known him I had never heard Arthur raise his voice. Nor had I ever heard him refuse a plea for help. Perhaps the grief and stress of the last few years was taking its toll. I felt profoundly uncomfortable, no matter that my eavesdropping was quite unintentional.

The Major was the only member of the household still at breakfast. He had some important War Office business with the local tribunal in town that morning, he told me. No doubt looking to snatch a few more men to be squandered by High Command. I lost my appetite again and went in search of more congenial company. The rest of the party had converged in the hall. Constance looked on edge as if she had been crying. Even with reddened eyes she was still beautiful. She was wearing a particularly flattering dress of royal blue.

'I can't remember,' she was saying. 'I'm sure I had them on Monday but they weren't there last night when I looked for them just before dinner. I wore my pearls instead. I've looked everywhere!'

'Those were our mother's.' Tristan was aggrieved.

'I'm always so careful.' Constance sounded defensive.

Clarissa appeared from the direction of the kitchens. Her hair was untidy and her cheeks were glowing.

'What's happened?' she asked.

'Constance has lost our mother's diamond earrings,' answered Mortimer.

'Oh, my dear, how dreadful you must feel,' said Evelyn. 'I would help you look, but I have some important errands in town for Sister Milton. Perhaps Clarissa might help you instead,' she suggested with a little smile. 'She's always so terribly good at being helpful.'

Clarissa flushed.

'I'd be happy to help.'

'Of course, Evelyn. Thank you. We mustn't keep you from your work.' said Arthur. He sounded distracted. 'In fact, Clarissa, you are just the person I wanted to see. I've some business to settle with Eustace just now and I'll need some help with some correspondence later.'

'Of course.'

'And I'm expecting an important letter. Please bring it straight to me when the post gets here.'

Arthur and Eustace Overbury went into the study. Arthur closed the door firmly behind them.

'I was hoping you could read with Percival later Clarissa, if you're not too busy?' asked Evelyn sweetly as she buttoned her cape. 'His eyes get tired so easily.'

'And which shall I do first?' muttered Clarissa.

Constance went upstairs and Mortimer headed for the dining room.

'I'll look in on Percival later,' offered Tristan.

I headed for the library across the hall, hoping that the bad-tempered undercurrents would not follow me there. The library at least had not changed. The old furniture, the familiar smell of dust and woodfire. I sat at the small table by the window overlooking the gardens. Men muffled in bandages and heavy overcoats were walking up and down the front lawn, closely chaperoned by nurses. I picked up the newspaper and idled through its pages.

A little later, I'm not sure how much later, my sanctuary was disturbed by Clarissa, who had clearly finished being useful for the time being. She looked displeased to find me there but said nothing. She settled herself at a table and busied herself with a pile of books and papers. Not long after the library clock had chimed the hour, I fancied I heard the post boy. I looked over at Clarissa, but she was completely consumed by whatever she was reading. I suppose I sympathised with the dependent position in which she found herself, which might explain why I stirred myself and went and checked the hall for the post. The other, more plausible explanation was that I was simply ill at ease and restless. My visit to the Grange was not proving to be the tonic I had hoped it would be. My reconnoitring revealed a brown paper parcel for Tristan, a postcard with a painting of a famous college beside a river (addressed to Clarissa) and three letters with typewritten addresses. One, on that brown paper favoured by H.M. Government, was addressed to Mortimer. Likewise, the thick packet of papers (from Messrs Chadwick Hoskins, N.C.). The other, addressed to Arthur, was franked by London County and Westminster Bank. I placed them on the console table to the right of the library door and returned to the library.

Moments later, I looked up, hearing hurried footsteps in the hall. I watched Mortimer shrug his way into his grey overcoat and adjust his hat in front of the mirror beside the study door. His appearance was obviously not to his satisfaction as he spent an inordinate amount of time lingering there, buckling his belt, adjusting his lapels and the dip of his hat. No doubt the business was running itself this morning. Eventually, he turned away from the mirror and towards the console table. He put his hand into the pocket of his overcoat. I watched as the mirror reflected the back of his neck flush an angry red as he pulled a pale feather from his pocket. I looked over at Clarissa. She was watching Mortimer, a smile playing across her face.

The front door banged. Mortimer had gone.

'Post's here,' I said to Clarissa.

She gave me an altogether unpleasant look and swished into the hall. There was a smear of mud on one of the heels of her boots. I wondered what had taken her outside so early in the morning. Bored by the paper and unable to settle I decided to go and look for Tristan who could at least be relied upon for uncomplicated conversation. I found him on his hands and knees in front of a flower bed. Constance was with him. She looked agitated. There was dust on the arm of her coat and the dew from the grass had stained her shoes.

'It's the only explanation,' she said. 'I haven't lost them. Look,' she pointed to footprints in the soil. 'It must have been a burglar. Climbed through the window. Arthur must have forgotten to lock it.' Her voice wobbled and rose, sounding panicky. 'I don't like it.'

She paced back and forth in front of the window. She started as a flock of birds rose from the woods down towards the lake and circled overhead their wings thrumming in the morning air.

'What if they come back?'

She shivered. I leaned over to look. Tristan gently lifted the crushed leaves from the mud.

'This one is completely destroyed,' he said. 'Although I think the rest can be saved, with a little care.'

For my part I thought that perhaps he should be more concerned about why someone might be loitering in the flower beds outside the study than the collateral trampling of the plants. He sat back on his heels and reached for his walking stick, manoeuvring himself awkwardly upright.

'Do you know,' he continued, 'we grew cornflowers and wild narcissi in France. And poppies and potatoes and celery. It's wonderful what will grow with a little encouragement.'

I nodded. I'd seen trench gardens and I could understand the need to hold on to beauty.

'Give a plant food and water and light,' he said. 'And it will flourish. So much less disappointing than people.'

Constance went back into the house. I was not sure that I was entirely convinced by her assertion that the prints in the flower bed had been made by a burglar. Nothing apart from the earrings had been reported missing. The footprints looked to me to have been made by someone with daintier feet than I would have expected of a burglar and there was a slight imprint of a small heel. Yet Constance had seemed most particularly agitated. Of course, it was really not my affair. She had a husband and new family to look out for her. However, I felt it behoved me to check the house and the outbuildings in case. I would at least have done the decent thing. A circuit of the house revealed nothing suspicious, no broken windows or tampering with locks and no footprints outside any windows apart from the study. Similarly, the outbuildings looked undisturbed.

As I was crossing the lawn I spotted Tristan returning from his hives in the orchard. I waved and called to him, but he didn't hear me. He carried on walking towards the house. Although, it then occurred to me somewhat uncharitably, that perhaps he had seen me because when I turned around, I was surprised to see Evelyn had appeared behind me. It was not inconceivable that Tristan had no desire for a tête-à-tête with his brother's aspiring fiancée. For me, there was no escaping the encounter. She greeted me with a smile. Where was I going, perhaps she would join me. Such a lovely day for a walk. She was a great walker, she indicated to her muddy boots. The fresh air lifts the spirits immeasurably. She always recommended it for her patients.

'Although,' she said archly, 'it makes a quite a change to have an active man amongst us.'

She carried on talking as we entered the grove of trees beyond the tennis courts, bordering the lake. She did so love the spring flowers. They were so beautiful. She always felt so hopeful at this time of year. There was a particularly lovely aspect, I simply must see it, she would show me. I forbore to point out that I had spent years roaming the grounds as a boy with Lionel and Percival and almost certainly knew them better than she did.

I had thought I was no longer capable of being shocked by violent death. Perhaps it was the setting. The silence, the carpet of primroses and the unsullied greenness of the grass on which the ruins of a man in a grey overcoat were laid. His right arm was flung out to the side, his fingers clasped around a revolver on the ground. His face had taken the force of the blast. He was unrecognisable. Evelyn stopped talking.

'Oh!' Evelyn staggered against me and clutched at my arm. 'Oh! How horrible!'

'Don't look,' I said, trying to turn her around. 'Don't look.'

'Mortimer,' she said. 'It's Mortimer! Why would he do this?' She clutched at me harder. 'Why would Mortimer want to kill himself?'

'Come away.' I half dragged her, half carried her away. 'Can you make it back to the house?' I asked. 'We need to telephone for the police.'

I had hoped to speak privately to Arthur, but Evelyn began shrieking and screaming as soon as we reached the house. I left her in the capable hands of one of the VADs. I seconded a couple of orderlies and a stretcher. Then the Major and Eustace Overbury took charge, dealing with doctors and police and whatever else needed to be done.

Arthur insisted on going to the copse himself. Major Hobson and Eustace Overbury accompanied us. To spare Arthur's pain I made sure to reach the body first. Mortimer's overcoat was unbuttoned, so I folded it across his ruined face while we waited for the police. I slipped the feather from the coat pocket into my sleeve. The grove was hushed and still as if holding its breath. There was no birdsong, no sign of life. Arthur refused to return to the house, to leave Mortimer there alone.

He seemed to diminish physically as we waited, until he was a shrunken, old man.

The police did not keep us waiting long. After they had viewed the scene and examined the body, Arthur was allowed to take his son home. The orderlies covered the body with a blanket and lifted it gently onto the stretcher. I took Arthur's arm to support him as our sorry procession returned to the house. I let the feather fall behind us as we walked. Later I sat with Arthur in his study.

'It's a terrible thing,' he said, 'to outlive your sons.'

The police did not intrude for long. Their superintendent was married to Eustace Overbury's sister and as a consequence Eustace was taken into his confidence. Out of consideration for Arthur, who was well known and respected in the community, the affair would be handled discretely and sensitively. The police spoke to us all in turn. A formality, we were assured. Not one of us could think of anyone who might want to harm Mortimer. And none of us had any reason to think that Mortimer was unstable.

After the police had gone, we left the family in peace. Eustace, Major Hobson, Clarissa and I convened in the library. Eustace relayed what he had learned from the police.

It transpired that I was the last person to have seen Mortimer that morning, in the hall, just after the post was delivered shortly after ten. This was confirmed by Clarissa. No-one had seen him after he left the house and his secretary confirmed he had not arrived at the office. As to our whereabouts that morning, I had been in the library (also confirmed by Clarissa) and later I had gone outside where I had seen Constance and Tristan (confirmed by both Constance and Tristan). I had then gone for a walk around the gardens. The sun was high in the sky for the time of year so it must have been around midday. I was unable to be more precise because I do not wear a wristwatch. I had not been walking long when I encountered Evelyn.

Evelyn, by her own account, had walked into town on an errand and was on her way back to the house when she met me. She had been with me when we found the body. We had returned to the house to raise the alarm and seek relief for Evelyn, who was becoming hysterical. Eustace had telephoned the police. The call was placed at twenty-three minutes past one. Then I had returned to the grove, accompanied by Arthur, Eustace Overbury and Major Hobson.

Constance had been in the house searching for a pair of earrings which she now believed had been stolen. Then she had gone for a walk, down past the tennis courts to the lake. There was a bench there she liked to sit on. Tristan could vouch for her. She had waved to him as he was returning from the orchard. Tristan, however, could not confirm her account. He had not been to his hives that day because when he went to the boot room this morning his beekeeping suit was missing. It was really very frustrating. He could not think who might have moved it or why they might have done so. Perhaps Constance had been mistaken. Or confused the days. She was upset after all, by the theft of the earrings. They had belonged to Arthur's first wife and she feared that Arthur's sons might resent the fact that he had given them to her. She was frightened that the burglars might return.

The gun belonged to Percival. He had kept it as a souvenir. He had no idea it was missing; he had not had it out for a while. No-one had seen Percival since the early morning, but that was not unusual as he liked to go for long hikes and would often be out all day. He'd walked as far as Thorpe Magna. No, nobody could confirm that, for obvious reasons he tended to try and avoid crowds these days. He had returned to the house at around eleven o'clock and had been resting in his room when the alarm was raised.

Arthur and Eustace Overbury had been in the study since after breakfast. They were going over Arthur's affairs. He was making a new will. He had recently married and wished to provide for his wife in the event of his death. A small endowment, but the principal beneficiaries were still his sons. Since Lionel's death, Percival was the eldest surviving son and certain adjustments needed to be made to the will to reflect that.

The Major was the one person who might have had an insight into a possible motive for Mortimer's drastic act. He recounted that Mortimer had received his call up papers that morning. However, he could not believe that he had chosen such a shocking course, rather than doing his duty to King and Country. Scandalous, when one considered what upstanding and patriotic men his brothers were. He wondered how Arthur could reconcile such a disappointment in a son. He himself had been in a tribunal meeting in town, returning shortly before one o'clock.

Reluctantly, Eustace Overbury revealed that he feared there had been some irregularities in the management of the business. Large sums of money were missing from the reserve funds. He and Arthur had been looking into the matter. Arthur had said nothing of any of this to the police. Eustace also noted that Arthur had been very anxious to receive a letter from his bank that morning, but the letter had not arrived. Clarissa could confirm that there was no letter from the bank when she collected the post.

Eustace confided that the police were not inclined to treat the death as suspicious, although they were not prepared to offer any particular theory as to why Mortimer might have wanted to end his life. It had most likely been a tragic accident. As we listened Clarissa grew visibly upset. She looked fearful and agitated, her fingers fretting at her handkerchief.

'Was it my fault?' she asked. 'I never meant for this to happen. I just wanted to upset him. He's always so beastly, talking about how this country is finished. How the future is in America. How could he say those things after what happened to Lionel and Percival? He seemed to think he was untouchable.'

'What did you do?' I asked, although I suspected I already knew. The trick with the feather.

'I wasn't to know,' she said, 'that he had actually been called up. I never would have done it. And now he's dead. And it's my fault!'

I reassured her that I would be extremely surprised if Mortimer had paid any real heed. He might have been angered and humiliated by the petty act, but to take it seriously would have run counter to his sense of his own worth and his instinct for self-preservation. The more I thought about it I found it hard to imagine Mortimer taking his own life. The Mortimer I knew would simply disappear, rather than face the music. He wouldn't kill himself. But unpleasant as he undoubtedly was, who would want to kill him? And why? Did it have anything to do with Constance's burglar? And why had Tristan lied about visiting his hives?

It occurred to me that I had seen Clarissa near the tennis pavilion early that morning and that was the one place I had not checked for signs of break-in earlier in the day. By her own admission Constance had also been nearby later in the day. I couldn't think what they might be doing there at this time of year. I left the others in the library and went to investigate while it was still light.

The pavilion was dusty and smelt slightly of damp. But on the bench at the side, I spotted a tin cup and an ewer of clean water. A plate and cutlery. The mystery of what had happened to the pie that Cook was assumed to have mislaid was solved. There was an Army blanket neatly folded and a pile of books. It looked as if someone was living there.

Clarissa appeared in the doorway behind me.

'He had nowhere to go,' she said. 'No-one ever comes down here. I didn't see the harm.'

'Who is he?' I asked.

'An old friend,' she said. 'I knew him from Cambridge, from before. We sang in a choir together. Before he was called up and I had to leave. He wasn't well', she said. 'He had nowhere to stay.'

If that were the case, perhaps he might be better in a hospital, I suggested, rather than camping in a damp tennis pavilion.

'No, he said he just needed somewhere where he could be quiet. He wasn't well,' she said again. 'He was,' and she paused, choosing her words, 'fragile.' She became evasive and I wondered whether her friend had parted company from the armed forces on entirely mutually satisfactory terms.

'Is it really awful out there?' she asked suddenly. 'No-one ever talks about it and I don't believe what I read in the newspapers. Apart from the casualty lists.'

I didn't know how to answer her.

'I'm sorry,' she said. 'I don't mean to be tactless. I know you're going back. You probably don't want to talk about it.'

She was right. I didn't want to talk about it, but I was strangely touched by her wanting to know. I had the sense that she might actually understand.

'Where is he now?'

'I don't know! I came to warn him to go away. What with Mortimer and the police and everything.'

'He's gone!' Constance appeared in the doorway behind us.

'You knew he was here?' accused Clarissa.

'Of course.'

'Gone where? He didn't tell me he was going.'

'He's safe.'

'But where has he gone?' asked Clarissa? 'Tell me!'

'I don't know. But he said he would send word. When he was settled.'

'Why would he tell you?'

'He's my brother.'

Clarissa looked winded. 'I don't understand,' she said, 'he had no money and no-where to go. If he's your brother, why didn't you just invite him to stay? And why didn't you just ask Arthur to help find him work?'

'I think you know why, Clarissa. Thank you for helping him.'

'Well!' Clarissa scooped up the books. 'I'll take these back to the house,' she huffed.

'You might return the crockery to Cook as well,' said Constance.

Clarissa looked dejected as she walked away.

'Poor Clarissa,' said Constance. 'I think she was enjoying having a secret friend.'

We were alone. We stood in silence. I looked steadily at her, re-committing the shape of her face to memory. She had tiny new lines at the corner of her eyes. She looked at me defiantly.

'I had to get him away from here. I was worried that he might be suspected of killing Mortimer.'

'You don't think that it was suicide, then?' I asked.

'A bit out of character, don't you think? If it were Percival, I might believe it.'

I could see that it did not look good for her brother. A desperate man might kill if he felt he had no other options. Or steal. Or even if he was innocent, such a man might be suspected of doing those things.

'Arthur refused to help him. I suppose I can't blame him,' she said. 'A coward and a deserter. And Arthur's sons are war heroes.'

'Did you really lose those earrings?' I asked.

'You have to promise me!' Constance caught hold of my arm. 'You have to promise you won't say anything. Arthur doesn't know he was here.' There were tears in her eyes. 'Please,' she begged. 'He's not well. They'll execute him if they find him.'

I could never bear to see her cry.

Naturally, it was a subdued gathering that evening. We were all feeling the after-effects of the earlier tragedy. No-one had any appetite for dinner. Eustace, Major Hobson and I attempted a little half-hearted conversation. Tristan was preoccupied and uncharacteristically terse. Evelyn appeared to have recovered from her earlier nervous shock but was still looking a little feverish. She was most attentive to Arthur, procuring and ordering such treats and restoratives as she thought might tempt him as if she were mistress of the house in place of Constance. She poured coffee for the rest of us and Clarissa carried round the cups. Arthur and I drank brandy. He spoke little. His suffering was painfully evident. His voice was hoarse and he took long shuddering breaths.

Constance sat quietly beside him. Every so often, she would reach over to him, touch his hand or his shoulder, reminding him she was there, in case he needed her. I saw to my surprise that she truly cared for him. She was watching Tristan with a hurt expression on her face. I guessed that she had thought that Tristan was one of her allies within the family. Clarissa said little, but I caught her looking resentfully at Constance once or twice. Even Percival made an appearance in the drawing room after dinner, leaning on Evelyn's arm. She settled him in the corner opposite the fire, adjusting the lamp and fussing about draughts.

Arthur retired early. The rest of us followed suit. I had a headache. These were commonplace since my injury and I reluctantly resorted to the powders that the doctors had given me. Although the pain wore off, rest would not come. I found myself replaying the events of the day, over and over. Was there something I could have done to prevent Mortimer's death, was there something I had missed? I must have slept eventually because I dreamed Lionel was sitting on the end of my bed in his cricket whites. He was excited and flushed as he described the perfect overs with which he had despatched St Anthony's First Eleven. Lionel was replaced by a man with no face looming over me. I cried out, but no-one could hear me. And then the face started to scream. And scream.

I woke sweating, my heart was a barrage in my chest. A woman was screaming. I flung open my bedroom door. The door to Arthur's dressing room was open and light was streaming out onto the landing. I rushed in. Constance was kneeling on the floor next to Arthur. He was unconscious. His breathing was laboured and his face and neck were swollen.

'Help! Someone help! Please! Get the doctor!'

'What's happened?' Eustace, the Major and Clarissa appeared behind me.

'I thought I heard a noise,' Constance sobbed, 'and when I came in, I found him like this.'

'Help him please, he can't die.'

I could hear the dependable Eustace on the telephone in the hall, asking for the doctor. It was an emergency, as quickly as he could please.

'Go fetch Evelyn,' I said to Clarissa. 'She might be able to help until the doctor gets here.'

Clarissa darted down the stairs and towards the hospital wing. Tristan appeared next. He had dark circles under his eyes and looked as if he had spent a restless night like my own. His limp was more pronounced than ever and he leaned heavily on his stick. He sank awkwardly to his knees beside his father.

'The doctor is on his way.' Eustace spoke calmly to Constance and Tristan.

Arthur coughed and convulsed. Constance wept harder.

'What's this?'

Major Hobson took a handkerchief from his dressing gown pocket. He leaned over and picked up something from under the collar of Arthur's pyjamas. He held out the handkerchief for us all to see. In the middle of the folds was a bee.

Tristan blanched.

'Do you think he's been stung?' Constance said. 'How did it get in here?'

'Was he allergic to bees?' I asked.

'No. I'm sure he wasn't. Do you think he would have bought them for me if he was?' Tristan sounded uncertain.

'I am,' said Constance shakily.

Clarissa reappeared, looking panicked. 'I can't find her,' she said. 'No-one has seen her. Her room's empty.'

By the time the doctor arrived, it was too late. Arthur was dead. The doctor conducted a brief examination. He would know more in the morning, but his initial finding was that Arthur had died of anaphylaxis. There was a small puncture wound on his neck and coupled with the swelling and the blueish tinge to his lips, a bee sting was the most likely cause. For the second time in less than twenty-four hours a body left the Grange. Constance was distraught. The doctor prescribed a sleeping draught. Clarissa helped her back to her bedroom and sat with her until she slept.

Tristan and I waited out the rest of the night sat in Arthur's study. We drank brandy and told each other stories, our remembrances of Arthur. We agreed to wait until morning, before we broke the news to Percival that his father had died and his fiancé was missing. Clarissa joined us just before dawn.

'He was so kind to me,' she said. 'I can't believe he's gone. I think I'll feel a little better if I can sit in here.'

Her dark hair was coiled loosely over her shoulder and her pale face was wet with tears. She went to sit at Arthur's desk.

'What's this?'

There was a letter addressed to Arthur on the blotter. Tristan tore it open. Evelyn regretted that she been called away on urgent family business, she was sorry she had not been able to wait until morning to say goodbye. She would send for her belongings in due course, when her plans were fixed.

'Can't say I'll miss her'.

Whilst Evelyn's precipitate departure might come as a relief, the timing was, to my mind, highly suspicious.

There was no answer when Tristan and I knocked on Percival's door a little later, Clarissa trailing anxiously behind us. The room was bare, monastic even, as if it had been emptied of all trace of Percival. The bed had not been slept in.

'Whatever has happened here?' Tristan looked shocked. 'It's usually such a mess.'

Apart from some charred fragments of paper in the grate there was nothing to suggest the room had been lived in.

'Look at this!' Clarissa lifted a scrap of paper from the grate. I could just make out *Westmin.*

'Was this the letter Arthur had been waiting for?' she asked. 'I know you saw it and it wasn't there when I went to fetch the post. I thought you'd taken it.'

'Why would I do such a thing?'

'I don't know, I just know there's something odd going on. Constance feels it too. She said something strange last night.' She paused, watching us both. 'She asked if I thought the bee was meant for her.'

'She was overwrought.'

'Maybe. But there is something. I know it. I just don't know who to trust.' She paced the room. 'Why would Percival take the letter? And why would he burn it? It doesn't make sense.'

'No,' I said slowly, 'it doesn't.'

'Wait here,' I said. I had just remembered the other letters that had been delivered yesterday morning. What had happened to Mortimer's call up papers and the packet from America? I was sure that I had seen him put them in his coat pocket, but they were not in there when we found the body. I hurried to Mortimer's room at the other end of the corridor. The call up papers were on his desk. The envelope with the American stamp was torn in half in the wastepaper basket. There was no sign of the contents. The only explanation was that Mortimer must have returned to the house yesterday after I saw him leave and before we found his body. Something was off, but I could not quite pin it down. I returned to Percival's room. The wardrobe door was open.

'Percival's clothes are missing,' Clarissa said.

'Why would he leave?' asked Tristan. 'Where would he go?'

We looked at each other. It did not make sense. After cloistering himself away since his injuries, why would Percival suddenly leave the safety of the Grange? I recalled his words from yesterday morning, 'It's not so bad here, now that the old place is full of other relics.'

'You can't think he killed Mortimer?' Only Clarissa was brave enough to say what we were all thinking.

'No.' I said, 'he didn't.' It was worse than that.

Wordlessly, I pointed to the bottom of the wardrobe. In the corner lay a tin mask, a painted copy of Percival's face. And under the bed was Tristan's bee-keeper's hat and veil.

It was impossible. Incredible. But the more I thought on it, the more I saw how it might have been managed. But the why of it? They say that a leopard never changes its spots. And thus it was with Mortimer. He was, as Clarissa had said, untouchable. He always did manage to side-step anything unpleasant or harmful to himself. From Eustace Overbury's testimony and Arthur's reticence to confirm the same to the police, it was clear that Mortimer was behind the money missing from the company. Despite Arthur's objections, he had gone ahead, diverted capital into investments in America. He no doubt thought he could bring Arthur round, in time. But his time ran out. His call up papers meant that he had to act quickly. If he did not join up, the Army would come looking for him. But if he did go, his fraud would have been discovered and he would have had to relinquish his grand American future. So, he had to disappear. And what better way to do that than to be seen to have died. Then conceal himself behind the tin mask of a respected veteran until such time as he had established an alibi and could leave without suspicion. Did he persuade himself that Percival had nothing left to live for, that he might be grateful for an end to his pain?

Percival himself had foreseen Evelyn's motive. She had not stayed for love, or pity, but plain old-fashioned greed. I knew what Percival must have done; I had done the same. His last will and testament, naming his fiancée as his sole heir. I remembered writing my own will in the early days of war. Not that I had much to leave, but at the time it had comforted me to know that the woman I loved would know that I had died loving her still, even though she no longer loved me.

And who better to busy herself with a patient's belongings than a devoted nurse? Evelyn must have found the will in his pocketbook. Then, when Lionel died, Percival was next in line to inherit the Grange. So Evelyn persisted, selflessly refusing Percival's offer to release her from their engagement. I wondered how long after their marriage Percival might have been likely to succumb to a sudden illness, leaving Evelyn mistress of the Grange.

But no one had foreseen that Arthur would remarry. Especially not to a much younger woman who could be expected to outlive him and for whom, naturally, he would want to make financial provision. Arthur had to die before the changes to the terms of his will could be finalised.

We will never know at what point Mortimer and Evelyn realised their interests aligned, when they made their deadly bargain. A brother's life, so that another might reinvent himself. And with Percival dead,

Mortimer was the oldest living son. For Evelyn, her future was assured. It was a simple case of swapping one brother for the other.

And, as for the 'how' of it?

Between the two of them, Mortimer and Evelyn must have monitored the conversation between Arthur and Eustace in the study. Had it been Evelyn, crouched under the window, crushing Tristan's spring bulbs? And then those useful footprints had been seized upon by Constance, to explain the disappearance of the earrings as the result of a burglary. And Mortimer lingered over long in front of the mirror by the study door, not out of vanity, but listening to learn how much of his fraud had been uncovered.

Percival's morning routine was well established. A walk around the lake, across the downs to the next village and back through the woods. Mortimer had simply to lie in wait and shoot Percival on his return from his walk, making sure to destroy his face. The two brothers were of a similar size and build, so Mortimer's clothes did not look out of place on Percival's body. It was audacious and not without risk. No-one had heard the gunshot, but Arthur was known to turn a blind eye to occasional poaching on his land. There were no groundsman or gardeners. The recuperating soldiers kept to the front lawn. Tristan's bees were in the orchard and his flower beds were close to the house. I doubted whether Mortimer or Evelyn knew about the man Clarissa and Constance were sheltering in the pavilion. They were fortunate. I did not like to think on what might have happened had either of them seen or heard anything.

In fact, I was the only wild card, my movements not part of the regular tapestry of life at the Grange. And I played my part. I walked right into their scheme, allowing Evelyn to lead me to the convenient discovery of the body which she instantly identified as that of Mortimer. The immediate suggestion that the death was a suicide had also come from Evelyn. Of course, if it had been staged as the murder it truly was, the police would have conducted a more thorough investigation.

Therefore, despite the damage to the family name and reputation, it had to be seen to be a suicide.

It puzzled me at first as to how Mortimer was able to return to the house without anyone seeing him, bearing in mind we had most of us been in the garden at some point that morning. Until I recalled a detail that had snagged in my subconscious. Both Constance and I were sure we had seen Tristan returning from ministering to his bees. But we had only seen him from a distance and he had not stopped to greet either of us. And that was when I remembered. The figure in the beekeeping clothes had not walked with a limp. Tristan had been telling the truth.

Once the switch was made, 'Percival' was back in his rooms after his morning walk. Along with the rest of us, he was interviewed by the police, who did not know him personally. He then had to overcome a greater test, to appear as 'Percival' before his family. He had not spoken beyond a murmured greeting. And Evelyn had ensured that he sat in shadow with the light behind him. Mortimer left the Grange as a reincarnation of Percival, taking with him Percival's belongings and the contracts which would assure his post war future in America. His own face was unblemished, so he had no need of Percival's mask. It must be assumed that he also took Percival's fiancée with him.

Later that night, the final part of Mortimer and Evelyn's devious plan was put into operation and Tristan's bees were to be blamed as the unwitting architect of Arthur's death. This time I believed that it must have been Evelyn who dealt the fatal blow, Evelyn with her nursing experience and access to the hospital dispensary, Evelyn who moved freely between the hospital and the family quarters. How easy would it have been to offer Arthur a drink of something to ease his distress, or to slip a sedative into his coffee, to ensure he was sluggish and tired? And then how simple to administer a prick of a syringe whilst he slept? Planting the bee was a masterstroke of misdirection. There was no need to look any further to explain Arthur's death.

Later that day, my leave was up. I reported for duty and returned to the front. I confess I felt a certain relief to be back. At least there the rules were clear. Although indiscriminate, death in war was at least honest. You knew that the person trying to kill you was in a trench just across the shattered landscape. I stowed away the events of the previous few days. There was no time for introspection, all was action and reaction. For myself, I neither cared whether I lived or died. I only knew that there was nothing left for me in England. I was reckless, volunteering for all manner of desperate and dangerous assignments. But fate had not marked me for death. I survived the rest of the war without a scratch. After I was demobbed I returned only briefly, to retrieve such items of personal value as were waiting for me. I took passage on a ship bound for Africa, where I was persuaded that an ex-soldier of middling years and limited ambition might eke out a living.

Eustace Overbury and Major Hobson proved to be staunch friends to Arthur in death as in life. I never heard the slightest suggestion of any scandal. They must have smoothed over any awkward questions or suspicions. The sudden death of Arthur P_ was attributed to an unfortunate accident. An extreme but plausible reaction to a bee sting. And his son Mortimer was tragically killed by persons unknown. There had been sightings of a suspicious stranger on the grounds, some earrings had gone missing and the family suspected burglary. Even the unwanted guest in the tennis pavilion unwittingly played his part, becoming a suspect, allowing Mortimer's death to appear other than as a suicide, for the sake of Arthur's widow and remaining son. The authorities never apprehended anyone.

I read the obituaries. I do not know whether it was apathy, or a sense of obligation, of respect for what the family had once been to me, but I have never spoken of the truth of the events all those years ago at the Grange. Apart from once, with my wife and after we wed, we vowed never to speak of the past again. But now I am the last left alive and I find myself compelled to reveal the full story of what happened. I have set it down in these pages, to be opened after my death.

We never completely severed our links with the past. We kept up through newspapers and journals, delivered to our farm in Rhodesia months after the news was fresh. The Grange was sold of course, we saw the sale particulars in *Country Life* magazine. It became quite a famous school. In the photograph Tristan's gardens looked resplendent in the Spring sunshine, just like they did before the war.

Ding Dong Dell

by Arthur Bernard

'Is there anybody there? Is there anybody there?'

Miss Miriam Lazarus' voice rang out forcefully. Her eyes were closed, her expression determined. Candles flickered on the table. Along with the embers of the fire in the grate, they were the only source of light in the room. There was a scent of wood smoke infused with incense.

Around the table with her sat four fellow villagers: Colonel Mostyn, Lady Rochford, Miss Finch and Mrs. Catterson. Colonel Mostyn was old school, clipped moustache and three-piece suit. He was seeking a chinwag with an old army chum, who had long departed this earthly realm. Lady Rochford was young, slim and elegant in a green silk dress, dripping with jewels and hair neatly bobbed. Her husband had died recently leaving her a rich widow and she yearned to know how he was faring beyond the grave. Miss Finch was the village's longest-standing resident, elderly, upright and Victorian in a high-collared black lace dress. She wanted news of her sister who had passed over some twenty-five years earlier. Finally, there was Mrs. Catterson, a tiny woman who was all sensible tweeds and dogs and anxious to keep her late husband on a tight leash despite his being dead.

'Someone is coming through,' said Miriam in a clear, shrill voice. The four guests expressed their delight, respectively grunting, purring, cooing and gasping.

'Yes, someone is coming, but I don't know for whom. Who are you, new spirit? Won't you tell your name? With whom do you wish to commune? Are you here for the Colonel? Or for her Ladyship? Or for Miss Finch, perhaps? Or maybe for Mrs. Catterson?' After a pause, Miriam shook her head—the spirit would not reveal.

Then Miriam spoke again, but in a quite different voice—lower, with a weird sing-song quality.

'The *skull,* that's where you'll find what you should seek—in the garden.'

For a moment the four guests glanced at each other, bemused at this cryptic utterance. Then Mrs. Catterson rose to her feet. She put her hands to her mouth in abject horror. Visibly shaking, she started to gabble.

'But it was an accident, I tell you, with the skull, he got too excited, it wasn't meant to happen.'

The Colonel, Lady Rochford and Miss Finch all stared at her as she folded back down into her seat. Miriam remained in her trance-like state, eyes still shut, but the others stood and gathered round Mrs. Catterson.

'Are you quite all right, Mrs. Catterson?' asked Lady Rochford.

'You were babbling frightfully, you know,' said Colonel Mostyn.

'What was that about a skull?' asked Miss Finch.

'Oh nothing,' said Mrs. Catterson, looking up at them and glancing nervously from face to face, 'It was from a dream I had last night, you see. I got confused. Sometimes, I suffer with my nerves.'

'I recommend a nice cup of tea, my dear,' said Miss Finch, 'That'll set you to rights. Perhaps camomile to calm yourself down. You must have had a funny turn—my sister had one of those back in 1908.'

Miriam emerged from her trance and declared that the spirit had quit the scene and was unlikely to reappear. The four villagers expressed disappointment and departed shortly afterwards. Miriam sat down in her armchair next to the fire. Well, that hadn't been hugely satisfactory! It was far better when a spirit got in touch and had a good old natter with one of the assembled. But she couldn't conjure up spirits to order. She was a serious medium, not a showman or crank. In fact she was the best medium in the village of High Hailsham, probably the best in Kent and quite possibly the best in the entire United Kingdom. This wasn't just her own opinion, either; it was shared by Inspector Cooling of the Kent Constabulary, who had availed himself of her services on more than one occasion (two, to be precise).

Winter on the North Kent marshes is no picnic. Of course, it isn't devoid of merit—not if you like splendid isolation, big skies and bracing walks. But on the other hand there are also floods, desolation and bitter winds. In 1936, the flooding was particularly severe. That was a problem in High Hailsham, which lay on the corner of a peninsula jutting out into the Thames. It was surrounded on two sides by estuary and on the remaining side by low-lying farmland. Thankfully, the villagers were used to adversity. A resilient lot, they knew to stock up and soldier on. This particular morning was overcast but dry, so Miriam could give Akhenaten his walk. Avoiding the flooded fields, the black Labrador bounced and barked his way through apple orchards and strawberry beds and along the sea wall.

Miriam strode along after him. She marched at a fair lick and her bearing was upright. She had a tall, slim figure. She wore a cloak of green tartan, a brown felt hat and robust boots. Her hat did not quite conceal her jet-black hair; she had a sharp nose, rosebud mouth and heavily-lidded eyes that burned with intellect. Sometimes village children said she looked like a witch, to which her reply was 'Yes, but I'm a *good* witch'.

The storms of late autumn had removed the final vestiges of foliage from the trees. Everywhere was muddy and a chilly dampness pervaded the air. Although Akhenaten was enjoying himself, Miriam was looking forward to the end of the walk and a return to a warm home.

She wondered about the words uttered by the spirit at the séance. Whose spirit was it? What was that about a skull? And in whose garden was the skull to be found? Mrs. Catterson's reaction was strange too. Somehow, it seemed like the voice of guilt. . .

The final stretch of the walk was a footpath taking them back to the village via a spot called Ghastly Gash. The place didn't merit its name. It was rather pretty really, in an unobtrusive way—a grassy spur of land extending out into the estuary. Ghastly Gash had as its focal point a stone well sited on a low knoll. The well was celebrated for its magical qualities, though its fame did not extend far beyond the village. People would throw in coins for luck.

Most days, Miriam did not bother to walk up to it, but today she noticed that the grid had been removed and now lay on the ground. That was odd. Boys from the village might have done it, but they were really rather well-behaved.

Miriam walked over towards the well. The grass was long and still damp. There were faint marks on the ground where some of the grass had been flattened. She could detect an unpleasant smell as she touched the rough stone and peered over.

She looked down and gasped. There was a figure at the bottom, lifeless. A tiny body—limbs and neck grotesquely twisted—was visible under the water. But the face was above the waterline and recognisable—features distorted, dead eyes staring out ghoulishly. . .

It was Mrs. Catterson. She was dead.

Miriam stood there for some moments. She felt shaken and had to grasp the stone surrounds of the well to support her. A faint noise made her turn round. It had become misty and out of the mist came

Miss Tremaine on her bicycle. Miss Tremaine was postmistress for High Hailsham and cycled in daily from her home in a nearby hamlet.

'Good morning, Miss Lazarus.'

'Good morning, Miss Tremaine. I couldn't trouble you to stop for a minute?'

Miss Tremaine applied the brake. In her middle years, she was a symphony in brown. Hat, coat, handbag, spectacles, even her bicycle, were all of a dun hue.

'One minute only. I need to open up.' She gave a good-natured smile.

'I'm afraid I've made a terrible discovery,' said Miriam pointing into the well.

Miss Tremaine leant her bicycle against the well and peered over.

'Oh my word,' said Miss Tremaine, 'Is that—can it be—Mrs. Catterson? But she's *dead.* This is too horrible, too nightmarish. . . poor woman. . . '

'It's not a natural death,' said Miriam.

'I think you could be right. Foul play does seem rather likely.'

'But why would someone kill her?'

'Good old-fashioned hatred, pure and simple,' said Miss Tremaine, 'And in our village! But why would anyone hate Mrs. Catterson? Such a harmless soul. It's quite unbelievable. It must be an outsider, surely.'

'It's a rum do, in any event,' said Miriam. 'People in the village need to be informed.'

'That won't be a problem,' said Miss Tremaine.

There is, as we all know, a great deal of chattering in an English village, and most of it emanates from the Post Office. Quite apart from this, Miss Tremaine had the village's telephone system at her beck and call.

'I'll also get young Larry to see to her dogs,' continued Miss Tremaine, 'They could be hungry by now.'

'And I for my part will contact the police. I'll telephone to Inspector Cooling at Rochester as soon as I'm home. I know him personally.'

'Good show,' said Miss Tremaine giving a serious look before setting off on her bicycle again. Miriam's gaze followed her as she vanished into the mist.

Back home, Miriam did not even shed her coat before rifling through her address book for Inspector Cooling's telephone number.

'Inspector? Miriam Lazarus calling.'

'Ah, good morning, Miss Lazarus. What might I do for you?'

'There's just been the most terrible *murder*, here in the village. One of our most respected villagers, Mrs. Catterson. I found her dead at the bottom of a well just outside our village.'

'You're quite sure it's not an accident?'

'That would be highly improbable. An out-of-the-way well which normally has a grille over it for safety's sake?'

'And not suicide?'

'It would be a very unreliable way of committing suicide, Inspector. It looks as if her neck broke. But if she'd thrown herself down there, she couldn't guarantee that outcome. She could have easily survived—in which case she'd have been in abject agony down there.'

'All right—suicide unlikely, then. Anyway, I'll be there straight away. . . Oh, hang on one moment. . . '

Miriam waited. She could hear Cooling conferring with other men.

'Ah, I'm informed the road is flooded. You're cut off. Can't walk there either; the fields are flooded as well. It seems High Hailsham can't be reached by foot or vehicle. You're effectively an island. Don't worry. I'll procure a dingy.'

'But that'll take hours. What should I do in the meantime?'

The Inspector hesitated for a few moments before replying.

'Well, I wouldn't propose this to any other person, Miss Lazarus, but why don't you have a go at investigating yourself? You've a good reputation for helping us, after all. I daresay I'll reach your place by late afternoon at worse. If in the meantime you can garner any information about the suspects then so much the better. Just poke around a bit. But safety first. Please don't put yourself in any danger.'

'But I hardly know these people, Inspector. Being seen as eccentric, I keep myself to myself.'

'Well, perhaps that's an advantage. You'll have fewer preconceptions and prejudices. *Get* to know them.'

When the call had ended, Miriam wondered whether to be flattered or indignant. Of course it's nice to get pats on the back. Inspector Cooling was clearly grateful for her help. So he should be. Her gifts had proved invaluable in the Argyllsham will fraud case. A young man called Jonny Heligan had forged his aunt's will and presented it at the probate office. The authorities were suspicious but had no evidence. At Cooling's suggestion Miriam had convened a séance in which she had contacted the late Vera Argyllsham. Miss Argyllsham was incandescent at her nephew's crime, and had revealed where she'd hidden the true will. Thankfully Jonny thereupon confessed to the forgery, so Cooling had no need to reveal his unconventional methods in open court.

Miriam had been no less helpful in the Lily Mandrake kidnapping case. Young Lily was abducted by an unscrupulous distant relative. This man had hidden Lily, bound and gagged, in a warehouse outside Maidstone. He had then gone to collect the ransom money, but had been in such a rush that he crashed his car and died. From the outset the police had considered him to be the chief suspect. Cooling had therefore requested that Miriam contact him in the afterlife in order to establish Lily's whereabouts. The miscreant was cross at having died and missed out on the money, but he was humane enough to want to help save the girl's life, so he had revealed where she could be found.

Miriam could quite understand therefore why the Inspector would want to enlist her help. But why hadn't he simply proposed that Miriam contact the murder victim in the hereafter? It was annoying that he hadn't. Why should *she* chase around? She sighed and looked out of the window at the village green. Actually, in fairness, she was in no state at present to contact the dead—she felt agitated when she needed to feel calm. As for the Inspector, she supposed that since this was a case of murder, a capital offence, it was far more likely to end up in court. Perhaps that was why Cooling wished to keep to conventional methods. In this narrow-minded world, he'd want to avoid any prosecution becoming a laughing stock.

A laughing stock! Hadn't that been one of her father's many insults? She looked up at her wall. She'd long ago removed her father's likeness as a result of a falling-out of immense proportions. Rabbi Lazarus who presided over Rochester Synagogue had disowned her some nine years ago, around the time of the General Strike. Contacting the dead, the Rabbi insisted, was incompatible with Judaism. Miriam had disagreed, and had accused him of being dogmatic and inflexible. This difference was enough to effect a permanent rupture, and father and daughter had not spoken since.

Oh well, that couldn't be helped. She must direct her attentions to the present problem. She needed a plan of action. Her female intuition told her that the death of Mrs. Catterson must surely be linked to the séance. That would mean that the other three people who had attended would be the chief suspects. So it was clear—she must visit each of them.

Colonel Mostyn was sitting in a deckchair on his terrace—a queer sight on a winter morning. He looked exhausted.

'Good morning, Miss Lazarus. *Terrible* news about Mrs. Catterson, eh?' His voice was puffed and wheezy.

'You've heard already.'

'Yes, it's all over the village, don't y'know.'

'You know I found the body?'

'Indeed so. Must have been an appalling shock. Dashed distressing. Do take a seat.' He rose and opened up another deckchair for her.

'Never good for a village, having a murder,' he continued, 'Always ends badly. Harms the sense of community. Candidly, I'm worried for the Constitutional Club; I help run it, you know. How many villagers will want to be convivial with a murderer in their midst! Anyway, murder in the village—bad show all round.'

From her deckchair, Miriam had a fine view of the Colonel's large garden. How dug-up were his flower beds! Of course, everyone gives their garden a good old dig in the winter but Colonel Mostyn really had done a most extensive job. No wonder he needed a sit-down.

'Care for a whisky? Under the circumstances?' he asked with a wink.

'Bit early for me.'

'Yes, perhaps for me too,' he said with a sigh. 'Idiot of a doctor says I should give up drinking altogether actually. Silly old fool. Can't stand that holier-than-thou attitude.'

'Why do you suppose anyone would want to kill Mrs. Catterson?' asked Miriam.

'Haven't the foggiest. Of course, she was a batty old thing. You got a good dose of that last night. Or were you "out for the count" at the time?'

'I rarely take in what I'm saying when I'm in a trance,' said Miriam. She was being untruthful, she always remembered everything. But she wanted to hear the Colonel's account.

'Well, she stood up and shouted something about an accident with a skull that wasn't meant to happen or some such nonsense. Oh, and someone having got too excited, whatever that meant. Then she sat back down again and was quiet. Couldn't make head nor tail of it.'

'An accident with a skull and someone getting too excited? How interesting,' said Miriam. But the Colonel shook his head sadly.

'Completely dotty, if you ask me! I reckon she'd have been carted off to the funny farm had she lived.'

'But what if those words *weren't* demented? What if they meant something, to someone else around the table?'

'Well, they meant nothing to me. Utter tosh. What *you* had to say made more sense.'

'What did I say?'

'That we'd find the skull we should be seeking—in the garden.'

'I wonder what that meant.' said Miriam. 'I only receive the messages, you see. I don't always understand them.'

She looked again at the dug-up beds. The Colonel had even taken out large lumps of perennials which were lying on the neat lawn. A robin was pecking fussily around them.

'You've been very thorough,' said Miriam, gesturing towards his efforts.

'Nothing like a jolly old dig. Does wonders for the fertility and good exercise to boot.'

Miriam raised a doubting eyebrow. Colonel Mostyn hesitated then exhaled loudly.

'Truth be told, I do have an. . . erm. . . *additional* motive, so to speak. . . for the digging.'

'What's that?'

'Gold Skull of Snod.'

'Come again?'

'You've heard of King Snod surely? King of Kent? Before the unification of England and all that rot.'

'Oh yes.' Miriam vaguely remembered Snod from lessons at school.

'Well, King Snod repelled a Danish invasion on this very peninsula. To celebrate the victory and defend his realm he built a castle here. It's long gone of course, but according to my research it was sited slap bang here, on the land that makes up my house and garden. Unbelievable, eh? Anyway, Snod filled the castle with treasures. The finest of them was said to be the Gold Skull of Snod. It's a skull fashioned entirely in pure gold! Of course, it would be almost priceless on the open market.'

'And you think from the séance that you'll find it in your own garden?'

'Well, the spirit *did* refer to a skull and a garden, so it's worth a try, what?' He gave another wink.

'You've gone about it with vim, Colonel,' said Miriam, gesturing towards the well-turned beds.

The Colonel gave a sigh.

'Truth is, I'm in a hole. I've mucked up my finances badly. I invested in some rotten shares and lost an awful lot of money. Got my fingers burnt.'

'I'm sorry to hear that. Do you suppose you've enough money to make ends meet even if you don't find the Gold Skull? It's just that it sounds like rather a long shot.'

'Oh, I won't starve if that's what you mean, plus this house is bought and paid for, thank God. But it'll be genteel poverty right enough. I'll have to forgo whisky and holidays by the sea, and relinquish my London clubs.'

'That's hard,' said Miriam.

'Still, it's got nothing to do with Mrs. Catterson,' said the Colonel sharply, 'I was digging *my* garden not hers. Anyway, it must surely be an outsider who killed her.'

'Oh, I don't know. I rather think it was someone who attended the séance.'

'Why do you say that? It certainly wasn't *me*. And why should it be a respectable lady like Miss Finch or Lady Rochford?'

'Well, a *woman* has a certain intuition, Colonel. . . female insight, female instinct. It's quite a scientifically-proven thing, you know.'

'Scientifically-proven? Well, can't argue with that, I suppose,' said the Colonel uncertainly.

'Besides, I have *the gift*, remember. And although it mainly attaches to contacting the dead, it can also give me a grasp of other matters.'

'No doubt, no doubt. All the same, I don't see how you can suspect Lady Rochford. She's refined, and now a wealthy widow to boot. All in all a most engaging woman.' He twirled his moustache rakishly.

'Was she happy with Lord Rochford?'

The Colonel shrugged in response.

'It was a *marriage*, my dear. One has to take the rough with the smooth and all that, or so I'm told anyway. I'd say they rubbed along tolerably. No, I don't see how she could have killed Mrs. Catterson. And as for Miss Finch, you surely can't imagine a dried-up prune like her committing a murder. Preposterous thought! She's a harmless old trout who lives in the past. She thinks of nothing but her family's heyday before the Great War. She's a bit disconnected, really. The one thing that animates her is that she's convinced her sister was dealt a bad hand by life. That apart, knitting and tea are her chief interests. I accept what you say about your female mystic powers and all that, but you're barking up the wrong tree if you suspect either of those two. It'll be some outsider, mark my words.'

The door at Hailsham Hall was answered by an austere butler.

'Her Ladyship is in the garden, madam, if you would care to step this way.' He led her through the hall and an elegant drawing room through French windows to a vast and splendid garden.

Miriam's neighbours were certainly choosing an odd time of year to be in their gardens! Perhaps, like Captain Mostyn, Lady Rochford had a special reason to be outside.

The butler seemed uncertain as to Lady Rochford's whereabouts. He led Miriam through an Italianate garden and a Japanese garden into a shrubbery. Her Ladyship was on her knees poking around a conifer with her trowel. Even when gardening she had an air of elegance. She was wearing a purple wool-weave coat, charcoal trousers and a sandy yellow beret tilted at a jaunty angle. Dismissing the butler, Lady Rochford got to her feet.

'Good morning, Miss Lazarus. I've heard the dreadful news about Mrs. Catterson. I can hardly believe it. We only saw her last night. It must have been terrifying for you, finding the body.'

'Yes, it was horrendous,' said Miriam. Her eyes lighted on a second trowel sitting unused on the soil. 'It would be a great help to me to talk about it. But I wonder—I don't like to be idle—would you like me to lend a hand with your weeding effort? I've a few minutes spare and I see you've an extra trowel.'

Lady Rochford seemed nonplussed by the offer, but handed Miriam the trowel. She also shared with Miriam the large rectangle of discarded rug, which she was using to protect her knees and coat.

'Why would *anyone* want to kill Mrs. Catterson?' asked Miriam as she knelt, 'She was fairly harmless, wasn't she?

'Harmless?' said Lady Rochford, 'I'm not so sure. You see, she really was a busybody of Olympic proportions. Granted there are always chatterboxes in a village, she really did stick her nose in.'

‘I suppose you’re right,’ said Miriam, ‘Then again it would be a miracle *not* to have nosy neighbours in an English village. I hope you never suffered personally from her gossip?’

‘Not at all. Not to my knowledge. Of course, one never knows *who* spreads *which* items of gossip in High Hailsham. But anyway, that’d be no reason for wanting the poor woman dead.’

Miriam smiled as she uprooted a stubborn clover. She noticed that Lady Rochford was not so much taking out weeds as poking around the bare soil.

‘We’re just weeding, presumably?’

‘Partly. Look—I’ve just extracted a swine of a ragwort.’

‘Partly?’

‘Well, to be perfectly honest I’m also *looking* for something.’

Gosh, wondered Miriam, is there a gold rush for the Skull of Snod in High Hailsham?

‘Oh yes, what’s that?’

‘Well, it’s because of what you said at the séance. About the skull and finding it in the garden.’

‘We’re looking for a skull?’

‘No, not as such. The skull’s a jewel, or rather it’s the macabre setting for a jewel.’

‘A jewel! And why would there be a jewel in your garden?’

‘Because my husband may have put it there. My *late* husband, I should say.’

‘Oh, how fascinating,’ said Miriam as she excavated the root of a stubborn dandelion. ‘Please do explain.’

‘Well, I met Lord Rochford when he was in India. He was high up in the Raj and much older than me. At that time, a famous jewel came into his possession, the Severndroog Diamond.’

‘That’s lucky,’ said Miriam. ‘Well, assuming it’s not one of those gems that’s famous for being *un*lucky.’

'Fortunately, it was the opposite. According to legend, the diamond bestows unbelievably good luck on whoever owns it.'

'Good luck? Tried and tested?' said Miriam uprooting an impudent daisy.

'Astonishingly so. For instance it was given to the son of a Maharajah. This young man was travelling through a jungle bearing the diamond and was attacked by a tiger. The tiger was about to bite his head off, but then it dropped dead of heart failure! Another time the diamond was owned by an Indian princess. One day crossing the desert she met bandits. She expected to be killed for her jewel. But the chief bandit fell in love with her and she reigned joyfully as queen of the bandits living to a ripe old age.'

'Remarkable. Still, I suppose for you it brought bad luck, what with losing your husband so young.'

'That's just it. I didn't actually *like* my husband. Not at the end. To begin with, I was very much in love with Steven, despite the difference in our ages. Some busybodies in the village insist I only married him for the money but it just wasn't true. Alas, things went downhill once we were married. Steven had a very domineering character.'

'Oh I'm so sorry,' said Miriam, pausing her weeding effort to look Lady Rochford in the face, 'Many a relationship *starts* well. Getting to *know* one's husband is a risky venture.'

'You're telling me! I found out too late that he'd insist on calling all the shots in our marriage. To me, that was intolerable. I need marriage to be a partnership of equals, not the husband controlling the wife. That's why my sympathies are entirely with King Edward marrying his divorcee. Divorce doesn't deserve the stigma. If a marriage doesn't work, it's better to end it.'

'But you didn't end yours?'

'Didn't need to,' Lady Rochford waved her hand testily. 'Steven died of a stroke. It was his own fault—he ate one vast dinner too many at his London club.'

'So if you didn't love him, why were you trying to contact him in the afterlife?'

'To find out where he'd squirreled away the gem! He'd hidden it from me. He'd given it to me at our wedding, but then he secreted it away somewhere, for fear of burglars.'

'So you thought he might divulge its whereabouts in the séance?'

'I felt it worth a try. I wasn't confident of the outcome. He might have derived pleasure by depriving me of the diamond forever. Some men are sadists. Then again he could sometimes surprise me and do the decent thing. But when you cried out about a skull being in the garden I had to assume he'd concealed it there. Hence the present effort.'

'Yes,' said Miriam, 'it was a strange message from beyond the grave—"the *skull*, that's where you'll find what you seek—in the garden"'.

'Less strange if you'd seen the setting in which the diamond sits,' said Lady Rochford. 'It's fashioned like a skull. Quite macabre. The previous owner evidently had strange tastes. He was an Indian mystic, I believe. I fully intended to have a new setting made, before my husband spirited the diamond away.'

'Well, I do hope you find it,' said Miriam looking at her watch, rising, and handing back the trowel. 'I'm afraid I must be getting on. Sorry we haven't found anything yet, but good luck with the search. In the meantime, do you have any theories as to who would have wanted to murder Mrs. Catterson? Would the other people at the séance have a motive? Miss Finch? Colonel Mostyn?

'Most of what I know about Miss Finch is hearsay from Mrs. Catterson. Apparently, she'd had a fair share of tragedy in her life.

Prim old-fashioned family. Miss Finch's mother had "married well", or so she thought. Father a strict disciplinarian. Then, in a fine show of nineteenth century hypocrisy, father ups and leaves them! That really dented the Finch respectability. The rest soldiered on—presumably the mother had *some* money—but the sister died, then the mother. Miss Finch really is remarkably cheerful given her hardships, though they were long ago.'

'And Colonel Mostyn?'

'He seems a public-spirited old buffer to me. Runs that awful club. Mrs. Catterson insisted he was a swindler, but I thought that was twaddle.'

Miss Finch's house was warm and dry after the cold and damp of Lady Rochford's garden. Too warm—Miriam unbuttoned her puce woollen cardigan.

'Yes, do feel free to shed a few layers. I like to be generous with the heating, Miss Lazarus.' Miss Finch knitted as the tea brewed. 'Of course, we were never allowed such extravagance as a well-heated house when my father was around.'

'A stickler for economy?'

'A miser! The Victorian age had many godsends, but it also had a blight—the curse of humbug! For years my father played the part of strict, upstanding parent—and then he abandoned us—my mother, my sister and myself—for a woman elsewhere! Of course, before the war desertion was seen as shameful for the family. But at least once he'd left, the house could be as warm as we liked.' She smiled gently.

Miss Finch's drawing room was in the style of the previous century. As well as the roaring fire there was a crowded hotchpotch of paintings and photographs on every wall, an array of ornaments and knick-knacks on every surface. Maroon wallpaper, brocade upholstery and rich rugs completed the picture. Miss Finch's house was on the edge of the village, and the views from the windows were of the calm, grey estuary. Miss Finch sat in an armchair close to the fire draped in a heavy shawl. It occurred to Miriam that Miss Finch, like many old maids, dressed to look elderly but was probably quite robust, a creaking gate who'd endure for years.

'It beggars belief that anyone would want to harm Kitty Catterson. Such a sweet woman,' said Miss Finch, her eyes moist. 'Of course I've known her since she was a girl. She liked to chatter, but then this *is* a village. The only objection to her would be her *dogs*.'

'You found them a problem?' said Miriam raising an eyebrow. Akhenaten had always played nicely with the Catterson pooches.

'Oh, *I* never complained. I'm talking about *other* people,' said Miss Finch as she speeded up her knitting. 'You know how her dogs love to yap and mess up borders and jump up on your coat with muddy paws. I find that keeping your garden gate shut works a treat, combined with the judicious use of the walking stick.'

'But you enjoyed her company?'

'Yes she was a good friend. Of course, like many talkative people she was prone to *exaggerate*.'

'She wasn't a woman of evil tongue?'

'Oh, far from it. It was all small village matters, minor tittle-tattle.'

'What do you suppose she meant at the séance? I mean that outburst about an accident, a skull and someone getting too excited?'

'I've no idea about the skull. Might it have been her late *husband* who got excited? Neville Catterson could be belligerent.'

'How did he die? It was before I moved here.' Miriam actually knew full well how Mr. Catterson had met his end, but she wanted Miss Finch's version.

'Most unfortunate. He fell off the sea wall after a night at the Old Bull. The Thames mud is awfully treacherous around these parts.'

'How tragic. And had it been a good marriage?'

'Well, it wasn't suicide if that's what you mean. Coroner said it was an accident. As to the quality of the marriage, let's say she kept him in order. He was slightly hen-pecked, or should I say bantam-pecked given that Mrs. Catterson was petite. I rather think he relied on drink to iron out the creases in his everyday life. He was awfully fond of drinking at the pub, and at the Constitutional Club as well.'

'Oh yes, the Constitutional Club. Colonel Mostyn is involved in that isn't he?'

'Yes. It's a great institution in the village even if the building's grotesque, and the Colonel tries his best managing its finances.'

'"Tries his best?" He doesn't quite succeed?'

'It's just a rumour. One I heard from Kitty Catterson, come to think of it.'

Miriam tilted her head inquiringly.

'Word in the village was that he's made a frightful muddle of the Club's finances,' continued Miss Finch, 'I've no head for figures so I can sympathise. I'm sure there was no *real* fiddling and thankfully the police haven't got involved.'

'That rumour must be vexing for the Colonel given that he puts so much work into the Club. And how about Lady Rochford? What do you know of her?'

'The Rochfords haven't been here long. The Earl of Sheppey had the Hall before them.' Miss Finch gave a nostalgic sigh. 'Of course, *she's* very nice. I know one shouldn't speak ill of the dead, but I was never very fond of Lord Rochford.'

'You haven't heard of the Severndroog Diamond, have you? It's owned by the Rochfords.'

'Oh, that huge thing she wore at the village fête? So *vulgar*. Lord Rochford bought it for her, the shallow, ostentatious fellow! Thrift's gone out—people are very showy these days.' Miss Finch tutted loudly.

'Do you suppose Lady Rochford married for money?' said Miriam starkly.

'Why shouldn't she?' said Miss Finch knitting fiercely, '"Gold-digger" is such an unjust term. It casts a slur on a woman for the crime of marrying well. But what's the use of marrying *badly*?'

'You don't think marrying for money is a little mercenary?

'Nothing mercenary about it!' said Miss Finch indignantly, '*You're* a modern woman who believes in independence and making your own way in the world. Well, *I'm* an old-fashioned woman. For me, being a wife is a woman's career—a wife manages her husband just as a modern woman manages her business—and so it's her *duty* to marry well. There's nothing wrong with that. A girl should make the most of her opportunities.'

'But you remained single?' queried Miriam gingerly.

'The Great War saw to that, my dear,' Miss Finch put down her knitting for an instant and waved a deprecating hand. 'Being a spinster wasn't by design. There just weren't enough men to go round. I was fated to become one of those "superfluous women". It was a good thing that I had a bit of family money. It makes spinsterhood far more tolerable. I was left enough, well invested. I'm one of the lucky ones. Mrs. Catterson, poor thing, had to penny-pinch after Neville. I never heard the end of it.'

'What if Lady Rochford had wanted to divorce Lord Rochford?'

'That I can't believe! Mind you, so many people have no *gumption* these days, no moral fibre. People should stick with their spouses. Marriage is holy. It should be for life. That's why I've no truck with the King marrying that Mrs. Simpson. Anyway, I don't see why either Colonel Mostyn or Lady Rochford would want to murder Kitty Catterson. Surely it must have been some desperate type—a prisoner, or a lunatic.'

But Miriam did not think that was terribly likely. High Hailsham was in the back of beyond, with the nearest prison and asylum both far away.

As Miriam left Miss Finch's cottage, she paused for a moment at the garden gate. She looked out at the estuary. It was such a vast stretch of water. On a normal day it was a struggle to discern the Essex side. Everything was grey today and mist obscured Essex completely. Then suddenly a Thames barge appeared out of the mist, its brown sail burgeoning. She could just make out the form of Inspector Cooling. He was with a couple of uniformed officers. As the boat approached, the Inspector's cheerful face became more apparent.

'Ahoy Miss Lazarus!' he hollered as he waved.

There was a quay at the tip of Ghastly Gash where the vessel moored. Once on dry land the Inspector greeted Miriam with a warm handshake. Miriam had half forgotten what a handsome man he was, tall and broad-shouldered, with his ready smile, regular features and shock of chestnut-brown hair.

'Thanks for holding the fort, Miss Lazarus. Now, perhaps we could start by viewing the body?'

'It's just a few paces away, Inspector.'

Once at the well Inspector Cooling looked down.

'Nasty,' he said. 'And what's also nasty is that we haven't the wherewithal to extract the body decently—not until the floods recede.'

'The well's been unguarded all morning,' said Miriam, 'I dread to think how many villagers have come to gawp.'

'We can end that malarkey forthwith,' said Cooling. He ordered his men to mount guard over the well until dark. He then walked with Miriam back to the village. She told him what had happened at the séance and of her interviews with the suspects.

'Great preliminary work. It seems we'll need to talk to each of them ourselves,' said Cooling.

'Really, Inspector, isn't that rather replicating what I've done?'

'Do you have a better suggestion?' asked Cooling with a good-natured smile.

'Yes, I do. Hold a second séance. Gather the three of them together and let me contact the other side.'

'A second séance, eh? And I suppose that will prompt the guilty party to spill the beans?'

'Exactly. I've got to do my bit. As a *genuine* medium, it's my duty.'

As luck would have it, it was the day of the winter solstice. By three o'clock it was almost dark. According to Miriam, dusk on the longest night of the year was a particularly potent time to attract spirits. Miriam had no problem securing the attendance of Colonel Mostyn, Lady Rochford and Miss Finch, especially once they were told that Inspector Cooling would be there and would appreciate their presence. Cooling's two constables maintained a discreet guard outside Miriam's cottage.

Everything was the same as the previous night save for Inspector Cooling replacing Mrs. Catterson. There were the figures sitting at the table, the dim candlelight, the glowing embers of the fire, and Miriam—chanting, incanting, beseeching the dead to appear. . .

'Is there anybody there? Is there anybody there?'

Immediately a rush of wind roared around the building. The candles flickered.

Miriam spoke again, but in a squeaky, quavering voice unlike her own.

'It's me. It's Kitty Catterson. I'm on the other side now.'

'Are you happy there?' asked Miriam in her normal voice.

'Never mind whether she's bally happy and all that bosh,' said the Colonel gruffly, 'Ask who killed her.'

'Quite,' said Lady Rochford, 'We're not here to pass the time of day.'

'Yes I am happy,' continued Miriam in Mrs. Catterson's voice. 'Happy after a fashion. . . .at least I've got dear Neville back. . . he's *quite* happy to see me—but I crossed over to the other side before my time. . . After the séance, I was upset. . . Miss Finch was kind, attentive. . . asked me back to her house. . . camomile tea, calming. . . I apologised to her.

. . should not have blurted out about the skull. . . Months ago. . . Rex getting over-excited, bounding into her garden, digging up the flower bed. . . a human skull. . . Miss Finch was careful to keep the garden gate shut after that. . . Something funny in the tea. . . I feel dreadfully drowsy. . . Where's Miss Finch. . . Oh. . . Why's she brought that wheelbarrow into the drawing room? *Aaagghhh!'* Miriam bent forward, pressing the side of her face against the table top.

'Whose skull, Miss Finch?' said Cooling angrily, getting to his feet.

Miss Finch paused, then spoke.

'Do you really suppose I'll confess to anything on the strength of this claptrap? The ham-acting of this charlatan?' She gestured contemptuously towards Miriam.

'Oh, we won't be relying on this séance, Miss Finch,' said Cooling. 'Far from it. We'll search every inch of your garden until we find that skull, and if you've reburied it elsewhere we'll find it elsewhere. Then there'll be dental records and all manner of checks. We'll leave no stone unturned—no clod of earth, either.'

He extracted a whistle from his pocket and blew it. The two constables entered. Cooling pointed to Miss Finch and they led her out.

'She's made a clean breast of it', said Cooling an hour later. 'The skull's her father's. He didn't desert the family before the war. The wife and daughters disposed of him.'

'I suspected as much,' said Miriam, 'Miss Finch said she'd been left money, well invested. That seemed unlikely. Where would the money have come from? The mother had "married well", meaning her side didn't have much. The father was mean. If he were swine enough to desert his family, he'd have taken the money with him—or certainly much of it. In truth, I think the father never went anywhere. The family did away with him—no doubt using poison, a woman's weapon—then told the village he'd abandoned them. They probably waited the seven years to have him declared legally dead.

'You see, Inspector, I never thought the murderer was someone who revels in carnage. I thought it had to be someone who was truly *desperate.* And even old ladies can become desperate if they have secrets to hide. When Mrs. Catterson let slip about the skull at the séance, that rather sealed her fate. Everything might come out! The prospects of public disgrace and criminal prosecution were too much for our murderer. Mrs. Catterson was doomed.

'By contrast, there wasn't a convincing argument for either of the other two suspects to murder her. Lady Rochford had committed no crime whatsoever as far as I could see. The Severndroog Diamond is undoubtedly hers, so what would be her motive for silencing Mrs. Catterson? Added to which, there's no question that Lord Rochford died a natural death. As for the Colonel, he made no secret of his desire to find the Skull of Snod. Again, it's hard to see how he could have acquired a motive to kill Mrs. Catterson.

'And then I asked myself: why would a spirit *bother* to issue that strange message? *"The skull, that's where you'll find what you should seek—in the garden."* We never established *which* spirit sent those words. It *could* have been Lord Rochford, referring to the diamond, but then again he and Lady Rochford no longer got on, so why would he go out of his way to help her? I hardly think anyone would bother to tell Colonel Mostyn the whereabouts of his artefact—and who'd know where it was anyway! No, my guess is that the message came from Miss Finch's father. Spirits tend to be acutely aware of how they met their end and what happened to their mortal remains. The father wanted his remains discovered. He sought earthly justice for himself.'

'Well, thank heavens we've got you, Miss Lazarus, with the perspicacity to solve this mystery for us.' Inspector Cooling gave her a broad smile.

'I can't take all the credit, Inspector,' said Miriam, 'I had my suspicions, of course. But I'd have been all at sea without our friends in the spirit world. *They* were the greatest help, believe you me.'

The Body in the Bathtub
by J.C. Bernthal

Before he was known as the 'Clerical Terror', Clarence Dorian was a soft-spoken, well-liked country vicar. He was, everyone thought, going to be a bishop.

No one in our village, probably no one in Suffolk, had any idea that he would become a detective novelist. Let alone one successful enough to have his own nickname. But I think he was inspired, if that's the right word, by real life. Without those horrible things that happened in the twenties, I don't think he'd ever have thought to put pen to paper—not for anything more than sermons, at least.

I've never told anyone what happened, out of respect for the family—especially dear Jenny. But she died last year. Standing at her funeral, her grandson said, 'She reached a ripe old age'. That had an impact—I'm ten years older! Which puts me in very real danger of shuffling off this mortal coil any day.

Then he went back to teasing his sister about the 'Spice Girls' and the 'world wide web' and I thanked God I am too old to need to keep up. In my head, it is 1928 and I'm still nineteen. No one expects me to go to university or better myself because middle-class families still employ staff.

You know, I can close my eyes, take a deep breath, and I'm back at the Hall.

'Dot!'

The light was sore against my eyelids. I kept them closed.

'Dotty!'

Still in sleep, I forced myself not to respond.

'Dot—it's *important.*'

Sleep was like a bad pantomime. It was time to wake up. Winching my eyes open, I let the sunshine do its oppressive duty and blinked several times to come to terms with it. I was in my usual room, dust dancing thickly between the bed and the window.

At the foot of my bed, a little girl tugged at my blanket.

'What is it, Jenny?' I asked, exaggerating my sleepiness ever so slightly. The idea with that was to incorporate some sort of lesson about how rude it is to wake people up.

'It's quarter to seven,' she replied, with absolute conviction. So clear and confident was she in her answer that I actually thanked her for letting me know.

Except. . .

'Why is that important?'

Jenny tutted as if I were the naughty child.

'Because you have to get me up at half-past seven. I thought you'd need some time to get ready.' She looked me up and down—or, because I was lying down—along. 'I should have given you an hour.'

To summarise: Jenny had woken up early and decided not to suffer alone. Surely, normal governesses didn't have to deal with this. Weren't most children simply dying to get away from their nannies?

'Give me a minute, Jenny. I'll be with you once I've washed and got a cup of tea.'

'But I don't want any tea,' said Jenny, simply. 'I'm only nine.'

I'd always liked Jenny. When they'd hired me, only that summer, the Dorians had warned me that she wasn't the easiest child in the world. Hence needing a live-in governess. *Of course we love her*, the mother had said. *But we have to. She's our daughter. Luckily, you don't have to love her. Just to keep her on a sensible path.* The father had rebuked his wife, but in a very mousey way. He'd said something about Christian kindness and asked if I wanted to see my room.

They hadn't seemed like bad parents, just people who should never have had children. Well, one child. What exactly made Jenny a difficult child, I hadn't yet ascertained. I suspect they needed a reason to hire one person instead of three—governess, tutor, and maid rolled into one. Or perhaps it was just that she had a personality. She asked questions. She wasn't afraid to wake me up because she was bored.

Well. She *was* clumsy and obstinate and easily led—I once made the mistake of saying, in her presence, *Toast always lands butter side up,* only to find her in the pantry at night, flinging buttered bread around, willy nilly, in the pursuit of science. I had then explained the concept of figurative speech. She had not cared for it.

I washed and dressed at my own basin and went down to the kitchen for some hot water. As I expected, Mrs. Dunn was there, with her own cup of tea.

'Good morning, Miss Snape,' she said, with that overdone friendliness that makes you think she doesn't like people and is ashamed of the fact. 'Sleep well?'

'Until I was woken up,' I smiled. 'Jenny must be keen to get started on her sums.'

'She's a good girl,' said Mrs. Dunn. 'Pre-cocious'. She sounded the word with an emphasis on 'pre', like it was a superlative. 'There's still water in the kettle if you want some tea.'

I did want some tea.

'How's Samuel?' I asked, pouring.

The cook-cum-housekeeper bristled. '*Mr. Dunn,*' she said carefully, 'is well. He's in the gardens.'

That made sense, for a gardener. Mrs. Dunn's husband was not a good gardener, and he would certainly not be in post had he not come with Mrs. Dunn. But the vicarage did not have rolling, expansive gardens. It was really little more than a lawn with a few trees. And a maze. Rather a lovely one, which he kept barely tended.

Samuel Dunn was in his seventies—a good two decades older than his wife—and, while she tried to hide her daily irritation, he positively embraced it. He rarely acknowledged other people and never me. He talked, more than anything, to the flowers, and they knew all his secrets.

There were rumours at that time of some scurrilous story about a society lady having relations with her gardener. The idea of Lady Dorian—the reverend's wife, she was from a noble family and absolutely knew it—and Mr. Dunn kept coming into my head and driving me near hysterical. I thought of it again and snorted into my hot drink.

'What was that, dear?' asked Mrs. Dunn.

'Nothing, nothing.'

We chatted briefly and glanced at the clock.

'I'd better wake Jenny up. Officially, I mean. Could you fix her some eggs?'

Teaching Jenny mathematics was my idea. She had, even then, a mathematical mind. Not that she was precise—quite the opposite—but when we worked at cooking and cleaning, she always looked for the formulas. She wanted to know how things worked. Well, I couldn't very well teach her chemistry, but I could help her with numbers.

It was our first lesson on division, and she wasn't grasping it. I searched my mind for real world examples and first tried her dolls.

'Now, imagine you have all your dolls lined up in three rows.'

This was a mistake. Because, of course, Jenny jumped up from her seat and started looking for her toybox, to set the dolls up.

'It's just an example,' I tried, to no avail. Then, as the playroom became impossibly messier by the second, 'Never mind the dolls. Let's think about something else.' I hesitated. 'Imagine Mr. Dunn's cabbages. He has three rows of three cabbages, doesn't he?'

Immediately, Jenny switched her attention to the window, which overlooked the garden. No harm in that. She couldn't actually see the cabbages from here, but she couldn't very well take me outside to investigate.

I continued. 'Mr. Dunn takes three cabbages from the garden. Let's say he is picking the first—'

'No,' said Jenny with resolution.

'No?'

'No.' She looked at me squarely. I think she genuinely thought she had caught me out in a lie. 'Mr. Dunn isn't picking cabbages. He's there, next to the maze. I can see him, talking to Mrs. Dunn.'

The Dorians had a small but beautiful maze in their garden. It gave the sensation of adventure, mystery, and escape, but was quite easy to navigate and its insides were fully visible from this side of the house.

I used the next second to ponder how to respond, and in that time Jenny reloaded.

'I imagine they're talking about Robin.'

Robin. It was a name, then. This was not a new name for me, but it was one I didn't know. When the Dorians had hired me, the reverend had given me some topics of conversation that were, in his words, 'off the dance card in all circumstances.' One was politics. I was not to discuss politics in the house, and especially not the rights of women. Another was any religion or philosophy outside the One True Faith (in this case, Anglicanism). The final point of no entry was a very specific bird—the robin. If a robin appeared in the garden at any point, I was to ignore it. I was, especially, not to use the word—not even to describe a bandit robbin' the silverware-in front of Mavis Dunn. I wanted to ask why but never dared.

Jenny, I realised, likely knew why. Still, I couldn't discuss robins. But Jenny had no such embargo.

I chose my next words carefully.

'What do you mean?'

'Oh,' Jenny blinked once or twice, and in this moment the natural instinct for gossip awakened in her. 'I'm not meant to know about Robin, but I hear things and put things together. I also ask questions.'

'Yes, dear. I've noticed.'

'Well, Robin—Robin was a baby. Apparently, we were born at the same time.'

'Twins?' I asked, involuntarily.

Jenny laughed.

'No. He was Mrs. Dunn's. She had him just before Mother had me. But he got sick and died. That's what I understand. Whenever they're alone or they think I can't hear them, nowadays, they talk about Robin. I think it would have been his birthday soon. It's my birthday in one week and two days.'

All of this was delivered with astonishing matter-of-fact-ness. For want of a better word, I was stunned.

'That,' Jenny concluded as I struggled to find a response, 'is my exposition. Is that the right word?'

'That is a very long word,' I said.

I didn't actually know what 'exposition' meant or if she was using it correctly, but I wanted very much to get the topic away from gossip. It had seemed like fun a few minutes ago, but now it was sad—and inappropriate. It was also slightly terrifying, how completely unphased Jenny seemed to be discussing the death of a peer. We spoke a little more about words. Did she mean 'explanation?' She assured me she did not. We went back to numbers and did not speak of Robin again.

While Jenny took lunch with her mother, I took myself for a walk. I had received a letter the previous morning, from Joe, the butcher's son who wanted to take me out. While I'm not and never have been a snob, I didn't think it was quite right. Don't governesses in books have designs on the man of the house, rather than servicemen?

Then again, governesses in books aren't addressed with their Christian name by their charges. But there was no way Jenny was ever going to call me 'Miss Snape', except in her father's presence.

'It makes you sound like an evil teacher in a bad book,' she'd said when I asked her about this. '"Snape"—snappy and snipey, something a lazy storyteller might come up with.'

'Like Edgar Wallace,' I'd said, smiling. Then I'd had to tell her all about Edgar Wallace and pulp fiction. She was such a curious girl. 'Snape is a good Suffolk name,' I'd concluded.

She had never called me 'Dot' in public, so I never minded and had no embarrassment being addressed like a common maid. Not that a common maid is any less of a person than me. But still. Certainly, I didn't think of myself as Joe's social equal—even if that kind of thing isn't real—but, I mean, in the eyes of other people. It didn't seem quite the thing for him to be writing to me as an equal—using my Christian name, too! Still, as I say, I'm not a snob, and I was seriously wondering whether to take him up on it.

He wasn't particularly good-looking, and I knew nothing about his personality, except that he always smelt of beef. In the letter, he said he danced well, and he had taken extreme care with his spelling. It reminded me of an activity I might have set my little brother or latterly Jenny, that letter. An exercise, and a fourth or fifth dedicated draft.

Joe dances, then. I do not dance. I was trying, mentally, to make a list. Pros and Cons, they say now. But I couldn't really think of much on either side. I just had no interest in romance or love or men or boys. Maybe that's why I got on with Jenny, too. I felt sure that, when she reached the age when the world and her parents told her she wanted certain things, she wouldn't go along with any nonsense.

What do I think of when I think of Joe? A bicycle that needs repairing and one shilling sixpence for a leg of mutton. Not the most auspicious first feelings.

But my thoughts were interrupted.

'You absolute sod!'

It was a shriek, and I thought it was a woman, until Samuel Dunn continued with a string of profanities. I looked up and realised, with a lurch, that I had strolled inside the maze. I wanted to retrace my steps, make my way out, but I'd clearly just turned a corner and had no idea from which direction. I looked around, blinkily, trying to find a way out of earshot.

There were two voices now—Mr. and Mrs. Dunn —overlapping and tense, and I couldn't think which way to go to avoid them. I didn't want to overhear anything that wasn't my business, but, more importantly, I didn't want to walk into them. I just wanted—needed—to get away.

'Bloody Robin! Always Robin. It's been ten years'

That pulled me up short. Robin—the Dunns' dead baby. I wished I could hear Mrs. Dunn, but she was speaking too quietly for anything to emerge but,

'Please, Sam.'

'I'm going to talk—no, shut up! Just shut the hell up! I'm going to tell everything I know. Everything.'

And I heard footsteps. Rapid, stormful, getting louder by the split-second. His face when he passed me matched them. Thunderous. I said something stupid about it being a lovely summer's day and he thumped his way through the wall and out of the maze.

Lady Dorian was taking her lunch, alone, in the drawing room. *The queen is in the parlour, eating bread and honey.* I tapped on the open door, and she looked up, genuinely confused to see me.

'Excuse me, ma'am.'

'What?'

'I just wanted to—'

'Make yourself useful and tidy this tea tray up.'

'Lady Dorian, I'm not the maid.'

I'd never spoken back to her before. Very possibly, she had never been spoken back to before. She thought for a second or two, then decided upon a course of action.

'Make yourself useful and tidy this tea tray up.'

I tidied the tea tray up.

'Ma'am, I wanted a quick word with you, about Jenny. Her look made me want to add, 'Your daughter,' but I forbore. She said nothing, so I continued. 'She is doing well with her numbers, but I think formal schooling might be more beneficial. The girl is distracted, easily, by familiar things around her. A classroom setting, and there are so many excellent schools for girls now, would put her among her peers, and. . . '

'And offer up more distractions!' said Lady Dorian, shortly. 'Anyway, you're wrong. She's not distracted. Distraction requires imagination. She is impressionable. She just takes everything very literally. If you tell her a novel is heavy-going, she will ask you precisely how much it weighs.'

I smiled. Lady Dorian did not.

'Was there anything else, Snape?'

It should have been 'Miss Snape,' but never mind.

'Well, candidly, Lady Dorian, I am a little worried about Mr. Dunn.'

One eyebrow went up a fraction of an inch. Face powder dislodged itself in the process.

'Don't worry about Mr. Dunn. Is he still banging on about—'

And this point was very embarrassing. At the same time I said, 'Yes, about Robin,' she continued, 'the geraniums'.

In less than a second, Her Ladyship's face became a mask of powder with nothing beneath it. Then it came back.

'Take the tea things away, Snape.'

The Reverend Clarence Dorian was, predictably, in his study, planning the weekend's sermon. Again, I tapped on the door and, again, was greeted with surprise.

He was much nicer.

'Hello, Miss Snape.' He gave me his vicary smile. Friendly, unconnected. 'How would you pronounce this name?' He handed me the bible he was reading from. It was open at Luke, chapter 2.

I read aloud from the point of his finger.

'And this taxing was first made when Cyrenius was governor of Syria.'

'Ah! You say "Psy-ree-nee-ous" too. So does the Bishop of Norfolk. But I wonder if it should be "Psy-reh-nay-us", if it comes from the Greek.'

'I couldn't say, Mr. Dorian.'

'No, I suppose you couldn't.'

This wasn't intended to sting. I have, after all, never studied Greek. I read on a little, to myself, those enduring words about the birth of Christ. The ancient world anticipating the saviour's birth and its petty officials thinking, first of all, about how they could use it to put up taxes, next about who they could kill, and only later wondering why anyone would need delivering from the sins of the world. The sermon Mr. Dorian was typing looked, from the glances I stole, much more along the lines of, 'listen to the angels (that is, your vicar or schoolmaster, or landlord) when they tell you something that needs to happen is happening.'

'You'd like to talk to me?' he prompted.

'About little Jesus—I mean, little Jenny,' I replied.

Mr. Dorian smiled his vicary smile again.

'Have you spoken to my wife?'

'Yes, but we don't necessarily see it the same way, sir.'

'Best to side with her,' said the vicar, and his smile had not shifted so much as a fraction of an inch. 'It's much easier that way. How are things otherwise?'

Now, I was taken aback.

'Things are very well, sir. Jenny is making excellent progress with—'

'I don't mean with Jenny Wren. I mean with you. Have you realised, yet, that you're hopelessly in love with the butcher's son? He calls round most mornings looking for a chance to see you, you know.'

This I did not know. I blushed. Dorian's smile became more genuine.

'If you ever want an afternoon off, to go to a matinee or whatever it is young people do, I'm sure Lady D won't mind.'

I blushed yet more and felt a silence begin to fall. I said the first thing that came into my head.

'If you don't mind, Mr. Dorian, I'm going to take Jenny to the park this afternoon.'

'Excellent idea, Miss Snape. Now, if you'll excuse me.'

He was already back with the shepherds, awaiting the delivery of Christ.

We took some bread from the kitchen to feed the ducks. Jenny was nervous, rolling crumbs into tight, angry balls and flicking them into the grass. I told her to stop, and she seemed surprised she was doing it.

'What are you thinking about, Jenny?' I asked.

'I don't know. But something doesn't feel quite right.'

Here is the strange thing. I knew what she meant. The sun was out, bright and defiant, and there were none of the portentous rainclouds of literature, but still it felt like there were. The air was clear and open, but something about the day was wrong. We met some other children in the park, but Jenny would not play with them.

'I don't have time,' she told me. 'You said we are to feed the ducks.'

The ducks were nice to Jenny, even queuing for their bread, but one of them tried to bite me.

It felt wrong. The whole afternoon had been soaked in a kind of foreboding, but as I climbed the stairs, I couldn't help drinking in something more tangible. The air was thick with something like secrets—something about to be uncovered. You know when you can just *feel* that something isn't right? I had that, abundantly.

I was slow on the steps. Jenny skipped up past me, towards the voices. She seemed excited more than anything.

'Door's locked,' Mr. Dorian was saying.

Lady D was tutting and fussing. They were both trying the door to her ladyship's bathroom at the very end of the corridor. Her private room, with tub and washbasin. The only bath in the house, and very nice at that.

'Give it a tug,' she was saying.

'For God's sake, woman,' his voice was raised now. If Jenny hadn't skipped so far ahead of me, I would have shielded her ears from the blasphemy. 'I've tried that. Jenny!' He noticed his daughter for the first time.

'Yes, papa?'

'Now, don't panic, girl. Pull yourself together and pay attention. Someone's in your mother's bathroom. We heard a splash about five minutes ago, but we can't get in.'

'You mean it's locked?'

'No pulling the wool over your eyes,' said the Reverend Mr. Dorian, sarcastically. 'You give it a go, Jenny. Give the door a good yank. We can't get it open.'

By now I was coming up to them and their voices were joined by the sight of them.

I saw Jenny straining at the door, but it wouldn't budge.

The vicar raised his voice one last time.

'If there's anyone in there,' he intoned, like someone reading the marriage bans, 'speak now. I'm going to break down the door.'

'Really, Clarence. . . ,' said his wife.

'Out of the way.'

Mr. Dorian pushed his weight inelegantly against the door. Then he did it again and it gave, easily. There is no smell of death. Well, I didn't smell anything unusual. Not on this occasion, anyway. But I knew, even before I saw their faces, before Jenny screamed, before Lady Dorian fainted, before I went in and looked for myself. Somehow, I already knew. I didn't need to see the water turned brilliant red. I didn't need to see the fully clothed body in the tub. And I certainly didn't need to see the drained and swollen face of Sam Dunn, waiting under the water. I took one look at the body and ran to Jenny. I shielded her eyes, but she'd already seen too much.

'Come on, Jenny Wren,' I said, using her father's nickname for her. 'Don't come in here. Let's go to your room.'

I tried to scoop her out, and walked straight into her father, who was looking at the door. The key was in the lock on the inside, and the latch was scuffed and splintered where he'd broken in.

'Watch out,' he said.

And I started to apologise for bumping into him, but he shook his head and pointed down at my feet. A penknife.

'Christ,' I said, and felt the absurd need to repent that word before this ashen-faced man of the cloth. 'Is that the—is that how he. . . ?'

Dorian shook his head. He glanced quickly at the—at the body. Another knife was in the man's hand, draped over the edge of the tub. This was a second, clean knife. Strange.

I started pulling the door inwards so we could get fully out, but Lady Dorian stopped me.

'We should leave everything as it is,' she said. 'For the police.'

Police?

'Police have to be called in any case of suicide.'

There was a silence. Because it was Jenny who'd spoken. She had just started reading detective stories—her weekly blood, she called it. I didn't realise she'd taken so much in. She was only ten! Let alone that, she knew the word 'suicide'.

'Come on, dear,' I said, feeling like a very young, untested, and unprepared nineteen-year-old. 'Let's get you to your room.'

The police arrived within twenty minutes, in the form of Inspector Catchpole and a constable whose name I didn't catch. The household—that is, the Dorians, Mrs. Dunn, and I—received him in the drawing room.

Catchpole was stationed in Ipswich. Many times, he told us that he was *really* near Felixstowe to visit his mother and that 'all this business' was most inconvenient. He was, it seemed, very keen to hand things over to the nameless constable and the local doctor. Nonetheless, he told us, he would take some quick statements and be out of the way 'before supper'. Lady Dorian winced at the vulgarity.

'Shall I fetch Miss Dorian?' I asked.

'Who?'

'My daughter,' said her ladyship, in a very strange and direct way. 'She's ten.'

'Nine,' Mavis Dunn corrected her. 'Miss Jenny is nine. Robin would have been ten.'

An angel passed—that's what people used to say in those days when a sudden, awkward and unexpected silence overcame a conversation.

Catchpole broke it.

'Robin?'

'Robin is nothing to do with you,' said Lady Dorian. 'And nothing to do with me, or Jenny. Enough about her. How shall we proceed?'

Even Catchpole, manifestly distracted, sensed something wrong here. He decided, I think, to channel his inner Lady Dorian and embrace dismissiveness.

'I shan't need to bother the kiddies—I mean, I shan't need to speak to any children.' He was adjusting his language to fit this ridiculous mockery of refinement. 'Robin, whoever he is, is not my concern. And I shall speak to the servants separately. You and you'—this to Mrs. Dunn and me —'are dismissed.'

Mrs. Dunn didn't look offended. She said she'd start working on dinner. 'That's what we call supper in this house,' she added to the inspector. I offered to help, which didn't fill her with glee, but she didn't stop me.

In the kitchen, Mrs. Dunn was inconsolable. She wept over boiling potatoes and wouldn't let go of the pan.

'It's not fair,' she said, through sniffs. 'First Baby Robin, now Sam—taken away before their times, the both of them.' She fixed me a searching, grief-hallowed look. 'You never knew Baby Robin, did you? You're too new.'

'I've heard about him,' I said, diplomatically.

Mrs. Dunn started crying again. A glob of something dropped from her nose and into the saucepan. Neither of us mentioned it.

'I don't much like that Inspector Catchpole.' She spat out the surname like a curse word, and flecks of spittle went into the saucepan. 'And did you hear the constable? Sounds like he were being sick in the bathroom.' Abstractedly, she watched the water boil over the pan and onto the hob, watched it collect itself, filmic. 'You saw the—the—the body. Was it very horrible?'

How does one answer a question like that? One doesn't.

'What was it like,' she continued, 'when you pushed open that door?'

'I didn't,' I said. 'They had to break it down.'

'Oh, my stars!'

Now she was sobbing. Deep, heaving sobs. I turned off the flame and sat her down. A glass of water was on the table—next to it, half a slice of bread, the crumbs rolled together in distracted sticky clumps.

'Have some water.'

'I can't,' she sobbed. 'That were Sam's last meal. You can tell he were distracted. He didn't even butter his bread.'

'I'll clear it away.'

'NO!' She grabbed my wrist, with predictable strength. 'Preserve the evidence, ain't that what they say?'

'Evidence? I don't think this is evidence.'

Her laughter was harsh, uncontrolled, and brief. It turned back to sobs.

Then the constable came in and asked us stupid questions. We weren't important enough, and neither was the deceased, for the inspector to bother with us.

As a rule, I had evenings to myself, barring twenty minutes when it was time to get Jenny to bed. No act of self-slaughter in the household would stop me taking my entitled time that evening. As soon as the doctor had gone, with the body—the police had not stayed long at all—I told Mrs. Dunn I'd be going for a walk. She looked crestfallen. Of course, she wanted—needed—company. But I needed the opposite. Seven decades on (good grief), I still feel bad about that.

The Hall was a vicarage, not a country house. There was only one way to leave the house legitimately—by the main doors. Out I went and walked directly into a man approaching the house. Joe. He had washed himself and put on a less tatty-than-usual cap. He gupped, fishlike, in my face.

'Hello,' I said. Which seemed as good a thing to say as any.

'Miss Snape.' The cap came off and he wrung it. 'I just heard from Dr. Carr. I wanted to say how sorry I am.'

The door was still wide open. I hesitated.

'I'm not sure Mrs. Dunn will want to see anyone, Joe.'

'I'm not here for her. I'm here for you. I wanted to check that you're coping.'

This seemed highly improper. It wasn't my husband that had died.

'Where are you going, Miss Snape?'

'Just for a walk.'

'Would you like some company?'

Suddenly, I realised that I would.

We strolled, like a couple in an Edwardian painting, in the slowly setting sunlight. Down to the pond where, just a few hours ago, Jenny and I had fed the ducks. It was quiet now. No ducks, no children, very few people. I pondered the ripple-less water.

'You know I think you're smashing,' said Joe, apropos of nothing. 'And I can't offer you much, but you must know that I'd like to see more of you.'

'I'm not that interesting,' I said, still water minded.

Then, as Jenny might have done, I said the first thing that came into my head.

'Ponds are nature's bathtubs, aren't they?'

It was, though I didn't realise at the time, a test. How would Joe react to this kind of unreasonable individuality in a potential mate? He reacted well because he engaged.

'I don't think so. You don't wash things away in a pond.'

'I enjoy your company, Joe.'

Now, he didn't smile as the vicar had smiled over his sermon. He grinned.

We talked gossip—not harmful Robin gossip but nice, normal polite scandal. We didn't mention the Dorians and we didn't mention suicide. We spoke of the barber's wife, who would come into the butcher's shop twice on a Wednesday—once for her husband and once for her tennis coach. We spoke of the church warden who seemed to acquire a new pair of expensive gloves every time a generous collection was taken (we absolutely did not speak of the vicar). In fact, Joe broke the spell by bringing up Jenny. A child's toy sailboat, lost or abandoned in the pond, floated past us and I said something stupid like 'Oh!', which prompted a giggle—an actual giggle—from Joe.

'Sorry,' he said. 'I was thinking of Miss Jenny.'

'My Miss Jenny?'

Yes, my Miss Jenny. It turned out that Joe knew her. In years gone by, his little sister used to play with her. Most kids in the village had played together not so many years before, all kinds of ages and no one gave a damn for social position because in a little place like this who else was there to play with? One Spring, they'd gone to the docks. She must have been about six, the same age as his sister. He'd been fifteen, acting like a very worldly guardian to the younger children, and—oh, never mind, it was a silly story. Not worth my time, he said. But the little boat had brought it to mind.

'Speaking of Jenny.' I searched for my watch. 'I'd better get back and read to her.'

Reading Jenny to sleep had transformed into a nightly ritual of jointly composing ridiculous stories about the events of the day until I was too tired to continue. But that night, things were much more sombre. We simply talked—of anything but what had happened.

'I saw the butcher's boy this evening,' I tried, as conversation started to dwindle.

'Joe?'

'Yes. He said he used to play with you.'

Jenny nodded.

'He told me he had a funny story about you and a boat.'

In an effort of remembrance, she frowned.

'The tugboat?' she asked at last.

Tugboat. Why was that significant? It was doing something to my brain. I realised I was meant to react, so I simply nodded.

'It's not really funny,' Jenny mused. 'Just annoying, really. We went to the docks at Felixstowe and Joe pointed to one and shouted, "tug-boat!", so I ran up to it and tried to give it a tug. That wasn't what he meant, apparently—so he shouldn't have said it like that, should he? I was only little way back then. I'm nearly ten now.'

'Yes, dear, I know.'

But my mind was going very quickly. *Tugboat. Tug the boat.* Of course she'd taken those words that way. She was a very suggestible girl. And it hit me in that moment that Sam Dunn had not killed himself. I thought back to the afternoon. The discovery and what came before it.

I remembered the words Jenny's parents had used. 'Give it a tug', 'pull yourself together', 'no pulling the wool over your eyes'. . . They'd waited for Jenny. Made her confirm that the door was locked. And how had she—that oh-so-impressionable girl—confirmed it? By pulling at the door handle. Because they'd planted a seed with their words. Like I had, when I told her toast landed butter-side up.

But what had Mrs. Dunn asked me? *How did it feel when you pushed open that door?* Jenny had pulled at a push door. It had never been locked. They'd made her try it just to prove a lie. That, I realised then, was why Clarence Dorian had gone straight to breaking it down. I was about to turn up—and I'm not easily led. The first thing I'd have done was try pushing the door. So, it had to be broken before I could think of it. Then slipping the key into the lock, messing up the latch with that penknife—the work of seconds, while I was looking at the body or taking Jenny away. Well, that was the second knife explained. And he couldn't hide it, because I'd stepped on it.

Both of them—the vicar and his wife. Both of them did this. And, I realise, the thoughts coming on top of themselves, I knew why. I caught Jenny's eye—wide, intelligent, with so much light and innocence. I couldn't look away as the pieces locked together behind my own eyes.

You, I said without saying out loud. *You are not Jenny.* Jenny Wren—a bird name for a pet name, like a grotesque clue in plain sight. *You're Robin.*

Like the inspector, I'd assumed that poor dead Robin Dunn was a boy. But what had Mrs. Dunn said? 'She ain't coming back.' *She*—Robin was a girl. And she was still alive. Hadn't the Dorians' baby had a difficult birth? Hadn't the baby not cried for the first few weeks? There had been problems, hadn't there, and the midwife had been dismissed? And the Dunns' baby—lovely, healthy, always under lock and key at the Hall until one day, word was spread that Robin had died—and all the staff, except the Dunns, dismissed.

How simple—how horrible but oh! how simple—to swap the babies: the living for the dead. How had they got the housekeeper and the gardener to agree to it? Money, probably. Not just hush money but the promise that, as Jenny Dorian, their little baby would have the best possible upbringing. Education, social position, a good marriage.

Had Sam agreed? I suspected he simply hadn't known. He was a drunk and couldn't tell one baby, even his own, from another. But then, years later, he'd worked it out. Something Jenny had said, perhaps, or done, that was so clearly and unmistakably an inheritance from her father. Rolling her breadcrumbs into a tiny, angry ball. Or maybe Mavis had just told him. 'I've had enough of secrets,' she'd said the night before he died. And he'd come to the Dorians. The kindly vicar who might be made Bishop. Perhaps he'd wanted money. Or justice. Neither would have been acceptable. Avoid scandal at all costs.

A private word in a private space. Lady Dorian's personal bathroom. A knife, taps drawn, and all that was left was to arrange the scene and fake the locked door. This, I knew, was what had happened. This was the truth. A lovely summer's day, but the vicar was writing a Christmas sermon. Who talks about the birth of Christ in July? A distracted man, planning a message he already knew by heart. Every clergyman knows his Christmas talk from end to end, because it is by far the best attended and the most remarked. With murder frontmost in his mind, he hadn't been able to preach anything new.

And still my eyes were locked on the girl's. I couldn't tell her. I could only say: 'Jenny, I'll always be here for you.'

I went to Lady Dorian and gave in my notice. I didn't tell her what I knew. I just said I needed to go. She looked at me as if she'd already forgotten who I was.

Jenny actually became a WREN in the second war. She dropped the nickname, though, and lived a quiet life. I followed her from afar, like a madwoman obsessing over a movie star. We met only once, in a post office. She didn't remember me, which made me happy because it means she didn't remember that time. I didn't press it. I never told her anything. But I went to her funeral and talked to her grandchildren. They probably thought I was a fan of her father's. Dorian's, I mean. There were a few there.

The Clerical Terror, a press invention of the 1950s. He wrote twenty-four novels, all set in English villages, all formulaic and predictable—never out of print. His first was called *The Body in the Bathtub.* And I truly think that, if he hadn't got away with murder, he wouldn't have thought to plan one out in prose. His books kept murder clean and bloodless, made it a game between reader and gentleman sleuth. I read the first few, out of morbid, horrified interest. There were a few servants, drifting about in them—mostly adenoidal maids and the occasional blisteringly stupid governess. No gardeners, though. His gardens fixed themselves.

People are trying to reclaim him now. 'Not cosy crime!' they're saying—not like that box office poison, Agatha Christie, but a forerunner to 'Cool Britannia' or whatever they're calling the current movement. He was all British, he was edgy, he knew about the darker side of life. They don't really have evidence for this. His real secret to success was that he kept on writing, so people kept on reading. But they made a film last year and it was all dark and sexy so now people are saying the books are like that. They're not. Still, the Clerical Terror did know the darker side of life. And he hid that knowledge by turning blood into sport.

Dorothy Snape, 1998

Midnight Blue Sonata
by Jorge Molina

Mortensen was not easy to surprise. Because of his profession, he always had to be one step ahead of everyone else. Deducing, piecing information together, making assumptions. Bringing criminals to justice hinged on those skills, after all.

But I somehow managed to surprise him with my birthday gift for him. Or, at the very least, he let me believe that. Even if he knew all along (and I heavily suspect that he did), he still played along and gave quite a believable reaction. That was nice of him.

I had gotten him tickets for a fiftieth-anniversary screening of *Midnight Blue Sonata* at the Starlight Cinematheque. I knew it would take something like this to get him to take an evening off from his restless investigations and crime-solving. Just me and him and his favourite movie of all time.

The film (which he had seen no less than a hundred times) revolved around a lowly cabaret singer who falls in love with a rich aristocrat in Francoist Spain. It was a landmark picture in the Golden Age of Hollywood, and the lead performance by Marianne Babette was considered one of the best in the history of cinema.

'She was the biggest film star the world has ever seen, or will ever see again,' Mortensen often said about Marianne Babette, undoubtedly his favourite star. 'She had more talent in the mole on her left temple than most actresses have in their entire bodies.'

Apart from the thrill of seeing the film again (a thrill that never faded no matter how many times he watched it), this screening was special because it would be introduced by Lucy Babette, Marianne's younger sister who was rarely seen in public anymore. The print belonged to her personal collection and had been screened only a handful of times.

A full house was sure to be expected, so Mortensen made us arrive two hours before showtime. I told him it was unnecessary, but he insisted. He wanted to be first in line. He wanted to make sure he would get his preferred seat, in perfect view of both the screen and the stage.

He was as elated as I was expecting him to be. He remained completely still throughout Lucy's introduction and barely blinked during the first act of the film, trying to take in every single frame at once. This was the biggest compliment he could give a movie.

Until something changed.

About forty minutes in, I noticed Mortensen relentlessly shifting in his seat. The pants I had ironed for him just that morning were now covered in wrinkles from his fidgeting. His yellow handkerchief wasn't neatly folded in the front pocket of his jacket anymore. He had taken it out to wipe his brow.

I recognised these gestures. I'd seen them many, many times before over the years. I could tell that a very particular side of his brain was being activated. I had just never seen it happen in front of a movie screen before.

'Is everything okay?' I whispered to him, breaking one of the seminal rules of our relationship. He did not respond. He was blocking any outside noise. Another sign I recognised. He removed his hat. The scar across his left eyebrow became more noticeable without it.

The scar that had a thousand origin stories, but refused to give a clear answer. The scar that, in normal circumstances, stood out as the only rough feature in an otherwise peaceful face. But Mortensen wasn't peaceful at the moment. Far from it.

I was not watching the movie anymore; my attention was on whatever was happening with him. He was completely focused on the screen. The images reflected onto his corneas. His face was a mirror of the scene playing in front.

But this was a different type of focus. It was not the sense of wonder, discovery, and total immersion that he usually brought into a theater. It was removed observation. It was objective calculation.

It was the focus he had whenever he was actively solving a crime.

Mortensen, my partner, was gone. And Mortensen, the Best Detective in the World, had taken over completely.

Something had gone terribly wrong. Just what I needed.

The Starlight was our preferred neighbourhood theater. The kind of refurbished nickelodeon movie palace where fifty cents would get you into every movie of the day. The theater where he fell in love with movies. And where I fell in love with him.

Of course, this was before Mortensen was making global headlines. Before the word of mouth about his investigative skills spread amongst tycoons and counts and heiresses. Before his yellow handkerchief and eyebrow scar turned iconic.

Before a local journalist named him the Best Detective in the World; a title that took off in the national press and catapulted him into the spotlight. What the national press was unaware of was that the local journalist was courting Mortensen, that the headline was meant as an inside joke just for us, and that he has taken it to heart too often since then.

Back then, we were just two young broke lads with nothing better to do than lose entire evenings at the Starlight. I was an unemployed writer, new to the city, and looking to fill time. Movies were a great way to fill it. Mortensen was an amateur investigator without any leads to follow.

He was in every show I ever attended. The handsome, mysterious man with a scar on his eyebrow. He fascinated me. So one day I sat next to him. *Midnight Blue Sonata.*

I'd never seen someone able to transport himself onto the screen like that. Starting a habit that I would repeat over and over no matter how hard I tried to stop it, I found myself watching him more intently than I watched the film. I like to believe he didn't notice, but he most certainly did.

I asked him for dinner when the film ended. We have never watched a movie apart since.

That night I learned that he loved film more than anything. Only matched by bringing a criminal to justice. Both scratched his particular itch for bringing sense into chaos.

I learned that films from the Golden Age were his absolute favourite. With their air of melodrama, slow push-ins, and wide pans, and the operatic score guiding the audience towards emotional catharsis. Their leading men with their Greek statue jawlines, the morally ambiguous dames with their unmatched glamour, and the Technicolor backdrops that somehow felt brighter than reality ever did.

And through the years, I learned (often the hard way) that he had a strict movie-watching code. He doesn't eat any movie theater snacks ('too distracting to the ear!'). He'd rather miss a film than take an aisle seat ('the screen needs to fully envelop you from every angle!'). And he *always* stays until the last credit rolled. ('A film is not done until the lights come up!').

But not tonight.

Tonight, Mortensen rushed outside as soon as the credits started rolling. I'd been chastised many times before for attempting to do the very same thing; this was a cardinal sin in his book.

I chased after him, still trying to grasp what had gone wrong. However, when I stepped out of the theater into the evening chill, I could not find him anywhere.

It wasn't until I walked a good two blocks north that I found him stepping out of a phone booth. I waved at him, with equal amounts of concern and frustration. I knew that whatever had happened, it would fall on me to get it out of him.

He came to my side and took out a cigarette that I then lit up for him. I waited for him to say something. He didn't. His mind was elsewhere. Not with the movie, where it would usually remain for an hour or two after we left a theater. It was somewhere else entirely.

I knew that look. It was the look he got when a solution had not appeared for him yet. When the pieces failed to fit together.

I put a hand on his shoulder, trying and failing to hide my frustration. 'Tell me what you're thinking. 'I learned early in our relationship it was best to not question or stop his mental processes. The only way I would get a response was asking him to bring me along with it.

'Marianne Babette.' He said, almost in a whisper.

I looked at him blankly. Did I hear him right?

'Marianne Babette? What about her?' Sweat was dripping down his brow. I handed him his yellow handkerchief. He mindlessly took it and wiped himself.

'It changes everything, darling. *Everything*. That one scene. It's all in that one scene. It's all been wrong. All this time. Marianne Babette. Everyone has been wrong.'

'Wrong about what?'

'Her death.'

I looked at him, not trying to hide my frustration and confusion anymore. 'Her death was an accident, Mortensen. You've read more about that case than anyone else in the world.'

'That was no accident.'

'What are you implying?'

'It was murder.'

Mortensen didn't ever get starstruck. He had handled cases that concerned the most famous movie stars, notable politicians, and renowned socialites. He believed the preconceptions that fame and admiration brought could easily cloud one's judgment.

However, earlier that evening, Mortensen had been starstruck by Lucy Babette. It was the closest he would ever get to the woman he had been idolising since he was a boy.

Lucy Babette was Marianne's younger sister; only slightly, by less than a year. She was now close to eighty-five years old, although she didn't look a day over fifty. She came to the theater wrapped inside a gigantic fur coat, wearing a pillbox hat of the kind that is not made anymore, and with a recently dyed, pitch-black bob haircut.

But most striking was Lucy's remarkable similarity to her sister. Not that it was a surprise. After all, Lucy did build her career being Marianne's double. It was hard not to imagine that this was how Marianne would look like had she survived. Only the mole on Marianne's left temple separated them.

'I must *thank* you all so *very* much for coming here *tonight.*' Lucy had a very particular speech pattern, where she highlighted seemingly random words. Besides the missing birthmark, that was the biggest telltale sign that this was not indeed Marianne. It was clear that her own career path did not involve diction training.

'Marianne would be *delighted* to see that her legacy *continues* after all these years.' She told the packed house. 'Her *biggest* wish was always to be immortalised *forever.* And I am happy to see that her wish has come *true.*'

She then proceeded to recount her and her sister's journey through Hollywood, a story Mortensen and I knew too well. How their parents immigrated at the turn of the century from Spain or Mexico or Argentina. I could never remember which.

Right away, their father saw a successful path in vaudeville for his daughters. He devised a double act, not before making them change their names from Mariana and Lucía Barrios to Marianne and Lucy Babette. 'No one questions a Frenchwoman,' he would say.

The Babette Sisters quickly gained popularity throughout the country: 'Marianne could *sing* and *dance*, while I did the high-adrenaline acrobatics. She had the personality. I had the *guts.*' Lucy continued. 'It didn't take long for *Hollywood* to come knocking.'

'But they only wanted *her*. They wanted the girl who *charmed* the crowds, not the one who *scared* them. I wanted her to take it. To go on without me. I was *exhausted*; I didn't know if I could *sustain* this lifestyle. But she wouldn't do it. She built it into her contracts that she would *only* do movies if I was her double. She even made them promise that we would *share* a dressing room, which we did until the very end. The rest is *history*.'

And indeed it was. Marianne Babette became a sensation; first in silent movies, and then into the sound era. Her voice was as enchanting as her face; her singing as fine-tuned as her acting. She supported her parents until their deaths and her sister until her own demise.

Marianne starred in nearly five dozen films (Mortensen could recite them chronologically at the drop of a hat). Her sister was her double in nearly all of them. She amassed twelve Academy Award nominations and won two of them.

'Her *presence* set everything on *fire*,' Lucy said, in awe of her sister, as if her image in movies had somehow surpassed her own memories of her. 'She was a star as *bright* and as complicated as they came.'

She was indirectly referring to the many rumours (some confirmed, most of them not) that Marianne Babette loved men, parties, and booze as much as she loved making movies. That she slept with every single man she ever shared a screen with. That she hated her family behind closed doors. That she demanded one bottle of gin per page of dialogue. That she died no fewer than three times in an ambulance before being revived.

Those were the facts that fascinated me the most about her. After all, there always tends to be some truth behind even the most vile of rumours. But those were the facts that Mortensen refused to entertain;

he was a bit of a stick in the mud when it came to his idol. 'Useless gossip used to tarnish her name. Inflammatory headlines that rival studios planted to try to lower her box office power. . . ' he would bicker.

'And although her life was *quite* extraordinary, bigger than most people can ever *dream* of, it is simply unfortunate that she is mostly remembered for the *tragic* way in which it ended. So I am *delighted* to share this little home video of mine with you, and I thank you all for coming to watch her as she *lived*.'

That's all she had to say before thanking the audience again and slipping to the back of the theater. That's all she had to say about the fire that ended her sister's life. The fire that happened on the last day of shooting the very film we were about to watch.

Midnight Blue Sonata was directed by Maximilian Wells, one of the most celebrated (and volatile) directors of the era. Maximilian was also Marianne's husband. They met during one of Marianne's early movies and maintained an on-and-off affair for years.

Their relationship brimmed with passion, oversized displays of emotion, and impulsive decisions. Marianne was Maximilian's muse, and for her muse, he wrote three movies, which became known as *The Magenta Trilogy* because of their pigmented titles: *The White Serenade, Red Velvet Rhapsody,* and *Midnight Blue Sonata.*

The films led to the best critical acclaim the pair would ever receive. Even I, who wouldn't put her anywhere near the top of my favourite performers (another sore spot in my relationship with Mortensen) cannot deny that she is nothing less than transcendental in the trilogy.

The third film was widely considered the best one, and it cemented Marianne as a legendary presence in Hollywood. But not just because of her performance, as Lucy had so coyly suggested in her introduction.

Although there are several, conflicting reports of what happened, it's now commonly accepted that on the last day of shooting *Midnight Blue Sonata,* while the cast and crew were celebrating with a party at the studio's canteen, Marianne fell asleep in her dressing room. A candle caught her room on fire and engulfed her before anyone could go in. Her body became unrecognisable.

Many believe she was under the influence of her infamous 'martini shots', another urban legend. No one knew what was in them, or even if they were real. It was said she took one every time she finished a movie to celebrate. But the autopsy revealed a lethal combination of pills and drugs that knocked her unconscious.

Lucy left Hollywood after the incident, unwilling to continue a career without her sister. Maximilian was also left bereft; of a muse, of a wife, of any creativity. In one of those twists of fate, Lucy and Maximilian found solace in each other, and a couple of years later got married and moved to Spain or Mexico or Argentina. I could never remember which.

Although rumours circulated about the timeline and true nature of their relationship, they led a happy life outside of movies. Maximilian died of a heart attack about a decade or so ago. And Lucy remained outside the public limelight.

Until this anniversary screening, featuring a mostly unseen print. A print that Mortensen was now demanding to see up close himself.

I chased Mortensen back to the Starlight. He was moving as fast as his mind. He rushed past a scared usher trying to close the doors and climbed the narrow stairs that led to the projection booth. Someone much bigger was now blocking his path.

'I cannot allow you to do that, sir. It is extremely sensitive material.' said an older man, as I finally caught up to him. I quickly identified him as the projectionist of the theater. He was about seventy, rugged and broad. He had probably handled more yards of film footage than there were bricks in the Great Wall of China. Watched more films in a year than most people watch in their lifetimes.

'You don't understand. This is an absolutely *pressing* matter.' Mortensen's voice was starting to break under the pressure of his own thoughts. 'This—this is cinematic history that's at stake!'

'Precisely. I cannot allow you to see, let alone handle footage this fragile. Miss Babette personally called us to schedule and programme this print. . . '

'But you don't—'

I squeezed Mortensen's shoulder. It was our private signal that adverted him that he was toeing the line. That reined in his worst instincts. It was another ritual that we had arrived at through trial and error. I could hear him take a deep breath.

'What is your name, dear sir?' Mortensen finally asked.

'Name's Broadbent. Stuart Broadbent' The projectionist said, responding to Mortensen's softening tone.

'Mr. Broadbent. My name is Mortensen. Detective James Mortensen. Perhaps you've read about me in the papers.' Broadbent's eyes widened in recognition. I knew that response too well.

'Aren't you. . . ? The one that was behind the—?'

'Yes, precisely. Mr. Broadbent, I may have been called the Best Detective in the World, but I consider myself a cinephile first. I can only assume you are one, as well. One has to be able to run a show as smooth and polished as you do every week here.'

Mr. Broadbent smiled. Looked back at the booth with pride. 'Nothing better in the world than losing yourself in the dark with strangers in front of a screen.' He beamed.

Mortensen smiled too. This was their language. A language I had become fluent in by marriage, but that was the mother tongue of them both.

'See, what you and I do is not so different, Mr. Broadbent. I consider film and crime two sides of the same coin. Both are puzzles to solve. Scattered information that only takes meaning after carefully assessing each separate element together.'

Broadbent was intrigued. I could see him leaning in. I relaxed my squeeze on Mortensen. Shifting into our own language now. He was doing good. This urged him to keep going.

'In film, the alchemy between the actors and the script and the costumes and the lights and the music create something singular, unmistakable and undeniable. It's that same alchemy that occurs when all clues and facts point towards the one, definitive solution of a crime. And you can help me right now to bring that alchemy to life.'

Broadbent took all of that in. He cleared his throat. 'What do you need, exactly?'

'I don't want to handle the film. I understand how precious it is. I am just asking you. . . no, *imploring* you to run it for me. Specifically, the balcony scene.'

'The balcony scene? Why that one?' Broadbent asked, genuinely curious now.

'I believe the truth about Marianne Babette's death is in that scene.'

We stood in silence for a few seconds, until Broadbent opened the booth for us.

'Come on in, it will take me a few minutes.' He said as he went into his office.

Mortensen turned to me. He was smiling. Frenzy had given place to pride. A very particular type of glee was bubbling up to the surface. He was now realising that the two things he loved most in the world were finally mixing.

He stepped into the office as I, the third thing he loved most, trailed behind.

The projection booth was cramped and at the same time incredibly tidy. Tins of canned footage. Vintage posters of movies that had been long forgotten. Framed archival pictures. It was the embodiment of what I imagined Mortensen's head to look like.

He was staring intently at an old framed photograph. He was switching back and forth from setting his attention on the image to losing himself in his thoughts. I could notice the almost imperceptible change in his blinking.

I looked at the framed picture. In faded, cursive handwriting on top read the words:

Midnight Blue Sonata, Wrap Party, Zimmerman Studios.

I'd never seen that picture before. And if I hadn't, odds were that Mortensen hadn't either. This tiny room above the theater where we'd spent countless evenings was now a time portal. A peephole into another time and place.

I stood next to him. 'Mortensen, can you please tell me what's going on? I'm frankly baffled at your behaviour.' The truth is I wasn't baffled. This completely tracked with his behaviour. I was annoyed that he managed to turn his birthday gift into a scavenger hunt.

He stayed silent for a few moments, and then said to me without turning, 'What do you remember about her death?'

'Whose death? Marianne's? Are you still on that. . . ?'

'Please, darling. Amuse me.'

He turned to me and smiled. He looked like a cat begging you to play with it, even though the last time you did, it left scars on your forearm. Against my better instincts, I played along with Mortensen.

'She died in a fire.'

'Oh, come on. Everyone knows that. What else? We've been living together long enough. Something must have rubbed off on you.'

'She died on the last day of shooting this movie. *Midnight Blue Sonata.*'

'Do you know what was the last scene they shot that day?'

I opened my mouth, but I actually could not recall that fact. It was one of many that Mortensen would throw my way that I just could not possibly retain.

'It was the balcony scene.' He said, anticipating my blank mind.

'What does that have to do with anything. . . ?'

The projector started to whirl, and in a few seconds, the film was being projected onto the theater below. 'There you go', Broadbent murmured under his breath, as Mortensen ran to the little window that showed the screen in the theater below. The beginning of the balcony scene was being projected onto it.

Marianne Babette and Elias Meriweather, her leading man in turn (and in my opinion, the most dashing Hollywood star of the time, perhaps ever) were arguing in the balcony of a palace. She would go on to take a tumble, hang from the railings, and almost fall. It was not the best scene of the movie, but it was an amusing display of screwball comedy.

'Do you want me to run it?' Broadbent asked.

'No, no. Let us play a little game of wits first.' He turned to me. 'What do you see?'

He'd reached the point of enjoyment. The point where he knew that he understood more than anyone around him, and he revelled in that feeling. He claimed it wasn't superiority; just pleasure in bringing others into the light. But it absolutely was superiority. I'd learned to ignore it, almost like white noise, but it was managing to seep through today.

'What is happening there?' he said, pointing to the screen.

'Well, Marianne is clearly in distress. She's just been rejected. Humiliated, in a way. She's probably thinking that—' I said, trying to cater to what I thought he wanted to hear.

'No. No. What do you *see*? What's in the frame?'

'Oh. Well, Marianne is leaning down from the balcony. . . ' I looked closer. 'The sun is setting. There are. . . rainclouds passing by behind her. They look like. . . a crab? I don't know what you want me to say.'

'You said the exact right things, darling. So now you understand?'

'What do you mean?'

'Marianne. And the clouds.'

'Mortensen, I don't know what you're talking about.' I hated looking a fool for him.

He smiled at me. A smile I knew well and I hated seeing. It wasn't frustration or anger. It was a loving form of pity.

'My darling. It all hinges on those two things. Let me ask you, are you absolutely certain those are clouds? And even more so, are you absolutely certain that is Marianne Babette?'

We went down to the theater, as I tried to collect my thoughts. The room looked vast without people eagerly taking their seats. The smell of popcorn had dissipated, giving place to floor cleaner and polished suede. It felt like we were trespassing on a sacred space.

The screen was still showing the balcony scene. Marianne Babette leaned down against the balcony, on the verge of falling. Or who I was certain was Marianne Babette, but now Mortensen had given me every reason to doubt myself.

Mortensen stood below the screen, looking minuscule under the giant actress.

'Darling, please look closer now. Look at the clouds again,' he asked me. Every inch of the frame was ten times as big up close. I focused my eye on the backdrop.

'I don't know what you want me to say, Mortensen. Those look like clouds. Thick clouds. Grey clouds. Grey clouds that look like a crab.'

Mortensen turned around and made a motion towards the booth. The scene kept playing, without any sound. 'Keep your eye on them.'

After a few seconds, I found something strange, but I couldn't pinpoint what it was. 'What am I supposed to be looking at?'

'Maybe it's the fact that the sun is not setting, even though the clouds are moving.'

I looked at the screen closer. Mortensen was right. While the heavy clouds seemed to be moving behind Marianne, the sunset never reached its conclusion. 'Maybe it's just a production trick. Actual fake smoke for the clouds, but a painted backdrop,' I said.

He came to my side and looked up alongside me. 'Darling, sometimes I wish you paid less attention to the way I look at things and more to the actual things I am looking at. Maybe you'd understand me better that way.'

I didn't know how to respond to that. So I didn't. I looked up again. Stared at the face of Marianne Babette. A face I'd seen countless times before, but that I was now doubting.

'I just don't see how you can say that is not Marianne, Mortensen. Her headshot adorned our boudoir for years. Until I finally convinced you that Mother held a bigger sentimental value and had a worthier place on there.'

'I'm still not sure about that, by the way.' He joked.

'But it's all up there. Her smile. Her eyes. You can even see her mole under the wig.'

'Ah, the *mole*. She had more talent in the mole on her left temple than most actresses have in their entire bodies.' He repeated his mantra.

'You have to give me *something*.'

'Let me say this. I'll tell you what went through my mind earlier. As I was watching, I had the most unnerving feeling that this was not a movie I had seen before.'

I laughed. 'But Mortensen, that's one of the things I like most about you. How you're able to watch something with new eyes. You must have seen this movie hundreds of times!'

'Precisely! That's why I'm so certain there was completely new footage. On *this* scene. The original version did not have any clouds. And the answer relies on *that*!'

Before I could say anything else, someone barged in.

'Sorry to interrupt. Mortensen. We're here. This better be good.' A hoarse voice exclaimed. A voice I knew extremely well.

'Ah, Inspector, thank you so much for coming.' Mortensen turned and approached Inspector Appleton, the head of the police department. He and Mortensen had been working in hesitant partnership for years. 'Were you able to do what I asked?'

'We did. And you were correct, she was about to head to the airport.'

'I'm glad I made that call on time!' he said to himself and then turned to me. 'Apologies for my hurried run after the screening. When I saw she hadn't stayed through the credits, I knew I didn't have much time. As much as it pained me to rush out like that.'

'Could *anyone* please let me *know* what this hassle is all *about*?' another voice echoed through the back of the theater. A voice with a particular pattern that had never seen a dialect coach.

Lucy Babette strutted through the aisle, far less pleasant than she had been earlier that day. Mortensen was, somehow, much less starstruck this time around.

'Thank you so much for coming, Miss Babette. I hope it was not too much of an inconvenience.' Mortensen said.

'Well, I'm afraid it *was*. I had previous engagements that I had to *cancel*. I may be *old*, but I'm still needed and *expected*. Who are you?' Lucy said, sitting in the front row.

'This is Detective James Mortensen. He has a few questions to ask you, ma'am,' said Inspector Appleton. I could see the tiniest reaction from Lucy at the mention of Mortensen's name. She knew who he was, but she didn't want to let him know she knew.

'A *detective*. Am I under investigation? Under *arrest*?' She took out a cigarette and lit it up. I immediately thought of how the ushers would have to get rid of the smell. I know Mortensen thought about that too.

'Well, let's hope not, ma'am. I just wanted to ask you a few questions about your sister.'

'Detective, I laid my sister down to rest *years* ago, and it was *hard* enough to bring her memory back earlier today. *Must* you make me walk down this path again. . . ?'

'All I want to know is where you were during the fire that killed your sister.'

Her eyes widened. She was uncomfortable. How could she not be? She shifted in her seat. Those seats had gotten their fair share of shifting this evening.

'It was such *tragedy*, of *course*. I was unable to get there in time. No one could.'

'A tremendous loss to the world, I agree with you. But where were you? Reports at the time said you claimed to be at the canteen for the celebration.' Mortensen pressed.

'I *was* there. I was *celebrating* with the rest of the cast and the crew. *Everyone* was there. There was music. There was dancing. We didn't want it to end.'

'See, there is just one thing I don't understand. Please, hold on a moment. . . '

Mortensen ran out of the theater, as everyone else watched, perplexed. No one moved or said anything until he returned. He was carrying something. A large frame. He was bringing with him the framed photograph from the projection booth.

Mortensen handed this to Lucy Babette. She remained totally quiet. ' *Where* did you. . . ?' was all she could let out.

'Ah, yes. It was believed most of these behind-the-scenes pictures were lost when Zimmerman Studios was demolished. Fortunately, a young projectionist working there at the time believed in preserving film history and made sure to save all paraphernalia. . . '

He waved back at the projection booth with a huge smile. The lights of the theater flickered. Broadbent smiled back at us from above.

'Now, can you help explain how, if you were at the commissary. . . ' Mortensen pointed to the photograph again. '. . . you are nowhere to be seen in this picture?'

The room went silent. Lucy Babette cleared her throat, trying to regain composure.

'I'm not sure I *like* what you are implying, Detective. It was a hectic day. People were in a *frenzy*. I. . . I must have been *away* when that was taken---'

'But you just said everyone was there. If you were not there, where else could you have possibly been?'

Mortensen started pacing. It was a big cliché of the profession, but I understood after watching him do it a few times that it was a way to let out bottled energy.

'You said it yourself earlier today. You and your sister shared a dressing room until the very end. Now, *that* seems like a natural place you would be in, doesn't it? But you weren't there. Or you would have seen Marianne. You would have sensed something was wrong. A candle dangerously dangling, or maybe one of those infamous "martini shots". . . '

'*Stop*, detective! I don't appreciate your insinuations! I can *promise* you with all certainty I was not with my *sister*. Now, I may not recall where I was, but it was *fifty* years ago. . . '

'Mortensen, do you have a point? I don't like where this is going. . . ' Inspector Appleton interjected.

'Just indulge me with one final question.' He motioned again to the booth, and the balcony scene was projected again. 'This print is from your personal collection, isn't it?'

'Yes, the studio gave *me* a copy after the *tragedy*. I keep it *dear* to my heart.'

'Have you ever done anything with it?'

'*Done* anything? What do you mean by that?'

'Tampered with it. Modified it in any way.'

'Of *course* not! Why would I mess with a *masterpiece*?' she exclaimed, offended. I have to admit by this point I was completely clueless to Mortensen's line of thinking. Maybe he had gotten too close with this one.

He then turned to me, with a smile. 'Darling, can you come here for a moment?' I obeyed, although I was confused. 'How did you describe the clouds in the background to me?'

'Oh. Thick. . . .grey rainclouds. . . that look like a crab.'

'I always loved how specific your choice of vocabulary is. You chose the right profession. Now, would you say that. . . ' he took the frame from Lucy. '*These* clouds in the edge of the photograph are also thick grey rainclouds that look remarkably like a crab?'

He pointed to a window in the corner of the photograph. The exact same cloud formation clearly appeared outside the studio canteen.

'I've seen this movie hundreds of times, Miss Babette. And I can assure you those clouds do not appear in other prints. Also, I'd dare to say that those are not cloud formations at all. They are too thick and dark for the type that would be made for a movie. No, I would bet that this is. . . *smoke.*'

I looked closer at the picture, and then at the screen above us. He was right. Those weren't dark clouds. That was a trail of smoke.

'Smoke from a nearby building that was burning down. Smoke that you would have *had* to see if you were filming the balcony scene; a scene that involved many physical stunts. But *why* were you and Maximilian Wells filming again after the movie had wrapped? While the cast and crew were celebrating? And why keep this completely new scene only in your personal print. . . ?'

Mortensen looked at me as he said this. And then it all clicked. I understood what Mortensen felt watching the movie. The frenzy that he had been put through. I was now surprised that he didn't spontaneously combust. I had a lot less restraint than he did.

'Oh my God! It was *her*. She started the fire! She killed her own sister! To get together with the director! The rumours were true!' I yelled, almost unconsciously.

Lucy stood up, infuriated. 'I am *leaving*! I cannot believe this. *This* is why I left the industry. The rumours, the insinuations! Do you *have* any actual proof?'

'Mortensen, this is starting to sound a lot like a gossip column.' Inspector Appleton was starting to get restless.

'You're right, ma'am. I have no proof that Lucy Babette killed her sister. Because that is an irrefutably wrong fact.'

I stopped in my tracks. What was he saying?

'But you are not Lucy Babette. You are indeed Marianne Babette herself!'

And in one swoop motion, Mortensen leaned in and grabbed onto Lucy Babette's brand new bob haircut, and pulled it. The hair slid off easily, to reveal a concealed wig cap underneath.

And among the shrieks and the gasps, what was made most evident was that on the left temple of that woman was a large, unmovable, iconic mole.

Mortensen kept pacing through the aisles as he spoke. I was motionless, following him with my gaze, trying not to miss a single detail.

'You always thought of Lucy as your second fiddle. An expendable toy. A shadow you could not rid yourself of. That story you told, about how you allegedly begged her to come to Hollywood with you. That wasn't you. That was your father. She forced her onto you. And you always resented her for being too eager to do it. . . '

Miss Babette was expressionless. She did not try to leave, or object. She was quietly observing and listening to the accusations thrown at her.

'You hated her all your career. There were hundreds of reports of your terrible feuds and jealousies. I always dismissed them as rumours. Mere tabloid fare. But there's always some truth buried underneath. . .

' he turned to me as he said that. Maybe something of mine had rubbed onto him as well.

'So she trapped her own sister on her trailer and set fire to it. . . ?' I asked aloud, being immersed in the mystery as if it was a movie I was watching.

'They celebrated together with one of your famous 'martini shots', but you made sure to make them. . . stronger than usual. Lucy had a lot less tolerance for hard substances than you, and after she passed out, a simple tumble of a candle made sure her body would become unrecognisable enough that it could feasibly pass as your own.

And to prove once and for all that you didn't need her, while the rest of the cast was celebrating, you did your own stunts for the first time in your life. Your husband, being the director and true love of your life, helped you. And the two of you kept the footage to insert into your copy of the film as a souvenir. . . '

He stopped. Silence filled the room. And then Miss Babette started to laugh, her cackles echoed as if they were blasting in surround sound from the speakers.

'I knew this would prove too irresistible for you,' she said. The random emphasis on the words was gone. A transatlantic accent that only someone who grew up among sound stages could know took its place instead.

'Detective, I really must thank you. You truly have proven yourself to be my most devoted fan. You've gone more times on the record about your love for me and my films than about any cases you have solved in your career. . . '

Mortensen blushed. I knew that, even in these circumstances, it did not bypass him that he was being recognised by someone he had been idolising for decades. 'So I was right. You carefully planned this,' he chuckled. 'The moment Broadbent mentioned that you personally called the theater to programme this print, I could feel the intention behind it. . . '

'For being the Best Detective in the World, you're quite easy to track down.' She smirked.

'I'm sorry, I don't understand what is happening.' Inspector Appleton said, echoing the questions in my own head.

Marianne Babette smiled. 'Let me explain the first rule you learn about Hollywood as an actress, Inspector. Your career has a shelf life. Thirty, thirty-five years. Forty if you are lucky. Especially back in those days. After that, you might as well be dog food. . . '

She had found an audience. And like one of the most talented actresses of her (and any other) generation, she was performing for them.

'I knew I didn't have long after Max wrote that final film for me. I was close to turning forty. The roles would stop coming soon. Even if he could keep writing me movies forever, the audience appeal and funding would disappear. But I wasn't ready to let go. . . '

She turned to the screen. To her own image, fifty years younger. 'One of the things about film is that it can give you something no one else can. You can become immortal in a piece of celluloid. . . ' she turned back to us.

'But it's one thing to be immortalised in film. And another to be immortalised in *history*. And what's the most sure-fire way to be remembered forever? By the way you *die.'*

She let the words hang. She knew she was sucking the air out of the room. She enjoyed it. 'I have to give Max the credit. He came up with it. Me and my sister switching places. Her dying instead of me. I got to see how the world would remember me. I would not let the industry push me out. I'd go out with a *bang*. . . .' She stopped, and grew grimmer.

'And it worked. For years, we looked from afar as the world mourned my death. Turning me into an icon. An irreplaceable star. . . '

'But then that stopped too,' Mortensen said, harshly.

'Hollywood is not what it used to be, Detective. There's no respect or reverence for the past. My work, my story, my persona. . . all got relegated to arthouse theaters and archival prints. My audience used to be millions around the world. . . .now it's just a handful of matinee seniors and overeager dandies. . . ' She looked at us with pointed bitterness.

'Then Max passed. And I was as lonely and forgotten as I always feared I would be. But then. . . then it occurred to me. . . who lives even longer than a dead icon?' She paused. 'A *resurrected* icon.'

Mortensen chuckled to himself. 'Hence The Starlight Cinematheque Presents: Midnight Blue Sonata. Fiftieth anniversary. Rare print in 35mm. With an introduction by Lucy Babette.'

'I couldn't have done it without you, Detective. Thanks to you, my career will live longer than I ever could have dreamed of. . . ' she said, as she laughed to herself. Out of reality. Or perhaps, embracing the new reality that was just settling in.

Inspector Appleton had heard enough. He took a pair of handcuffs out of his pocket and tied them around Marianne Babette's wrists. She willingly went along with him.

I looked at Mortensen as he watched her go. There was a flicker in his eye. The credits were rolling in his mind, and he was staying all the way through.

Mortensen and I sat at our usual table at our usual restaurant. The one we always went to after the Starlight. The one we chose on that very first evening.

'When did you know?' I finally asked him. There were many questions circling in my head, but that was the first one that came to mind.

'She said it all from the start, darling. In her introduction. 'Marianne's *biggest* wish was always to be immortalised *forever*,' he said with a glimmer in his eye. 'I told you, darling. You have to watch what I'm looking at just as closely as you're watching me.'

'Why didn't you say anything? Why let me doubt that it was Marianne?' I asked, curious.

'I never said that it wasn't her. I just made you look into your own reasoning. You hate it when I give you the answers right away. You like to get there yourself.' He was right. 'I have to give it to you, though. You truly memorised her face. You were convinced it was her up there, and you were right.'

'She was important to you. So I made her important to me.'

We kept quiet for a few more moments. The dessert arrived. We always shared a gelato.

'I'm very sorry your idea of Marianne Babette is gone,' I said.

'I just watched her give her last and perhaps best performance ever. This turned out better than I could possibly have imagined. Thank you for those tickets.'

He dove his spoon into the bowl, focusing his joy on the sweetness in front of him. I would try harder next time, but tonight, I still enjoy watching him a lot more than watching whatever thing he is looking at.

Murder on the Honeymoon
by Claire Tyler

Susan Everly, a young woman for whom death was no stranger, stood in the hotel room she shared with her husband, gazing out from a large window in the cheery mid-morning light, waiting for him to finish dressing for breakfast. They made a handsome young couple; Susan, with her wide Botticelli eyes and a practiced air of composure that lingered even through grief; and Kenneth, as charming and attentive a young man could practically be, sporting neatly combed blond hair and an easy smile that could have caught the attention of anyone he set his sights on, which, as fate had it, had turned out to be Susan.

Susan knew, and bore this knowledge with no real emotion one way or another, that Kenneth Everly would not have become her husband two weeks prior, and perhaps not ever, had it not been for the shocking and untimely death of Wilson Hughes, her beloved older brother. A newly bereaved sister and a newlywed, Susan had embarked with Kenneth directly from their wedding in London to their honeymoon in a charmingly small but beautifully furnished hotel, formerly a manor house, in the Cornish countryside. Susan had insisted upon the location, having spent many a happy childhood holiday there with her parents and brother. Of the four of them, she was now the only one left.

It had been well over a decade since her last visit, and from her vantage point on the second floor, she looked down over the hedge garden that was planted behind the hotel. The window itself was bordered on either side by the waxy leaves and encroaching tendrils of vines growing up the trellises that lined the back wall of the hotel. In the centre of the garden stood a stone fountain adorned with carved vases, and rows of boxwood hedges meandered around four individual flower-beds, each planted with a thoughtful variety of flowers such that no matter the season, there would always be flowers blooming. Now was the time for roses, and Susan imagined she could smell them even through the closed window.

Beyond the garden lay a vast expanse of sloping hillside. Looking to the south, Susan fixed her eyes on the familiar sliver of ocean that lay just below the horizon, feeling a familiar longing she could not quite articulate. The sea was, to her, as a lighthouse is to a ship. An icon of relief—distant, yet always present, if only one is close enough to see it.

'Darling, are you quite ready?' Kenneth called from the wash-room.

Susan blinked, and then replied that yes, she was. Soon Kenneth emerged, and, seeing her turn to face him, raised his arm for her to take. He looked the perfect gentleman in his cream-coloured linen suit, his hair combed suavely to the left, and Susan chastised herself for not feeling more comforted by his presence. He had been good friends with her late brother, and yet she still couldn't bring herself to explain to him how empty everything felt now that he was gone, and how it seemed that she was seeing the world through smoked glass. She knew how hard he was trying to ease the burden of her sudden loss, and so she took his arm and returned his smile, the one that put a slight crinkle at the corners of his pale blue eyes, as best she could. After all, he was her husband.

Arm in arm, they descended the ornately carved wooden staircase that led to the chequered tile lobby on the ground floor. A magnificent crystal chandelier hung from the centre of the tall ceiling, and with sunlight streaming into the room through the latticed windows set into the wall of the hotel's main entrance, the space seemed to take on an enchanted glow.

The pair strolled to the back of the lobby, opposite the front door and past the reception desk, just as they had done every morning for the past two weeks, and entered the dining room. As usual, the two large French doors at the far end of the room stood open, allowing the fresh air and the birdsong from the hedge garden beyond to lighten the atmosphere inside. The room was decorated in a traditional countryside manner, with wall sconces and deep burgundy curtains and small dark-stained wooden tables and chairs, most of which were already occupied.

As tends to happen with guests spending long stretches of time at a hotel, routines set by happenstance had solidified into daily habits, and many of the tables had become unofficially claimed by various parties. At a table near the front of the room sat—as always, as far as Susan and Kenneth were concerned—Mrs. Benson and her young niece. Mrs. Benson, a well-mannered lady of a respectable age, was quietly reprimanding the girl for some small thing or another, and the girl, who had apparently long grown accustomed to this sort of interaction, did not seem to be listening very closely.

In the middle of the room, near the right wall, sat Mr. and Mrs. Tremaine. Mr. Tremaine was an older gentleman who looked as though he had enjoyed many a glass of port in his youth, as well as in his middle and current age, and for whom the word 'whiskers' could aptly be used in a casual onlooker's description of his beard. Mrs. Tremaine, in contrast, looked to be at least two decades younger than her husband, an impression accentuated by the deep crimson lipstick she wore at all hours and the lustre of her carefully curled blonde hair. The little laughs and smiles she made at her husband's oft-repeated anecdotes seemed to Susan to be waning in believable authenticity with each passing day.

Seated across from the Tremaines on the left wall was Colonel Perkins, a man slightly past middle age, who was rarely seen without a pipe in his mouth. He had a casual, almost boyish air about him, and would often, with a note of genuine wonder and joy in his voice, point out how lovely or marvellous a simple thing would be; a bird alighting on the fountain, the cherries served atop an evening dessert, or perhaps the pillows on the lounge sofa on the second floor. He tended to initiate conversations with the other guests whether they were expecting him to or not.

Of the two tables near the back of the room by the open French doors, one sat unoccupied, and at the other sat Mr. Templeton, a gentleman of uncertain age who was traveling alone. He kept mostly to himself, apart from exchanging the usual pleasantries with the other guests, often sitting alone in the lounge or the garden and writing in the little brown notebook he kept in his breast pocket.

Susan and Kenneth took their usual seats at the empty table next to Mr. Templeton, and they had barely settled into their chairs when a loud *slam* echoed in from the lobby. A faint 'terribly sorry!' could be heard above some indistinct clatter, along with a couple of hushed admonishments. The dining room, which had fallen suddenly silent at the noise, quickly picked up its chatter, and a few minutes later a new set of guests arrived through the door.

More specifically, a large, playful black spaniel trotted into the dining room, followed by a thoroughly unamused-looking elderly man in a wheelchair pushed by a young man with slightly messy hair and a look of mild overexertion about him. The two men bore a slight resemblance to one another, if one were to look at the right angle. As the spaniel circled the room, happily nosing at the guests at each table, the young man wheeled the older man to a table near the centre of the room and positioned him so that he could look out to the garden beyond.

The initial commotion was short-lived, and table by table, the room's occupants returned to their own affairs once more. Susan turned to Kenneth, about to ask whether he had enjoyed the French toast he'd ordered the day prior and whether perhaps he thought she ought to try it, but found his gaze fixed on the table with the two newcomers. His brow was creased, and he appeared lost in thought.

'Good heavens. Susan, I know those men. Old man Atkinson used to work at the office with Wilson and me. Mostly before our time, though. Retired ages ago, but that son of his still wheels him in from time to time. God only knows why.'

'He brings him to the office, you mean? With nothing to do? Whatever for?'

Kenneth shrugged. 'Sometimes people can't let their old lives go—maybe he'd grown attached to it all, didn't want to admit his own obsolescence or something.'

Susan gazed at the elder Mr. Atkinson. 'I see. Do you think he knew Wilson?' Kenneth's attention snapped back to Susan at the mention of her late brother.

'I daresay he did, yes. Not that he'd be able to speak with you about him now, though, darling. He doesn't say much at all these days.' With that, Kenneth cast his eyes around the room. 'You might try the French toast, dear,' he said as he located and waved over the attendant.

As the attendant approached Susan and Kenneth's table, there was another sudden outburst from the newcomers. The elderly man was speaking quite loudly and pointing, it seemed to Susan, to her husband, though his words were largely incoherent.

'Darling, I think he recognizes you,' she said, suddenly uncomfortable.

'Heavens, what a scene,' muttered Kenneth. He made a curt wave to their table in acknowledgment and raised an eyebrow slightly at the younger man, who saw him and quickly shook his head apologetically at what he understood to be an offer to come see what the matter was.

'No, father, I don't have your cane,' Susan faintly heard the younger man say in a practiced soothing tone over the older man's continued slurred words. 'You know you need more than a cane now. No, you are *not* able to walk with just a cane. . . '

Once breakfast was served, Susan and Kenneth ate in mostly silence. As they were finishing up, Kenneth placed a hand over Susan's, which had been resting on the table.

'Darling, I know I said I'd put all business on hold during our honeymoon, but seeing dear Mr. Atkinson just now reminded me there was one thing I'd meant to take care of before the wedding that completely slipped my mind. I'll just nip down to London tonight and I'll be back before you know it.'

Susan looked up at him more in apprehension than disappointment. 'Not to gamble,' she said, her voice so quiet that she practically only mouthed the words.

'No, no,' he chuckled. 'That's all in the past.'

'I know, I do trust you, my dear. I just hope you won't be long.'

'Just until teatime tomorrow, I promise, my plum cake. Don't fret.' He gave her hand a squeeze, and she returned his affable smile as best she could.

As they made their way to the lobby, Susan could just make out the younger Mr. Atkinson saying, 'Father, I already told you, we didn't bring your cane.'

Her husband was gone before Susan knew it. She had spent a fairly uneventful day walking around the grounds, reminiscing to herself about the times she'd successfully clambered up those vine-laden trellises to her room as a young girl, and then relaxing on a bench in the hedge garden, reading a weathered copy of a period novel she'd found abandoned in the lounge. She had always loved to read, finding that she enjoyed losing herself and her own worries in troubles that belonged to other people. As a child, she often lost all sense of time and space when she fell deeply enough into a book, needing to be called several times for supper before she heard. Kenneth had joined her for her walk, then left to pack a few of his things before evening fell. Some time later, he found her in the garden where he gave her a quick kiss on the forehead and a few sweet parting words, and left by cab for a brief visit to the life that Susan dreaded returning to.

To Susan, London still held the shattered promise of her brother's dreams and successes. She remembered how proud he'd been to show her the placard with 'Wilson Hughes' engraved in gold letters on the door to his office at the bank. Their parents had left each of them a not unsizeable amount of money, but Wilson had still wished to make a name for himself of his own accord, perhaps to prove to himself that he didn't need an inheritance to make his way in the world. Susan supposed it was quite lucky that he'd found such a fine business partner in Kenneth so early on in his career, for now she had a husband who shared her fondness for him. After her brother's accident, though, the city that once seemed full of life now struck Susan as cold and impersonal. Kenneth's sudden departure to London struck a note of sad inevitability into her psyche. She couldn't stay in the countryside forever, she knew. She'd have to face her real life again, with Wilson no longer in it.

She decided to stay in the garden and read her book until it was time for tea, no matter how chilly it became. Overhead, the sun slowly slanted down along its daily course, and the air took on the cool damp wind traveling inland from the sea. Only when Susan noticed how badly she was shivering did she close her book and begin to walk, somewhat stiffly, to the lobby door.

Once inside, Susan had just begun to climb the stairs and consider the merits of a warm bath when she heard voices raised, several voices, coming from the lounge. Concerned, she quickly changed direction and approached the lounge door. She could now hear, in addition to the shouting, a stream of terrible, indescribable noises coming from beyond it. She quickly pushed the door, which was already ajar, further open. Mr. and Mrs. Tremaine, along with Colonel Perkins, were standing and looking at something in the far corner of the room, where the point of commotion apparently lay, but she couldn't see past them to see what it was. Then, suddenly, she felt someone take her arm, and found herself being led back through the door.

'My dear Mrs. Everly,' said Mr. Templeton, who had until that moment not spoken to Susan except in polite greeting as they passed one another in the halls, in a hushed voice quite close to her ear. 'Why don't we leave this room for the time being?' He led her back out into the lobby, gently closed the door behind them, and, placing her hand on his arm, began to walk briskly to the reception desk, Susan obediently trotting alongside him to keep up.

'Call an ambulance at once,' said Mr. Templeton as they approached the desk, the tenor of his voice carrying the authority required to impel the receptionist to pick up and start dialling with no hesitation. 'It's the old gentleman, the one who just arrived this afternoon.'

'Mr. Atkinson,' Susan offered in a voice that she did not allow to tremble. 'His name is Mr. Atkinson.'

'Mr. Atkinson,' repeated Mr. Templeton, looking down at Susan somewhat quizzically, as if he hadn't expected her to know more about the man than he did. 'I'm afraid he won't make it; they must come at once.' With the receptionist now busy relaying the relevant information to the emergency line, Mr. Templeton began to walk Susan to the stairs she had just begun to climb a few minutes prior.

'Why don't you go up to your husband, my dear?' he said. 'I'd hate for you to stay down here. Terrible business.' Susan released his arm and looked up at him, finding that even up close, she could not determine his age. His dark hair had just begun to speckle with white at the temples, and he carried a depth in his eyes. He was dressed in a suit finer than was necessary at a small hotel so deep in the countryside.

'I was about to go up to my room anyway,' she replied, still shaken, slightly too evenly to sound natural. 'Though my husband had to leave on business this afternoon. Kenneth. I must introduce you when he returns tomorrow.'

'Yes, you must,' replied Mr. Templeton, who had already begun to turn back to the lounge. 'Goodnight.'

'Goodnight,' said Susan, and kept her eyes turned upward toward the second floor as she ascended the stairs so as to not accidentally catch a glimpse of the scene unfolding in the room below through the open door.

The next morning, Susan was greeted in the dining room by silence broken only by the gentle clinking of silverware by the uncharacteristically quiet hotel guests, and by the low murmur of conversation between the younger Mr. Atkinson, whose eyes were red and sleepless, and a police officer who had joined him at his table. She knew at once what must have transpired. *Poor Mr. Atkinson,* she thought, and felt a terrible sense of weightlessness that she wished she could relieve by reaching for Kenneth's hand, but he wasn't due to return until the afternoon. Instead, she walked past them and took her usual seat at the back of the room.

She was quite absorbed in her own thoughts when she heard footsteps approaching, and she hoped it was the attendant to take her order and not the police officer, though she didn't know why the police officer would want to speak with her, but when she looked up she found it was neither; Mr. Templeton stood before her table, his little brown notebook in his hand, and he gestured with it toward the empty seat usually occupied by her husband.

'May I?' he asked in an undertone. In the relative silence of the room, all noise seemed louder than it really was. Susan hesitated then nodded quickly, extending her hand toward the seat in invitation. Mr. Templeton sat, set his notebook down at the table, and turned his attention to Susan. 'I'm afraid I never properly introduced myself. My name is Henry Templeton. I'm a writer—or at least, I like to think I am. Hence the, ah. . . ' he trailed off and gestured to his notebook. 'Useful thing to have on hand, you know, for when the right thought strikes.' He paused there and waited for her reply, but when there was none forthcoming but for a polite nod, he carried on. 'I hope you didn't think it rude of me to usher you away from the lounge yesterday evening, not having previously made your acquaintance. I just couldn't imagine allowing you to stay in that room when. . . well. I'm sure you've guessed how that turned out, poor fellow.'

'There's no need for an apology, Mr. Templeton. You were very thoughtful. And very quick thinking, to call for an ambulance, even if. . . well.'

'Yes. All a person can do in these cases, sometimes, and you have to live with it.' As he said that, they each turned their attention to the middle of the room, where the young Mr. Atkinson had now stood up and was following the police officer out of the room, the black spaniel trailing at his heels. After they left and the door had been closed for a few moments, a soft murmur began to fill the room as almost everyone began to talk to their table partner at the same time.

Mr. Templeton turned back to face Susan, and leaning toward her slightly, he said, in a conspiratorial whisper, 'I suppose you might be wondering why the police are here.'

Susan's eyebrows shot up. 'Oh! I hadn't considered. I've been so. . . ' she paused, and Mr. Templeton tactfully nodded. 'But please do tell me, if you know.'

'It seems,' he said, 'that there was a break-in, yesterday, before the tragedy occurred. The younger Mr. Atkinson says someone had forced the door to his room open, though it seemed nothing was taken. He didn't think much of it at the time, but of course, now, considering everything. . . so he called the police.'

'Good heavens! Surely—well, I suppose we can't be sure of anything. How horrible.' Then she added, slowly, 'Mr. Templeton, what did occur yesterday? I mean—how did it happen?'

Mr. Templeton sighed. 'Are you sure you'd like to. . . ?'

Susan nodded. 'I've lost both my parents, and a month ago, I lost my only brother. My husband is the only person I have in the world, and yesterday he recognized Mr. Atkinson and told me he had known my brother. Though he apparently couldn't speak about him, or about anything, Mr. Atkinson knew him. He knew Wilson,' she said, somewhat defiantly, knowing her voice would waver as she said his name, and it did. 'I would like to know how it happened.' Mr. Templeton held Susan's steady gaze, his face entirely unreadable to her.

'My dear girl, I am so terribly sorry. Life can be so cruel, and to the least deserving people.' He opened his mouth as if to say something more, then stopped, then began again: 'It was some kind of medical event. I don't know the details, and that suits me just fine, but I get the idea, from what I've heard, or perhaps rather overheard, from the poor man's son, is that his pills were supposed to have prevented it. And the thing is. . . ' Mr. Templeton again leaned over the table, and this time Susan leaned in as well, awaiting his now-familiar hushed tone, 'the pills were in his room last night—during the apparent break-in. He's convinced someone tampered with the pills. He thinks,' Mr. Templeton now said in a whisper, 'he thinks someone murdered his father.'

Susan gazed at Mr. Templeton, aghast. 'Surely. . . !' But the intractable man merely shrugged and sat back in his chair.

'Don't ask me,' said Mr. Templeton.

'But who would. . . ?'

'It's a terrible thing, but at this point, if anyone were to have done it,' mused Mr. Templeton, 'it would be the person with the most to gain, which would be, in this case. . . ' He glanced toward the door.

'Not his son!' hissed Susan, with a note of genuine alarm. 'That's a terrible thing to suggest!'

'Well! Not his son, then,' Mr. Templeton gracefully conceded. 'Though I imagine the old gentleman was quite well off, and he'll be leaving his rather beleaguered son quite a lot of money. . . '

'You seem to be rather content to make speculations,' said Susan.

'My dear lady, you asked me to,' he replied.

'Well, I. . . I suppose I did.'

'And if wasn't the son,' Mr. Templeton continued, 'and it wasn't a mere accident, or a fluke of medicine or the human body, then who was it?'

Susan glanced guiltily around the room. Mrs. Benson was helping her little niece to some more hash browns; Mr. and Mrs. Tremaine were dully staring at their plates; Colonel Perkins was contentedly slicing a row of sausages.

'I can't imagine it being any of them,' she said. 'They don't seem the type, and what reason would they have?'

'Precisely,' agreed Mr. Templeton, and at that he flipped open his notebook and jotted down a few words. 'Leaving your husband, and myself. And you, of course.'

'Mr. Templeton!' cried Susan in her quietest voice of consternation.

'Mrs. Everly!' he wryly demurred. 'It's a simple matter of facts, I'm sorry to say.'

'And there's the staff,' Susan added, 'and possibly someone came in from outside and we'd have no idea who they were.'

'Doubtful on both counts,' he said, thoughtfully. 'I think someone would have seen a stranger, not to mention notice any cabs arriving that were unaccounted for. It's such an insular place. As for the staff—what reason, like you said? He'd only been here a day, and it's unlikely that anyone knew him beforehand.'

'It's unlikely that my husband would have known him beforehand, but he did,' said Susan, and then she stopped, considering. 'That is odd, I admit, but it certainly wasn't him,' she said, anticipating an inquisitive glance from Mr. Templeton, but his eyes were gazing into the distance.

'No, that is unlikely, isn't it? I'll have to defer to your judgment on him,' he said, with a note of amusement in his voice.

'You can defer to my brother's judgment then, too,' said Susan, almost defensively. 'I've only known Kenneth for about a year, but he was Wilson's business partner at the bank for three years, and they were close friends. They were nearly as close as brothers. Both blond, too... not that they looked anything alike,' she added, 'unless you were quite blind. So when Kenneth told him he wanted to propose to me, Wilson gave his blessing. I know my brother would never misjudge a man's character, so I know I can trust him.'

'I see,' said Mr. Templeton, cautiously, not wishing to overstep. 'I'll place my trust in your brother's judgment as well, then.' Susan smiled faintly, and then as a thought occurred to her, she reached into her handbag and pulled out a carefully folded sheet of paper. She unfolded it, then, tenderly, she held it out to Mr. Templeton.

'That's the last letter my brother wrote to me—he wrote it just one day before he died. I'm so glad Kenneth found it in his work things, since Wilson didn't get a chance to mail it to me before. . . well.' she said. 'He was keeping late hours at work and had less and less time to spend with me at the apartment we shared after our parents' death, so he'd write me letters. This is the one in which he told me Kenneth had asked for my hand in marriage, and that he heartily approved. He was the most thoughtful man. . . '

'Goodness,' said Mr. Templeton, looking at the letter as if it were an artifact from a cherished museum collection. 'May I. . . ?' Susan nodded, handing him the letter. He read it carefully, thanked her for her confidence, then asked, 'that little mark at the bottom, I take it that's his stamp?'

'Yes,' said Susan, accepting the letter back and folding it before returning it to her handbag. 'Our father gave him his signet ring shortly before passing away, and about a year ago he started using it to stamp his letters to me. It was a little joke we had, that the stamp made them official correspondence.' She smiled wistfully. 'In the end, it was work that was the death of him. He never had enough sleep, and one day he was so exhausted that he tripped while running to his office with an armful of papers and fell. . . ' Susan began to struggle to speak. 'He tripped over a bannister and fell two stories to the lobby below.' At saying this, a tear rolled down her cheek, and she began to apologize.

'My dear Mrs. Everly,' soothed Mr. Templeton. 'Do not apologize for your grief for your brother. The world would be a better place if we had all had a brother like him, I am sure.'

Susan sniffed, nodding. 'Thank you,' she said. 'I didn't mean to tell you all this. . . I'm not sure how—'

'Never mind that,' said Mr. Templeton. 'You need a breath of fresh air, and so do I. Come with me to the garden.'

Outside, the crisp breeze struck Susan as somewhat extraordinary. She felt as though she were feeling the cool, damp air for the first time in weeks.

'I suppose it wasn't you, then?' asked Susan as she and Mr. Templeton strolled slowly past the last bed of roses and out onto the sprawling fields beyond the hotel.

'That's quite a thing to ask me now, all the way out here,' he replied.

'Don't tease me, Mr. Templeton, I've been through quite a lot lately,' Susan said drily in mock reproach.

'No, no, you're quite right, of course. And no, it wasn't me. I'm far too boring for all that. I have half a mind to say I think it wasn't anyone at all—that it just happened of its own accord.'

'And the break-in?'

'He could have been mistaken about having locked the door earlier. I don't know.'

'How dull,' mused Susan.

'Quite,' agreed Mr. Templeton. 'What do you think that outburst was all about, yesterday at breakfast? All that babbling?'

'I've no idea. He said something about his cane; maybe he wanted to go somewhere on his own? But his son kept saying he wasn't able to.'

They finished their stroll mostly in silence, both gazing out at the little spot of sea on the horizon before heading back through the garden and into the lobby, where the unfortunate young Mr. Atkinson and his dog were bidding goodbye to the police officer, whose demeanour remained inscrutable.

'Oh,' Susan said to Mr. Templeton, 'I was hoping to speak with the son. Maybe he knew my brother as well—and I'd like to offer him my condolences in any case. I'll see you later, Mr. Templeton. Thank you for being so kind. I look forward to introducing you to my husband this evening.'

Mr. Templeton bowed his head wordlessly, smiled, and walked upstairs to his room. Susan approached young Mr. Atkinson in the lobby, and the two of them spoke quietly for a short time. After they said their goodbyes, and Susan had once again offered him her sympathies, she returned to her room, where, looking decidedly shaken, she placed a phone call to London.

As evening fell, a sense of normalcy finally began to return to the little hotel nestled in the countryside—people spoke in tones unhushed about topics unextraordinary, and occasionally laughter could be heard—so it came as an unwelcome shock when a single shot was heard echoing in the garden just as the guests had begun to gather in the dining room for supper.

Colonel Perkins leapt into motion with a cry, and together he, Mr. Templeton, and the hotel attendant struggled to push their way through the French doors and into the garden, finding themselves temporarily hampered by a heavy potted plant that had been placed in front of the doors. After a minute or so, the gap in the doors was wide enough to fit through, and the three men rushed out into the falling darkness. Mrs. Benson, her young niece, and the Tremaines remained in the dining room, stunned, where they were soon joined by a breathless Susan, who had just run downstairs past the bewildered receptionist. They struggled to see what was going on outside; from inside the dining hall, the light was too dim to see very far beyond the windows.

Susan rushed past the other guests toward the French doors, reaching them just as Mr. Templeton re-emerged from outside, his face a mask of worry. As soon as he saw her, he took her shoulders in his hands and hurriedly and decisively turned her away from the doors. She struggled to look past him, and despite his best efforts to orient her toward the lobby, she could see, unmistakably, the lifeless figure of her husband slumped against the fountain.

The next few hours felt, to Susan, unreal. The disbelief; the hushed, soothing words from everyone who spoke to her; return of the police officer; the questions; the fear. The complete, utter loneliness. The loss, amplified by the horror. And, to Susan's shock, nothing but the most cursory suspicion that her husband's death had been a murder. The consensus, though she couldn't believe it, was that her husband had killed himself.

The police officer, along with Mr. Templeton, explained everything to her. How the gun they found was her husband's; how it was found in his hand, with the associated bullet in his temple; how he hadn't gone to London on business after all, that he'd actually been gambling; how he'd left a note saying he'd lost everything, and that he was sorry, and he couldn't see another way out, that he loved Susan, and regretted all of this; how he'd taken the gun from the safe in their hotel room after returning from his final round of gambling, where it had been safely stored along with Susan's jewellery; and how she was alone, now, yes, but that she needed rest, and that she would be okay.

Susan couldn't believe it. Her mind kept tracing the possibilities, relentlessly, during the minutes that trickled into hours she found herself spending staring past people as they spoke to her in words she couldn't hear.

How could he have done such a thing? And: Two deaths in two days in a small hotel. How could they be unrelated? Why wasn't anyone linking them together?

And she kept on thinking until finally she hit upon the one thing that proved her husband could not, beyond a shadow of a doubt, have been the one to pull the trigger.

A soft knocking brought Mr. Templeton to his hotel room door, late though the hour was, and his eyes were soon met by Susan's frightened gaze. She seemed, despite having been the one to appear at his doorstep, uncertain about whether or not she should accept his somewhat bewildered invitation to come inside.

'Mrs. Everly,' he repeated. 'You must know me well enough by now. If I can be of assistance. . . '

'I can prove who did it,' she said in a hushed, broken voice. 'I can prove who killed my husband.'

'My dear Mrs. Everly,' Mr. Templeton exhaled, after a moment passed. 'Please. Come in. We can't have you standing around in the halls alone now, can we?' At this, he ushered her inside and locked the door behind her. 'You are. . . certain?'

'Yes,' said Susan, allowing Mr. Templeton to lead her to a chair beside the fireplace where a small fire crackled. She sat and gazed straight ahead at nothing in particular. In the firelight, her hair seemed to cast its own ember glow, and she folded her hands neatly in her lap, her expression maintaining more than a glimmer of her usual composed demeanour despite the flush in her cheeks and her nose, and despite the slight quiver in her chin. Mr. Templeton knelt beside her.

'You must know how dreadfully sorry I am,' he said, and waited. It seemed that minutes passed before Susan spoke again, just barely above a whisper.

'I'm afraid I won't be able to tell you who killed him,' she said, slowly. 'Though I feel I must. I know I must, for my own sake. But, Mr. Templeton. . . I'm frightened.' Her words trailed pitifully into a soft, pleading pitch.

'Frightened? Why? Surely we can just tell the police, and they'll—'

'It isn't that simple. He wasn't that simple,' she said bitterly, shaking her head.

'But Susan,' he said, perplexed. 'Surely you're safe now, here, with me? I won't be letting anyone in this room, I can promise you that. And I have no idea where you are, if anyone asks.'

'You promise?' She looked at him, suddenly, through a glaze of tears.

'Of course I promise. Of course.' After a slight hesitation, he reached forward and placed his hand over hers. 'I promise.' At that, the tears that had been forming in Susan's eyes began to roll down her cheeks.

'Thank you, Mr. Templeton,' she said, her voice catching on his name.

'Please,' he said. 'My friends call me Henry.'

'Henry. . . ' she smiled, accentuating the sadness in her eyes. 'Henry, you've been so kind to me, and I feel I owe you the truth, even if that means. . . ' She turned away from the warmth of his inquisitive expression. 'I. . . it was me. I killed him.'

The gentle crackle of the fireplace softened the deep, sudden silence that filled the room.

'You killed him,' said Mr. Templeton. 'My dear, I trust you had a good reason.'

'A good. . . ' Susan was astonished. 'You believe me, then?'

'I believe you,' he said, taking both of her hands in his and holding them gently. 'And I believe you have a good reason for coming to me and not the police. Why did you do it?'

Susan began to cry in a muddled confusion of guilt and relief, and Mr. Templeton simply sat with her, waiting, occasionally running his thumb over the back of her hand in a gesture of comfort.

'He lied,' she gasped, suddenly. 'He lied about everything. The letter I showed you. . . it was fake. Wilson never gave him his blessing to marry me.'

'But. . . the stamp, surely?'

'That's what got me thinking about it, showing you the stamp. I couldn't let it go. I asked Mr. Atkinson. . . the son, in the lobby after we returned from our walk, I asked him if he knew Wilson, and he did. Closely enough, apparently, that Wilson told him, the day before he died, that he'd lost the ring. . . weeks ago. Just happened to mention it to him. It was one of the last things they'd spoken about, apparently, which is why Mr. Atkinson mentioned it to me. Just a little anecdote to illustrate the terms they were on,' she said, her tone incredulous. 'So he didn't have it the previous day, the day the letter I showed you was dated. Obviously, Kenneth didn't know he knew.' Mr. Templeton nodded, his eyes fixed on hers.

'So that letter. . . '

'Kenneth must have written it after Wilson died, and stamped it with the ring he stole from him.' The tremble in her voice had begun to turn from devastation to anger.

'Susan,' Mr. Templeton said softly, 'I believe you, but how can you be sure?'

Her words tumbled out quickly now. 'Kenneth told me, weeks ago, that he'd sent Wilson's belongings to a safe deposit box, including the ring. And so tonight, after Mr. Atkinson told me that Wilson had lost the ring before he could have written that letter, I called the bank to enquire about the ring, and they told me they had it. It was there! It was never lost; Kenneth stole it and must have placed it back with his things after killing him, and he counted on me never finding out that it had gone missing in the first place. So then I called Kenneth—he was at his favourite gambling parlour, wouldn't you guess—and told him everything I've told you.'

'And he confessed?'

'No. Of course not," she laughed bitterly. 'He tried to charm me, as he charmed everyone, including my brother, I see now. But it wasn't just the ring. Theoretically, you know, Mr. Atkinson could have been wrong about the dates. . . no, it was also what you'd asked me about on the lawn. What old Mr. Atkinson had been shouting about. The way I shortened what I'd heard. . . I kept playing it back in my head, and that's when I realised. The words we heard weren't the words we thought we'd heard.'

Mr. Templeton nodded slowly, visibly confused.

'His cane. He kept talking about his cane; and his son said he wasn't *able* to walk with only a *cane*. Those two words. Cane . . . able. . . '

Mr. Templeton made a noise of amazement and squeezed her hands. 'Cain and Abel! My god!'

'It's absurd, isn't it? The truth was under our noses all along. I did tell you that a very blind person might think that Kenneth and my brother were brothers, and Mr. Atkinson. . . ' she trailed off. 'I never could quite believe that Wilson had fallen over a banister,' she said quietly. 'Mr. Atkinson must have been there at the office that day and seen it, seen him push my poor brother. . . ' Susan stifled a sob, and Mr. Templeton wiped a fresh tear from her cheek. Then his brow creased, and after a few moments his eyes suddenly widened.

'Good lord! Does that also mean—' he started. At this, Susan's eyes filled with tears again, and she nodded, pulling her hands from Mr. Templeton's grasp and burying her face in them.

'Yes,' she croaked. 'My dear husband killed Mr. Atkinson too. He realised he'd been witnessed.' She wiped her tears and placed her hands back in her lap, squeezing them together so hard that her nails dug into her skin. 'He must have heard the true meaning right away, tampered with the pills, then left before the man could actually die. Can you *imagine. . . ?*' And then, more quietly, 'Henry, I was married to that man.' She shuddered, and Mr. Templeton took her hands in his again, gently loosening her painful clasp.

'He was no man, Susan. He was a monster.'

Susan nodded, drawing in a shaky breath, and having finally allowed her hands to relax, now took his hands in hers.

'He only admitted it when I confronted him face to face. I'd asked him to meet me in the garden when he came back so we could talk in the fresh air before supper, but. . . I was prepared. I thought of everything, Henry. I brought his gun and the note, I moved the planter in front of the doors, and I knew I could climb the trellis to our room, just like I used to when I was younger, before anyone could get through the back doors.

'And he admitted it! He finally admitted it when I told him I knew what Mr. Atkinson had realized about him; what he must have seen. And he *laughed.* He laughed, and he said the police would never believe me. And I knew he was right. And then he said. . . he said eventually I'd learn to be grateful to him, because now I get Wilson's share of the inheritance as well as my own. In that instant, I knew why he married me. That was the moment. . . that's when I. . . and now he's dead. What does that make me?' Her voice began to choke up. 'I feel sick.'

'Oh, Susan,' he said, his voice a medley of immense sympathy, deep admiration, and latent anger. 'That makes you the bravest, most clever, and most resourceful person I know. Dead is the best thing for that man to be. Death is what the bastard deserved, by law and by nature.'

'What shall I do now?' She looked up to him, her eyes finally clear of tears.

'Absolutely nothing.'

'But the missing piece—'

'No one suspects any pieces are missing. Do nothing, my dear, and when the police leave, you'll begin your life anew. You're free now,' he said. 'Your life is your own. You'll be fine. I promise.'

'But. . . he's left-handed,' she insisted, her eyes wide, 'and I shot him from the right side; and the gun, it was in the safe, and only I knew the combination to open it before he had a chance to get back to the room after returning from—'

Mr. Templeton placed a single finger to her lips. 'No missing clues, my dear. The police have already sorted it all out. Besides which, I could have sworn I saw him writing with his right hand in the lounge just last Tuesday. And I cannot think of a single missing clue.'

'Can't you?' she asked, a fresh mist forming in her eyes.

'Not a one,' he replied, and Susan knew that for the first time since her brother's death, she was no longer alone.

Vaulting Ambition

by David Hill

'Tell me everything you know about Jocasta Samson.'

Still mulling over 'Polymath enslaved within a capital city,' I lower the crossword book to my knee.

'I'm sorry?'

'Jocasta Samson,' he says, turning in his chair to look at me. 'What do you know about her?'

Hardly the most auspicious start to one of our cases, but so often that was the way with Alistair Davenport. Impatience flushes across his face, so I rack my brain. Despite my father's best efforts when I was a child, I never took much interest in sports, but nonetheless, even I could recognise the name of one of Britain's foremost gymnasts. A flurry of facts scattered through my mind—was it the silver or bronze she'd taken home at last year's Summer Olympics? Davenport receives my untidy report with vague approval.

'You missed out one important thing,' he says once I've finished, throwing a plain folder onto the wooden coffee table between us. 'She's dead.'

'*Dead*?'

I quickly scoop up the folder and flick it open. Whenever I caught him reading of these folders, it invariably meant the involvement of the police, and that in turn usually heralded at least one death. But all the same—could this really be *the* Jocasta Samson?

Any doubts I might have had were annihilated by the folder's contents. Jocasta Samson, 24, entered the gymnasium of her family home, The Eyrie, Colton, Surrey at eight o'clock on the evening of Friday 6th November, for her usually nightly training session. At twenty past nine, her coach, Anthony Porter, had noticed that her session had overran by twenty minutes; upon entering the gym, he had found her lying in the centre of the room.

'No obvious wounds,' I say as I scan over the document, thinking aloud. 'It seems she was found to be unresponsive, but alive. Declared dead about two hours later in hospital.'

I replace the folder on the table. 'It's sad, but I don't see your interest in it.'

'You don't think her death's unusual?'

I shrug.

'You'd be hard-pressed to find an athlete these days who isn't pumping their body full of God only knows what.'

Davenport just gives me one of those looks—eyebrow slightly raised; head tilted back.

'I see. Well, let's just hope my instincts are more reliable than yours. Are you doing anything today?'

'Well, I,'

'Good, because we've got a train to catch. We need to be in Guildford by lunchtime.'

And with that, he glides into the next room, presumably to stuff a few pieces of clothing and one of his beloved Jane Austens into a rucksack.

'Could I at least finish the crossword first?' I call over to him.

His head pops back through into the living room.

'Depends,' he replies airily. 'Have you got Athens yet?'

Four hours later, we're arriving at Guildford. I've never been a great traveller—beyond the M25, I might as well be in Kuala Lumpur—and the busy, clammy train didn't help matters one bit. Davenport was fine, of course; he simply spent the journey nestled into a corner, sucking on mint humbugs, sipping black coffee and thumbing through *Sense and Sensibility* for the hundredth time. (This was once we actually *got* onto the train—I'm sure he won't mind me sharing that we almost missed it because he insisted on queueing for a ticket and paying with cash, rather than simply using a card like every other Londoner does. Tradition, or paranoia? Reader, you decide.)

As we step through the doors, there's a young man waiting for us—a bright-eyed, strawberry-blond Geordie.

'Mister Davenport?' he asks. 'DC Connelly. I've been sent to escort you to the scene.'

He shows us a warrant card, though heavens know why he bothered to. If you were to give me six hours alone with a microscope, I still wouldn't be able to tell you if the card was real or not. But it seems to be good enough for Davenport, so minutes later, we're plodding through the Guildford traffic.

In the six months or so I've been working with Alistair Davenport, I don't seem to have taken much time to describe him physically, aside from my first impression of him as a 'Misanthropic, mop-haired skeleton' (See 'The Man in the Long Black Coat', 8th July). However, now seems as good a chance as any to amend this void. He's a touch taller than average, but his slight build makes him appear even more so. Forever marked with stubble and crow's-feet and premature wrinkles, his thin face is practically ripped from a Brontë novel; his hair is a dark shock of unruly black curls. The only splash of colour about him is the red poppy still dutifully attached to his lapel, despite Remembrance Sunday being two days past, and despite the fact that he last smoked over a year ago, he's forever haunted by the smell of stale cigarettes.

'The DCI's a fan of yours,' Connelly says as he drives us out of Guildford. 'Doesn't let on, like, but he is. Don't think he'd have let you in on this, otherwise.'

'Maybe there is something to be said for publicity,' I say to Davenport with a grin.

'Aye, it was that case with the chess game and the politician, he loved that one.' (See 'En Passant', 19th September.)

Before the narrative gets much further underway, I also feel that this would be an opportune moment to reply to some of the feedback these publications have received. 'Why are all of Davenport's cases so unbelievable?' railed one righteous commentator. 'Why do they always involve locked rooms, and celebrities, and complicated alibis? Where are all the *normal* cases?' The answer is pleasingly prosaic. Out of the fifty or so cases that Davenport has handled during my time shadowing him, less than a dozen have made it to print, as it were. Some saw him fail to reach any satisfactory conclusion; some overlapped with complex, ongoing investigations that might take years to fully resolve; and some were of such a public and intimate nature that even anonymising it would likely cause no end of anguish to those involved. But in honest truth, the vast majority of these cases were simply *boring*. If any of my readers is thrilled by the idea of a seven thousand word blog post about a night spent lurking in a Citroen Saxo, waiting to see if Mrs. Jones was right about Mr. Jones sneaking away to Miss Smith's house of an evening, then you're more than welcome to it. Personally, I'd much rather have the one about the international film star, with the mysterious South American poison, in the billiards room—and I suspect most of my readers would too. Here endeth the lesson.

Ten minutes later, we're on the outskirts of Guildford; another fifteen, and we're in open countryside. As fond of London as I am, I'm grateful for the chance to escape the concrete and the people and the taxis and the noise—the noise! A week had passed since Bonfire Night, and yet someone on my street was still letting off fireworks until the early hours of the morning. Before long we're pulling up to the Eyrie. As I haven't yet fallen to the murky depths of working for a real estate agent,

I won't waste time describing its modernistic contours, or its homely yet charming appearance, or the lush, rolling green lawn spread out over the front. It was—to my entirely untrained eye—a standard country house and looked exactly like any other country house you might visit on a quiet weekend. As we cross through the wrought iron gates, there's a small shack to our left; what was once the gatehouse, presumably. The gravel driveway clacks and crunches underneath the car as we pull up by the main entrance.

A man comes up to greet us. From my brief reading of the file that morning, I recognise him as Anthony Porter. He's slightly shorter than I anticipated, which does no favours whatsoever for his rotundity, but there's still a *presence* to him. He's like a bear, just woken from its rest—a little slow, and ponderous, but still not something you'd hurry to upset.

'Afternoon,' he says to us, blinking out the sun. 'You must be the private detective fella, right? Davidov?'

'Davenport.'

'That's it.' Porter swallows, then looks uncertainly between the three of us. 'It's, er, just through here,' he adds, leading us into the house.

'Actually, before we start,' Davenport says, 'am I alright to just use your toilet quickly?'

Normally, I wouldn't have deigned to include such a detail—I mean, you never hear about Sherlock Holmes stopping mid-case to answer a call of nature, do you? But the moment Davenport's out of earshot, Porter suddenly springs towards me and Connelly.

'You never said were bringing him in,' Porter hisses, leaning in close.

Connelly frowns.

'Something the matter, Mr. Porter?'

'This is a private matter,' Porter answers, after a moment's thought. A beat passes; he calms a little. 'We don't want every journalist and nosey parker sniffing around, do we?'

Davenport returns to our party, and any trace of Porter's outburst has completely dissipated.

'Right, gentlemen,' he says, rubbing his hands together. 'Shall we crack on?'

'Big place for three people,' Davenport remarks, as we're herded up a staircase.

The four of us are moving in two rows of two—Davenport and Porter at the front, leading the way, with Connelly and myself trailing after them.

'It's been in the family for a while,' Porter explains. 'Time was the whole family was packed in here. Then some of them moved away, and of course, the parents passed away. There's this firm, in Woking. They keep sending letters, wanting to buy the place and make it into a hotel, and after what's happened, I can't see Eleanor turning them down again.'

'That's Eleanor Samson, Jocasta's sister?' I offer up.

Porter stares at me.

'No,' he answers, 'Eleanor Rigby. Of course it's her bloody sister.'

He throws another look of disparagement in my direction, and suitably chastened, I move back to rejoin Connelly. At the top of the stairs is the home gymnasium. The room just originally have been a library, or a study of some kind; crimson leather-bound volumes still line two of the four walls. In the middle of the room, though, is a large gymnastics mat. Miscellaneous gym equipment is spread out around it. (As I previously mentioned, I'm no great sportsman, so if you were hoping for some more specific detail, 'miscellaneous gym equipment' is all you're getting, I'm afraid.)

'That door there is the only one way in, only way out,' Connelly tells us, pleased at finally having something to do.

'There's a keypad,' I say, thinking aloud.

'Pretty secure for a gym,' Davenport says.

'Erm, yes.' Porter flushes slightly. 'But if you see.'

Without even looking at the keypad, he presses on the door to the gym; it swings open easily.

'The locking system broke a year ago,' he explains hastily. 'We've been meaning to get it fixed, but,'

'Why did you even get it in the first place?'

'It got put in after the thing with the stalker a few years back. Jocasta was having a bit of a panic, so these locks got put on this place, her room, that sort of thing.'

'Stalker?'

Porter just shrugs.

'All came to nothing as far as I know—this fella kept sending her messages, dodgy emails, all that. It a bit before I started as her trainer, though. Eleanor'll probably know more about it than me.'

Davenport gives a brisk nod and looks around the room. 'Is Eleanor at home?'

'She is, but she was out last night. Fundraiser thing for. . . ' Porter shakes his head. 'Homeless children or dying cats or something. She'll probably be up in an hour or so.'

'And where were you while Jocasta was in here?'

'In my room, reading.'

'The Blue Room,' Connelly offers.

'Tell you what, mate,' Porter says to me, conspiratorially, 'I lucked out there. Size of a cathedral, cracking view of the front lawn. It's even got an en-suite.'

Davenport wanders about the room. I'm sure many of my readers would be fascinated to hear about his deductive process, but frankly, they'd be disappointed more than anything. They say still waters run deep, and that seems especially true when it comes to Alistair Davenport—five minutes of silent prodding and poking and measuring, barely even *breathing* audibly, whilst countless thoughts rattle through his mind like a tombola. As he works, Porter, Connelly and myself stand around awkwardly. It's just as I'm inspecting one of my fingernails when Davenport turns to us.

'How would you do it?' he asks, more at me than either of the other two. 'If you were to murder someone, in here—how?'

It's a question Davenport's put to me more than once before now, but each time I struggle for an answer.

'Poison, probably,' I answer lightly, giving the first thing to come into my head.

His face lights up.

'Exactly. Maybe there's hope for you yet. Poison,' he goes on, now more to Connelly and Porter. 'Easy to make look like natural causes. No struggle to think about, no gaping wound to tidy up and the only weapon you need to worry about is *that*.'

He points to the pieces of equipment, the vault, I believe it's called. It's the one about waist-height, and you're meant to sort of leapfrog over it, if you follow me. Davenport leads us over, his hands in his pockets.

'Look underneath,' he tells us.

On top and along both sides, the vault is made from a light brown, downy sort of material. The underside, however, is hollow, ridged with little crevices and folds in the metal framework, and just visible in one of the ruts is a small glass cylinder. Connelly puts on a pair of light blue rubber gloves and reaches over, gingerly, as his hand returns, it's carrying a hypodermic syringe.

'Bloody hell.' Porter looks between the three of us.

'I'm guessing you had no idea this was here?' Davenport asks.

'None. What is it?'

Connelly inspects the needle as he bags it.

'There's no markings,' he answers, peering at the side.

'It's definitely just the three of you here?' Davenport asks Porter. 'No gardener, or boyfriends, anything like that?'

'There's a woman who comes in on a Friday to do some cleaning, get shopping, that sort of thing,' Porter continues, 'but she's away at the moment. Staying with her sister in the Algarve.'

'We've checked with immigration,' Connelly pipes up, 'she's definitely out of the country.'

'And no boyfriends, or girlfriends or anything? At all?'

'No. Nothing. At all.'

Davenport takes one last look at the gym, then back to Porter.

'Could you go and get Eleanor for me, please?'

'Why poison?' I ask, once the three of us are alone.

'No signs of any trauma or asphyxiation.'

For once, I've overtaken the great Alistair Davenport.

'You're going the wrong way. You're making the facts fit your theory.'

'Go on?'

'If she *was* murdered, then yes, poison seems the most likely option. But go from the start. If you were going to kill her, would poison be your first instinct? She's a gymnast, so not exactly hard to overpower. If it's a premeditated murder, then you could do anything. Throw her off a bridge, drown her in the bath, anything. Poison'll probably leave a trace. You might get the dose wrong. It's messier.'

There's a twinkle in Davenport's eye as he looks at me.

'It's a good point. Two in one day; you're definitely improving.'

Porter returns.

'She's in the kitchen downstairs,' he tells us.

'Can't she come to us?'

Porter shrugs, and Davenport turns to me.

'If Mohammed won't go to the mountain,' he mutters.

Porter ushers us down to the kitchen, where Eleanor Samson is nursing a coffee and aspirin.

'Who's this again?' she asks, her head in her hands.

'The private detective I was telling you about.'

If she's interested, she's hiding it well. She drains the last of the coffee and sets about making herself another. Porter slips away.

'You were here the night your sister died, right?' Davenport asks, settling on the seat opposite her.

'I was the one who phoned for the ambulance. It was, what, about nine o'clock, wasn't it? Something like that?'

'Something like that. Did your sister usually spend time alone in the gym?'

'An hour every evening, and most mornings, as well. Sometimes she'd let Anthony in with her, but not very often.'

'Tell me about these hate messages she got.'

'Messages? Oh, *that*.' She waves her hand, like the question is a swarm of midges.

'That was just nothing. A storm in a teacup.'

'The police didn't seem to think so.'

'Of course *they* wouldn't. They've got to take it seriously, haven't they? It wasn't even anything that serious. She got some funny messages, that's all. My friend had a stalker once, an *actual* one, and he used to send chopped-up bits of animals to her house. She came downstairs one morning to find half a pigeon stuffed into her letterbox.'

'So you think Jocasta was making it up? Exaggerating?'

'Well, I don't know about the first ones, but the newest lot, at least.'

'Newest ones?'

Eleanor blinks at us.

'The new messages. They started a month or so ago.'

'Porter said it was years ago, before he joined.'

'Yes, *those* ones were.' She rolls her eyes. 'Five years ago, someone was sending Jo a bunch of angry messages, we spoke to the police, they died down. Then just recently, they started up again. We spoke to the police again, and would you believe it, they stopped again. Have you got it now?'

I sit up.

'But Porter didn't,'

'Sorry,' Davenport says amiably, 'long train journey. I'll wake up in a minute. So you don't think these messages were anything serious? A jealous ex or something?'

Eleanor snorts.

'You must be joking. The only person Jo needed in a relationship was herself.'

'What about Anthony Porter?'

'*Him*? That's an even bigger joke.'

'I don't know. People live together, spend a lot of time together, anything could happen.'

'Not with that ogre, thank you very much.'

(If the conversation seems to resemble a court transcript by this point, you must forgive me—I'm a stickler for accuracy, and there are only so many times I can mention Eleanor sipping her coffee, or Davenport scratching his cheek.)

'So what do you think happened to your sister? Do *you* think she was taking something?'

Eleanor swallows.

'I wouldn't have said so. She barely even drank coffee, let alone anything harder than that. And like I said, it's not as if she ever *went anywhere*.'

'I meant more along the lines of performance-enhancers,' Davenport explains uneasily. 'That sort of thing happens a fair bit, doesn't it?'

'I wouldn't know.'

'I've done a bit of research myself.' Davenport opens his notepad, and somehow makes sense of his scribbles and scrawls. 'There's a diuretic called furosemide, which limits the amount of water in your body, that seems to be pretty popular. Meldonium, that's another one, it improves your blood flow.' He looks up at Eleanor. 'Either of those two ringing a bell?'

She looks square back.

'Jo wouldn't even take paracetamol when she had a headache,' she says evenly.

'If she had taken them, though, that'd a competing ban, right? Two, three years? If *anyone* were to find out, that'd be the end of her career.'

Eleanor folds her arms.

'Surely if Jo *had* taken anything, the doctors will be able to tell.'

'Eventually, yeah. But that takes time. You can't just snap your fingers and have a toxicology report back in your hand. And in the time it takes them to find out whatever the hell was in her system, her killer has a head start on us.'

'To do what?'

'To dispose of evidence. To take care of witnesses. Anything. So just to be sure you don't know *anything* about your sister taking performance-enhancing drugs?'

'Nothing. Oh, this is a waste of time. Why do I need to tell you this? I've already told all of this to that man from the police, anyway.'

'Who, Connelly?' Davenport points over to our companion.

'No, the one who phoned me.'

Davenport blinks.

'A police officer phoned you?'

'Yesterday morning. I was getting ready to go out, I've a new Ralph Lauren, and I've just been *dying* to show it off, when the phone rang. The man said he was from the police, and that had some questions for me about what happened to Jo.'

Davenport leans in. '

Can you remember the number?'

'Erm. Not really.'

'Did it end with 770?'

She thinks for a second.

'No, I wouldn't have said so. So anyway, I told them more or less what I've just told you now.'

'And you're sure it was a man's voice?'

'Positive.'

'These messages,' Davenport says, 'can I read them anywhere?'

'We printed out them out for the police when they first started,' Eleanor replies. 'I think there's still a copy in the office. Now, is that everything? My head feels like there's an elephant sitting on it, and there's a shower upstairs calling my name.'

Eleanor takes a fresh mug of coffee upstairs, leaving the three of us alone.

'Whose number were you thinking of?' I ask. '770?'

'Nobody's—first three numbers I could think of. I already had a pretty good idea of what's happened, I just needed to confirm it.' He looks at me, and I swear to God, he's almost pitying me. 'The police withhold their numbers these days. The fact that Eleanor had to think about the number at all tells me that it wasn't them she spoke to.'

'So it was someone pretending to be the police.'

'Well, it could be a police officer trying to go off the record, but most likely, yes. But if Eleanor's involved, then me asking if the number was withheld would clue her in. At least this way, it might lead her on the wrong path.'

'Might be a reporter,' I say.

'You heard what Eleanor said, she's doing an interview about it tomorrow. She's not exactly being coy about it, so why the underhand tactics?' Davenport turns to Connelly. 'And your lot *definitely* haven't spoken to her about it yet?'

'It's the first I've heard of it.' Connelly clicks his tongue as he thinks. 'I'll radio the station, mind, see what they say. Do you think this really is poison, then?'

Davenport makes sure the three of us are definitely alone.

'In all likelihood,' he answers. 'Furosemide would be my bet.'

'How would you get hold of it?' I ask. 'I don't imagine they sell it in Boots.'

'It's amazing what you can buy on the internet these days. First things first, though I think you'd better begin a search of everyone's rooms.'

'We already have.'

Davenport looks over at Connelly.

'You have?'

'First thing we did. The SIO's a bit of a goer, you see. Doesn't like to let the grass grow under her feet.'

'And you didn't find anything?'

Connelly seems to falter a little under the torrent of questions.

'Not, not that I know of. We did a thorough job, like.'

'Were you there?'

'I was, yeah.'

'Was it raining?'

'Raining?'

Davenport blinks.

'Was there *water* falling out of the *sky*?'

'It, erm. Yes, it was! I remember now. It didn't look too bad at the start of my shift, so I'd left my good coat at home, but by the time,'

Davenport shuts off the recount with a wave of his hand.

'Right, I want to have a look at these messages. The office, she said, didn't she?'

The office turns out to be little more than a cupboard. A poky little box room with an admittedly sleek computer and reams of disorganised paperwork.

'I can't see either Jocasta or Eleanor being in here that much,' I say, as Davenport settles himself behind the desk. 'Gymnasts and socialites don't usually have to do much paperwork.'

Davenport begins rifling through the papers.

'Are you going to help me,' he asks under his breath, 'or just stand there watching like a lemon?'

With my help, we soon find the documents in question.

'Text messages,' Davenport says, glancing over the sheets, 'sent from a withheld number.' He looks at me wryly. 'Maybe it was the police.'

I look at the messages for myself. *Talentless slut. Just do the world a favour and die. Nobody'll miss you.*

'You can see why that might upset someone,' I murmur to Davenport.

Not to the same degree, obviously, but my own articles have received their share of vitriolic comments—most frequently, I am bemused to say, calling for me to retire the 'dull, irritating narrator character'.

'Porter said they were emails,' Davenport says absently.

'Did he?'

'Yeah. These are text messages.'

'He probably just made a mistake. Some people still aren't used to computers. My aunt keeps turning her laptop Russian whenever she tries to check the weather.'

'Ten years ago, maybe,' Davenport replies, 'but nowadays? Everyone and their dog's using a computer these days, you'd think Porter would know the difference.'

I accept his point, and Davenport moves on.

'Look at the rate they come in. The first one is sent on Monday 11th October, and straight away, there's three, four a day.' He goes to the end of the messages. 'Tuesday 26th, that's when they spoke to the police, look, there's a copy of the report here and the messages stop almost overnight. Why?'

'Maybe they found a new target. Someone else to bully and harass.'

'Maybe. But get into the mindset for a moment. To send these many messages, this often, this hateful, you'd be *obsessed* with the person. And I don't mean a little bit obsessed, I mean "searching through their bins and collecting their fingernails" levels of obsessed.'

'That makes sense.'

'So why stop? These are the sort of people who see restraining orders as a challenge. It just doesn't ring true.'

'I see. You think they're fake?'

'It's a bit convenient if they're not, isn't it? Onslaught of messages, at all times of the day, and then the second Jocasta speaks to the police, they stop.'

'Maybe the police managed to track the number,' I say. 'They found the sender, cautioned them or whatever it is they do, and that scared them off.'

'In two days? Even I'd struggle to do that. And besides, there'd still be some record of it. You don't honestly think if the police had managed to actually solve a case for once, they'd keep quiet about it, do you?'

'Okay, point taken. So why did the messages stop?'

'It's obvious, isn't it?'

He looks at me, silently. Waiting. He'll do this, from time to time: insist on waiting for me to catch up and fill in the blanks. In another life, I feel that Alistair Davenport would have made an excellent teacher. Teaching *what*, God alone knows. Besides criminology, his only talents seem to be cooking Spanish omelettes and swearing but he'd have the right temperament, at least.

'Eleanor told us that Jocasta didn't want the police involved,' I say. 'You can see here that Eleanor's the one who reported it to the police, and anyway, we could verify it with Porter if needs be. So Jocasta didn't want anyone knowing. Maybe she didn't want them to worry about her or didn't want the attention or whatever.'

'So why would she send hate messages to herself, and then try to cover them up?

'Because she didn't. Someone else did.'

'We have a suspect list of two.'

'Three; you're forgetting about Mrs. Mopp, the cleaner. But to be fair to you, I think we can probably rule her out. Porter says she comes around on a Friday. They decided to speak to the police on a Monday, made the report on Tuesday, and the messages had stopped by the

Wednesday, so unless they went out of their way to tell her, which let's be honest, isn't exactly likely, she wouldn't have had time to hear about it.

'So, we're back down to two,' Davenport goes on. 'Eleanor and Porter. By all accounts, Jocasta didn't speak to anyone else.' He leans back in the desk chair, blowing out his cheeks. 'Toss a coin? It's a one-in-two chance.'

'There's a third option,' I say, and I'm proud to see a flicker of confusion across Davenport's face. 'It's both of them.'

'No.'

'It could be.'

'You heard her back there, the way she was talking about it.'

'Oh, come on. Did you not think she was laying it on a bit thick?'

'Oh, I *see*. The lady doth protest too much, is that what you mean?'

'It's been known to happen! Maybe Jocasta found out about the affair, and that's why they killed her.'

Davenport scoffs.

'What affair? It might make a conflict of professional interest for him, but it's hardly Charles and Camilla, is it? And besides, the most that would happen if she *did* blab about it would be the end of his career, which at most would only serve to drag Jocasta's down with it. She'd be cutting off her nose to spite her face. Jocasta Samson was many things, but she wasn't stupid.'

'But she, '

'And if it was *Eleanor* being blackmailed over this so-called relationship, then for what? Having it off with her sister's middle-aged gymnastics coach? There might be a touch of the Elektra complex about it, but that's all.'

Mollified, I cross my arms over my chest.

'Alright. Since you have all the answers, who did it? Eleanor or Porter?'

Popping another mint humbug into his mouth, Davenport sits back up in the chair, rapping his fingertips on the chipped desk.

'I don't know,' he says, after a moment. 'Yet. But it's only a matter of time.' He checks his watch. 'It looks like it's going to be a long job. I'll speak to Connelly about finding us a room for the night.'

'We could always stay here. They're not exactly crammed in like sardines.'

'And risk having our throats cut in our sleep, or someone putting weedkiller in the morning coffee?' He flashes a wolfish grin. 'No, I'm sure there's a nice little bed-and-breakfast just around the corner.'

The thought doesn't exactly fill me with hope. Davenport might be able to sleep all night through on a slab of cold concrete, but I need a decent mattress if I'm to get my full eight hours. If our previous cases are anything to go by, I'll tossing and turning all night on a bed about as big and as comfortable as a second-class stamp.

'He's just on the phone to them now,' Davenport says, as we reunite in the hallway. 'Apparently, he knows a cheap place nearby from a case. The previous owners made a dodgy batch of chicken madras, gave all the guests salmonella.'

'Sounds lovely,' I reply in a deadpan.

'But before then, we've got one last thing we need to do. Should only be a quick job.'

Porter descends the main staircase to join us.

'PC Plod said you wanted to see me,' he says, hands stuffed into his pockets.

'That's right. We've got a job to do, I thought you might be able to help us.'

'Oh?'

'That gatehouse, out by the. Well, by the gate. It's out of use, right?'

'That's right. There was a storm last year, and a tree fell through it. They've been meaning to knock it down properly ever since, but you know how it is.'

'I thought so.'

Porter tilts his head.

'You think there might be something in there?'

'Whatever that needle was filled with, it must have come from a vial, or a bottle, or something. I don't think the police would have thought to check for it there, and even if they had, a pile of rubble is a pretty good place to hide something. And you probably know better than anyone what's *meant* to be in there.'

'Many hands make light work,' I add.

This seems to win Porter over, as with a momentary glance at Davenport, he agrees to help us.

'So how long have you been working for the Samsons?' Davenport asks, as we troop across the sodden lawn.

'It would have been five years next summer.'

'Were they happy with you?'

Porter smiles.

'I'd like to think so. We were only at the Commonwealth a few weeks back, she did alright.'

'Even so, you're probably going to be looking for a new job now, right? I can't see Eleanor keeping her sister's old gymnastics coach around for nothing.'

'Eventually. I thought I might take a bit of a break. I've got a friend who moved out to Singapore a while back, I'm always meaning to go and stay with him. See some of the world while I still can.'

'Is money not a bit tight?'

'It wasn't bad pay here, and I'm not exactly a spendthrift. No, I've got a nice little bit tucked away for a rainy day.'

I'll happily admit that Porter's mentions of Singapore invoked a pang of jealousy in me. So far in my life, I'd rarely even left the South-East. The furthest I'd ever gotten to international travel was the case Davenport and I had taken on Alderney (See 'Murder by Starlight', 19th August). The idea of simply upping sticks and leaving everything behind for a new life was certainly an alluring one. We approach the gatehouse. I look down in despair at the mud caked over my boots, and a thought hits me.

'That's why you asked about the weather! It would have been muddy that night as well.'

'Exactly. If you were investigating something like this, your first thought would be to discount the gatehouse entirely. After all, how would you run across that lawn, hide the weapon, and run back into the house without looking like you'd just crawled through a field? The problem is, if that's your *first* thought, the *second* should be how prime a hiding-place would be a result.' He turns to look at Porter. 'The police can never look past the end of their nose at the best of times.'

As Porter pointed out, the gatehouse is really little more than a shed with soot-stained bricks, grimy windows, and the roof caved in by a fallen branch on one side. Davenport pulls at the door, and the hinges break away from the rotten wood. Inside, various items have been piled together haphazardly. Light blue wallpaper peels away from the cracked wall, and a cracked electric chandelier hangs uneasily from the ceiling.

'Doesn't look like anyone's been here recently,' I venture. 'Looks more like a bomb's hit it.'

'Best place to hide a book is in a library,' Davenport murmurs. 'Best place to hide a murder weapon is. . . Well, whatever this is.'

With that, we start our search of the gatehouse. I'm breathing through my mouth the whole time, but even so, the stench is stifling. Collar pressed firmly over his mouth, Davenport's sifting through the detritus with his free hand like a bloodhound, tossing aside anything not of interest—a rusty garden chair here, a sodden photo album there. Porter and I do our best to help, which, given the circumstances, isn't much.

'Why wouldn't they dispose of it?' I ask. 'Rather than stuff it away like this.'

'Dispose of it *how*?'

'There's a reservoir down the road,' Porter offers.

'And suppose the police are this second sifting it. You've no way of getting it back before they find it, have you? Same again if you'd thrown it in the rubbish, or buried it in the garden, or, well, anything. You need to be able to keep an eye on it.'

'They might have destroyed it.'

'Possibly. But I think they'd hold onto it,' Davenport answers. 'After all, who's to say they won't find *another* use for the weapon?'

Through the grubby window, I make out a grey silhouette approaching from the house.

'It's Connelly,' I tell the others, peering closer through the glass.

Davenport stands up erect, dropping the ancient puncture repair kit he was examining with a crash.

'At last,' he says and sails out of the gatehouse, Porter and me once again at his heels.

'Any joy?' he asks the constable.

Connelly just nods in response, then his gaze falls onto Anthony Porter.

'Mister Porter,' he says plainly. 'Would you care to explain what this is?'

He holds before him a transparent evidence bag. I crane my neck to get a better look; inside are a few boxes of tablets.

Porter looks dumbly at the bag. 'What?' he asks, squinting at Connelly.

'We found this in your room, the Blue Room, that is yours, isn't it?'

'It is, yes, but, '

'Well then.' Connelly pauses. 'Take your time.'

'You need a warrant to search through my belongings,' Porter says at last. 'You need a warrant.'

'It's Eleanor's house,' Davenport replies coolly. 'If she says we can search one of *her* rooms, then who are you to say otherwise?' He turns to Connelly. 'What are they labelled as?'

'Furo,'

'Can I?'

Davenport reaches out a hand for the bag, and Connelly hands it over.

'Furosemide,' Davenport announces, reading the label through the plastic. 'Two of them are still sealed, so they've probably not been switched over, but even so, I'm sure they'll want to verify the contents. Do you know what furosemide is, Anthony?'

'Of course I do.'

'Do you want to explain why you have it?' Connelly asks.

'I don't. It's not mine, it's.' He looks straight at Davenport. 'You lied to me, you *swine*!'

Davenport and Connelly exchange a look, and I'm sure any able reader will know what Connelly did next.

'Have I ever told you that you're a conniving sod?' I ask Davenport an hour later, as we're waiting for our taxi.

He's sitting at the Steinway, ringing out some dolorous bars of Rachmaninoff absently.

'Now and then,' he answers, between chords.

'That whole business with the gatehouse, it was just a diversion, wasn't it? We were keeping Porter occupied while Connelly was having a nosy.'

Davenport looks at me like butter wouldn't melt in his mouth.

'I thought you knew that,' he said. 'After all, if I really did think there was any evidence in there, I wouldn't exactly let a suspect tamper around with it, would I?'

He closes the piano lid with a *slam*.

'No,' I concede, 'but all the same, you could have *told* me.'

Davenport grins back at me.

'Where would all the fun be if I told you *everything*?'

Three months have passed since that day at the Eyrie, and in the meantime, the case was mostly consigned to my desk drawer. Anthony Porter's car was searched, and a burner phone was uncovered beneath the spare tyre. Naturally the police managed to recognise it as the number

Eleanor failed to remember in our interview. The gymnastics community was briefly set alight when the news of his charge was broken, but as these things usually go it eventually dissipated just as quickly. I hastily compiled my notes into the manuscript you've just read, gave it a peremptory title, *Vaulting Ambition* which is no *Murder on the Orient Express*, is it? and saved it away in a file on my laptop, ready for upload the moment Porter's trial finished. At time of writing, his trial concluded three days ago with his conviction.

The date is now Friday 24th April. At four o'clock this afternoon, I left work and, as was my usual routine, headed immediately to Alistair Davenport's permanent residence at Flat 7, Alderbrook Mansions, Streatham, SW16 1BH. He was in a state of some disarray as I arrived.

'Won't be a second,' he explained, 'just keep yourself busy.'

This again was nothing unusual. I pride myself on being a punctual person, and Davenport's mastery of time is loose, to say the least. Fortunately, having some straight from work, I still had my laptop on my person. As far as I can tell, Davenport is unaware that I'm writing this, by now, he is well used to the constant pattering of my keyboard. I attach my previous account of the prior investigation into the murder of Jocasta Samson in its entirety.

Throughout these chronicles, I've always put myself in the background. My natural maladroitness aside, it made for good business sense; people read these to hear from Alistair Davenport, the master sleuth not Dave Hill, second-rate English teacher and third-rate writer. Now, however, I must reverse our positions.

As I have already explained, I was left alone in the living room of Davenport's flat, whilst he readied himself for the evening. After a social engagement the previous week, I owed Davenport a small amount of money, about twenty pounds, over the last round of drinks. As was our routine, Davenport refused to accept the difference from me, despite his income being considerably less than my own. As a result, my usual answer was to secrete the owed money into the pocket of one of his black overcoats.

It should be clarified that my choosing of that pocket was sheer serendipity. Davenport has a number of such black coats, all identical, save for some frays and patches in certain areas. The pockets of each coat are invariably filled with receipts and mint humbug wrappers and stubbed-out cigarette butts. I chose the coat nearest the door and opted for the right-hand outside pocket. As expected, it was filled with all manner of detritus, which I emptied into my open palm. Among the litter was a crumpled train ticket. Idly, I inspected the details. Paddington to Guildford. At first, I simply took this as a memento of the Jocasta Samson case. But then I read the date. 06/11/23. It's funny how some dates just stick in your mind, isn't it? In a moment, I could see Davenport's poppy. I could remember complaining to him about the fireworks on the way to the train station. We hadn't travelled to Guildford on the sixth, it would have been later. I was certain.

I went over to Davenport's collection of case files, if only to corroborate my thoughts. I quickly found the folder for the Jocasta Samson murder. It was empty. The copies of the original police reports, the newspaper articles, Davenport's handwritten notes, my account of the investigation, all of it, gone. As untidy as Davenport usually is, his cases are a source of unerring pride for him. He would never be so uncaring as to displace them like this.

At least the account on my laptop would still be there. I scroll back, my words flying across the screen—*Jocasta Samson, 24, entered the gymnasium of her family home, The Eyrie, Colton, Surrey at eight o'clock on the evening of Friday 6th November, for her usually nightly session.* I was right.

Have you ever left work after a long day, and made it all the way to your front door without realising, made the entire journey on autopilot? That's how I can best describe that afternoon in the gymnasium. Did I see Davenport find the syringe? I vaguely remember talking to Connelly at the time or had it been Porter? Surely I would have seen Davenport reaching into his pocket? Surely even I would have noticed that? But if he *was* responsible, when was he meant to have planted the vial in Porter's room? The sixth? The police had already searched the rooms that evening and didn't find anything. And I was by his side the entire time we were there. We never even went *near* Porter's room. No. That moment, when we first arrived, Porter's room overlooks the front, it will have been just over the entrance hall. When Davenport slipped away for a moment, to use the toilet could he really? The sound of Davenport's shower just died away. The ticket, the file, what do these mean? And then like a thunderclap, I'm thinking of Anthony Porter's parting words to us.

'You lied to me, you *swine*!'

Not at Connelly, not at myself, at Davenport. If my suspicions are right, then the safest course of action is to send this document to you, Martin. What Davenport's reaction to my discovery will be, I can't say, but this information would surely be safer with you. If you hear nothing else from me by tomorrow evening, then make it public, take it to the police, do whatever you can. If I'm wrong, then this message will be followed a self-effacing email, apologising for giving you a fright. It will be an amusing coda to the latest Alistair Davenport case. The time I played detective, and mistook my friend for a murderer. I hope I am wrong.

The Cookery Show Conundrum
by M.E. Reynard

My sergeant accelerated through a green light while I brought up my emails and read out the one titled *Confidential. Detective Inspector Amelia Flynn & Sergeant Jade Jones.*

'There's evidence someone is targeting the live cookery show, *Britain's Best Homemade Menu*.'

Jones made a shocked sound which I silently agreed with before continuing.

'Two dangerous incidents have occurred at the *HM* house. An oven fire two weeks ago and a microwave explosion early this morning. Of the sixteen contestants who started in the *HM* house thirteen have been eliminated from the show and our inquiries, leaving Dave Fiddle, Hannah Crook, and Tristan Steels in this afternoon's final. It's feared that one of the finalists is trying to sabotage the others for the cash prize of fifty thousand pounds. The judges, Brandon Lux and Teresa Cavendish, may also be in danger. However, the incidents could simply be accidents. Utmost discretion is needed given the high-profile nature of the show and the possibility someone could be seriously hurt, or worse, during the live broadcast final. You must discover and arrest whoever is behind the incidents or determine if they're merely accidents.'

I finished reading out the email.

'All right,' I said with a heavy feeling, 'Here's what I know. Teresa Cavendish is the queen of desserts and wine. She owns bakeries, fine food and wine shops in major cities here and across Europe, with

London and Paris being her flagship stores. Brandon Lux got started in the late nineties by winning the food contest, *Master Dish,* with his now world-renowned seafood pie. Over the last twenty years Brandon Lux has gone on to become *the* gourmet food king. He owns a hugely successful chain of international restaurants including ten in the United States along with several high-end hotels across the globe. Not to mention he stars in his *own* cookery show, *Restaurant Rescue*, fixing failing restaurants.'

'Oh my goodness I *love* Brandon and his seafood pie!' Jones enthused, her cinnamon cheeks dimpling. 'I order it every time I go to *Brandon's Brasserie* in town. King prawns, crab, lobster, mussels, and salmon in his secret sauce, oh it's delicious.'

From Jones' enthusiasm I could almost smell the delicate seafood combination and creamy sauce. I swallowed and re-focused.

'I couldn't agree more,' I said. 'Now, along with most of the country, I watched the live semi-final of *HM* last week. I'm really pleased Dave got through as he certainly deserves his place in the final. That starter of roasted bell peppers stuffed with cardamon infused cous-cous and garlic sauteed bacon along with his main of individual beef wellingtons with goat cheese sauce were inspired.'

'True, but for me his wine poached apricots, candied pecans and lychee ice cream sealed it. Mind you, making those wellingtons looked really hard.'

'Very tough wellies,' I smiled. 'Chewy.'

Jones rolled her eyes at my amazing humour while I continued.

'Hannah and Tristan were already through on points but here's the interesting part. According to the rules, if any contestant fails to compete in the final or drops out during the final itself, whoever is left carries on. However, if there's only one contestant left, they win by default.' I sighed. 'Meaning any of them could be trying to sabotage and scare the others into dropping out. Or worse.'

Jones shot me a look.

'Fifty thousand pounds is an awful lot of money, Boss.'

'People have killed for much less,' I agreed.

In the *HM* house's formidable lobby, we were introduced to Tori Gregory, producer of the show. She was in her late twenties, petite, with a dark, razor-sharp bob and worried blue eyes.

'I'm so glad you're here,' she said in a breathy, little girl voice that was at odds with her tailored trouser suit and perfectly painted nails. 'Everyone's on edge. It's just an awful atmosphere.' She looked ready to cry but rallied. 'I've got the judges and contestants waiting for you.'

'Thank you,' I replied, glancing about. 'I never realised how huge this place was.'

Beside me, Jones studied the old art deco building and like me I was sure she noted all the places for concealment and nefarious goings on.

'We don't film most of it,' Tori explained as we walked. 'It used to be a hotel but it fell into disrepair in the early noughties. The production company bought it about six years ago. We upscaled the bedrooms and converted the downstairs for cooking, filming and communal living.'

As we followed her deeper inside, the air became laced with the delicious ghosts of dishes and I drew an appreciative breath. Tori eventually led us into a gold and cream sitting room which was clearly meant for the judges during filming. The air of luxury bestowed by the furniture and thick carpet was at odds with the utilitarian décor of the off-camera hallways we'd come along. As we entered, I saw Brandon Lux sprawled across a sofa with his pale blue suit and wolfish looks uncharacteristically rumpled. Teresa Cavendish curled delicately in an armchair sipping coffee and looking tired beneath her make-up. Her sleek, chestnut hair was a stark contrast to Jones' blackberry curls and my ginger locks. Tori murmured introductions, glancing at Teresa before spooning six scoops of coffee into a small cafetière, adding hot water, and leaving.

'It's about time you got here,' Brandon growled with his well-known scowl that had once made a contestant cry over her soggy bottom.

'Now, Bran,' Teresa said while putting down her tiny cup. 'Don't be rude.'

Brandon merely grunted with his scowl firmly in place. Teresa smiled at us and gestured to the sofa opposite to the one Lux lay on.

'Please,' she said, 'have a seat.'

We settled onto the soft leather and Jones gave a small sigh of pleasure.

'Tell us about the microwave incident,' I said without further preamble. 'It happened in the common room, didn't it?'

'Yes, and oh my goodness the explosion was terrifying,' Teresa said, shaking her head with an unsettled expression. She pushed the fresh cafetière plunger, refilling her cup and inhaling deeply over the black liquid before adding two lumps of brown sugar.

'I could've been killed,' Brandon muttered.

I glanced around, my gaze lingering over the plush fittings and fixtures.

'Why were you even in the common room?'

'I got in early and was getting my morning latte from the pod machine in there.' Brandon gestured to a space on a nearby sideboard. 'Our one in here broke last week.' His chiselled jaw clenched and unclenched. 'If I'd taken a bit longer,' he trailed off.

'And the fire a couple of weeks ago?' I prompted.

'Everyone thought it was an accident,' Teresa said, sipping coffee, her expression oddly neutral at such a sweet, strong taste. 'It was during a practice session. Hannah's oven caught fire, incinerating the lamb loin she was cooking as well as her starter.'

'Practice?' Jones queried, frowning. 'But the show's live.'

'Indeed, it is, but the contestants have to practise their dishes. Otherwise, it would be a complete disaster on air.'

Jones looked stunned and I continued, hurriedly.

'Mr. Lux, you know the pressures of participating in a food contest. How are the finalists handling it?'

'They're holding it together, I think. Some better than others. Mind you, my experience was years ago.' He looked away, his expression inexplicably sad. 'And it all became a bit of a blur afterward.'

We asked a few more questions before Tori took us to the contestants, who were together in the dining room. It was a wide room containing three long tables with bench seats to accommodate all sixteen contestants before they got whittled down as the series progressed. The dining room was separated from the common room by a pair of closed French doors. Through the glass panels I could see the common room and the forensics team in protective suits painstakingly processing the scene. The burnt wall and blackened, twisted microwave remnants were sobering. Despite this the faint smell of bacon and coffee lingered in the air, making me hungry, but I ignored the pangs and studied the contestants as we approached. Skinny Tristan, the quiet type with wild, buttery blond hair, who was in his mid-twenties with a flair for making traditional dishes with a twist. Hannah, a middle-aged lady with dark eyes and a wicked smile who enjoyed fusion flavours. And Dave, a short, egg headed, jolly chap with a fascination for seafood recipes. We settled at the familiar table which featured in many episodes where the contestants were filmed eating together or just hanging out. Their dramatic relationships only added to the addictive dynamics of the show. After the introductions, Tori quietly left us again and I asked about the microwave incident.

'I was only in here half an hour before the explosion.' Hannah shook her head her expression bemused. 'I was getting an early breakfast.' She glanced towards the common room and grimaced.

'I slept in,' Tristan explained, 'but heard the explosion and ran out of my bedroom, bumping into Dave in the hallway,'

'Same,' Dave confirmed. 'Heard the noise and ran out of my room.'

'What about the oven fire?' I asked.

'That was horrible, just horrible,' Hannah breathed. 'There was smoke everywhere. My lamb was destroyed. My starter burnt to a crisp. It happened just before my sample taste with one the judges. Luckily, no-one was hurt.'

'What about my marinated quail legs?' Tristan grouched. 'The smoke ruined them along with my quince jelly.'

'*Everything* smelt like it'd been barbequed including my seared tuna and pear chutney.' Dave chuckled, then sobered. 'But it *was* awful. Boom! Suddenly flames and smoke filled the kitchen, and the heat was intense.'

Hannah shivered. Dave put his arm around her his usual cheery demeanour replaced with a worried air. His concerned gaze found mine.

'What happens to the final if all our cooking is ruined?' he asked.

'Hannah would win,' I said. 'She's ahead on points.'

'But the final's definitely going ahead?' Tristan asked, looking anxious.

'Until we determine if the incidents were deliberate or not there's no reason to cancel it,' I said, despite my personal misgivings. 'However, there will be a hefty police presence in the house and while we investigate.'

The contestants all looked each other with the same evident relief. I felt a flare of frustration unable to tell if it was due to the final going ahead or the police presence. No obvious suspect there then. Next, we donned protective suits and investigated the common room itself. Which apart from the scarred wall and microwave shell held no clues and any testing on the appliance would take weeks. The kitchen likewise had been thoroughly cleaned and the destroyed oven replaced. We had officers trying to recover the damaged oven but there was little hope of finding it in anything other than pieces, if at all. We then interviewed the crew but made little headway with no-one seeing or hearing anything out of the ordinary before either incident, or after. Throughout our investigations Jones' expression grew increasingly sour.

'What's the matter?' I eventually asked.

'I can't believe they practise!' she exclaimed. 'I actually cried over Hannah's anxiety when she was cooking her fennel crusted lamb loin, blanched spinach puree and pomegranate reduction live on air.'

'Come on, Sergeant. You don't seriously think non-professionals pull off such complex dishes live, without practise?'

'No of course not, but I thought they tried out recipes at home. You know, perfecting their cooking skills before they got here. When I think how Tristan struggled with his slow poached eggs, gammon foam and parmesan hollandaise on screen, I feel betrayed.'

She stalked off and I shook my head, pouring myself some coffee, and settled to watch previous episodes of *HM* including behind the scenes footage. Sometime later, a much calmer Jones re-joined me.

'Have you seen anything interesting?' she asked.

'Not really. It's mainly Brandon having his make-up re-done every five minutes, Teresa constantly blowing her nose which is probably due to the hot, spicy dishes she seems to favour this series, and Tori being everywhere. On the plus side, I've developed a hankering for pan roasted duck with ginger sauce and salted caramel cheesecake.'

'Well, I finished the background checks,' Jones said, waving her tablet. 'The judges have no financial problems. *HM* is lucrative. Teresa's bakeries and shops are award winning. Two of Brandon's restaurants recently achieved Michelin stars and *Restaurant Rescue* is about to start filming its fourth series.'

'Did you look back at the, *Master Dish* final Brandon won?'

'I did, and you were right. Something did happen afterwards.'

I took the tablet, reading about the man's triumph on the show, sadly mixed with tragedy. All around us, the kitchen was bustling with the crew preparing for the final. Seemingly everywhere at once, Tori sailed past us, gripping her clipboard with long nails digging holes into the back. She stopped nearby looking tense while giving orders and surreptitiously watching us. I ignored her and sipped my drink, suddenly recalling Teresa's extra strong, sweet coffee earlier.

Is she having trouble sleeping? A guilty conscience keeping her up, perhaps? I mused.

I thought back to Teresa's behind the scenes footage with all the nose blowing and how she favoured intense flavours this series.

Some kind of new direction she's going in? I shook my head feeling I was missing something.

'Jones, we need to dig more into the judges and Tori. It feels like something odd's going on there.'

'What's their motive?'

'Not sure, but I've a couple of ideas cooking.'

Jones raised an eyebrow.

'Really, cooking?'

Grinning, I continued perusing her background checks.

'Well, this is interesting,' I said. 'Tristan's in a lot of student debt and he's trying to start his own restaurant. Meanwhile Hannah's looking to invest in a bakery, while Dave's starting a wine import business. So, it appears as if each finalist has fifty thousand reasons to sabotage the others.'

I looked at Jones, seeing her grim expression and knowing it matched my own. I re-read the background checks and thought through everything I'd seen and heard since arriving. Slowly, I pieced together all the disparate information and happenings but still the answer remained frustratingly elusive; were the incidents accidents or dangerous sabotage?

By mid-afternoon, officers were stationed around the *HM* house with paramedics on standby. Jones and I had spent the last few hours digging even more deeply into everyone. I now felt the answers were just out of reach, needing only the final pieces to complete the puzzle. Feeling tense but trying not to show it, I stood just off camera with Jones and Tori with an unrivalled view of the kitchen set. Brandon appeared looking relaxed wearing an aubergine-coloured suit that was striking with his blackberry locks and cool grey gaze. But from my vantage point, I could see the anxiety beneath his make-up. He took his place next to Teresa, whose honeycomb hued dress complemented her peachy complexion and chestnut hair. However, little frown lines kept appearing and disappearing on her forehead. Then the spotlights hit, and the cameras rolled. Instantly, the two judges turned their megawatt smiles on as if nothing were amiss and announced the contestant's final menus.

Tristan's starter was cider and butternut squash soup with sourdough bread. His main was a saké glazed salmon featuring elderflower sauce and cucumber relish on sun-dried tomato rice. For dessert, a lemon and lime curd tart with raspberry coulis accompanied by rose and lavender Turkish delight.

'Ambitious,' murmured Jones, and I nodded in agreement.

Hannah's starter was tiger prawn and oyster tostadas with pomelo and apple dressing. Her main a macadamia crusted chicken, rosemary salted roast potatoes and braised red cabbage with dates. Dessert was a baklava accompanied by butterscotch syrup and peach sorbet.

'I'd eat all of that,' I whispered, feeling hungry, and it was Jones' turn to nod in agreement.

Dave's starter was pan fried trout, sauteed asparagus with hazelnut and truffle cream sauce. A main of lobster and gruyere souffle, steamed leeks with walnuts, sauteed baby potatoes and crispy lemon crumbs. His dessert was chocolate mousse cake with fudge sauce and caramel ice cream.

In the starter round, Tristan's soup gained the most points meaning he took a one-point lead. For the main course Dave's souffle was a triumph so he drew level with Hannah. I didn't need Jones' whispered confirmation to know whoever triumphed in the dessert round would be the overall winner and fifty thousand pounds richer. We went to a break and, despite everything going smoothly, I felt the set was more tense than a final should be. Tori returned from overseeing the dessert plating, her eyes darting everywhere and knuckles white around her clipboard.

'Maybe those incidents *were* just accidents,' the producer whispered.

'Maybe,' I murmured.

Broadcasting resumed and tension on set snapped like a trap, belying the delectable smells and gorgeous desserts. The judges and contestants soldiered on. Teresa called Hannah's baklava masterful. Brandon said Dave's cake was magnificent. Both agreed that Tristan's tart was outstanding. Then Teresa whispered in Brandon's ear with an almost imperceptible gesture toward a dish dotted with rose and lavender dusted sweets. Lux nodded, plucking a Turkish delight from Tristan's plate, and popping it in his mouth. Suddenly, he gasped red face contorting, and spluttering uncontrollably he collapsed gasping and retching. Teresa screamed and fainted. The set was in uproar, and I struggled to get through the panicking crew to the writhing Brandon. Someone shouted that the live feed was cut, and we were off air. I finally reached Brandon. His eyes were closed, sweat sheened his face and his breathing rattled harshly. Bending over him, I caught a whiff of something bitter just as the paramedics rushed in.

'No-one leaves,' I yelled to the constables. 'Brandon Lux has been poisoned.'

I moved away, noting that Hannah was crying, comforted by Dave. Tristan, paler than ever, was visibly trembling. Tori was frozen, staring wide-eyed at Brandon with a look of panic. A paramedic was trying unsuccessfully to revive Teresa with smelling salts. I studied the unconscious woman, and the final piece of the puzzle dropped into place.

Much later I dismissed the crew and gathered the contestants—Brandon, Teresa and Tori—around a dining table. A pale faced Brandon had refused hospital treatment, but I'd been assured he'd recover fully, the Turkish delight having shot from his mouth when he collapsed. Sitting next to him Teresa held Brandon's hand, looking concerned. Dave continued to support Hannah with his arm around her shoulders while Tristan sat with his head in his trembling hands, staring at the tabletop. Tori, still clutching her clipboard, perched rigidly in a chair across from Brandon, staring anxiously at her star turn.

'So, who wins?' I asked pacing the length of the table.

Tori dragged her gaze to me.

'No-one,' she said, 'until the judges announce how the dessert round scored.'

'Well, we can't do that,' Teresa said. 'Clearly someone wanted to sabotage the whole show. Either of us could've eaten that Turkish delight.'

'So why did you encourage Mr. Lux to eat it?'

Teresa's hand flew to her mouth.

'How could you even think such a thing?' she whispered. 'I'd *never* hurt Bran.'

'I believe you, Miss Cavendish. However, having scrutinised previous episodes, I've noticed you've been championing the more intensive flavours, bit of departure from previous series' and then there's your coffee habit. Earlier today you took it so strongly and with so much sugar it could strip paint, but that's the only way you can even begin to taste it, isn't it? You see, I believe sampling those delicate Turkish delights today was impossible because you're losing your sense of taste, aren't you?'

Teresa turned white as dough.

'My reputation,' she managed.

'And I further believe someone found out about your condition,' I continued. 'Someone who knew you'd never eat the Turkish delight because you'd have to make up what you thought of their taste. A judgement that could have clashed with Mr. Lux's correct assessment of the sweets. Such an obvious mis-judgement would undoubtedly raise unwanted questions not just amongst the crew but the viewing public.'

Teresa suddenly wept into Brandon's shoulder while he patted her hair looking stunned.

'Tristan,' I said, 'what poison went in the Turkish delight?'

Tristan's buttery head bobbed up and he looked whiter than ever.

'None,' he blurted out. 'Why would I need to do that when was winning?'

'Why indeed?' I murmured.

I turned to the other two finalists huddled together looking worried. Under my gaze, Hannah swallowed while Dave's egg head suddenly peppered with sweat.

'You can't think it was me?' he said. 'I'd never hurt anyone!'

'Nor me!' exclaimed Hannah. 'I promise.'

'Such a conundrum,' I sighed, gazing around the room where constables stationed along the walls awaited my signal. 'Each finalist with the same motive. All with the opportunity to poison the Turkish delight. I looked at Tristan. 'Who among you sought to sabotage the show and win by default? Or perhaps it was a team effort to split the money,' I stared at Hannah and Dave, who shook their heads. 'I can't say any of you are coming across well at this point, so maybe it was a three-way split?'

Dave erupted into loud denials. Hannah and Tristan stared at me in mute appeal. Teresa kept crying. Brandon looked shaken. Tori's fingers gripped her clipboard, her long nails digging in so much it might snap.

'Brandon,' I called, silencing Dave with a raised hand, 'please tell us how your seafood pie and secret sauce came about.'

Teresa lifted a tear-stained face looking confused. Brandon's gaze darted about then he sighed.

'I'm not sure why you're asking but it was such a long time ago, I don't suppose it matters now. Back then I was barely twenty-one, living on a shoestring and engaged to a wonderful woman called Vicky Turner. We were very happy together and lived not far from here, actually, in a little two-bed place with her child from a previous relationship. Now, I'm incredibly talented don't get me wrong but Vic was a *brilliant* cook. Innovative and creative but she was very shy especially with strangers and in social situations.' He shook his head with that sad look I'd noted earlier. 'It was why I entered *Master Dish,* and she didn't, couldn't truth be told. But we invented the seafood pie and secret sauce together specifically for me to cook on the show.' Hannah gasped. Teresa looked bewildered. Everyone else appeared stunned. Brandon continued quietly, 'She died in an accident the day after I won *Master Dish.*'

'What happened to Vicky's child?' I asked gently.

'After Vic's death the girl's father got custody. He made sure I never saw her again.'

'And the child's name?'

'Vic named the girl after herself, Victoria.'

Tori suddenly rose, white faced and trembling.

'You liar! You *stole* the recipe! *Stole* my inheritance!'

Everyone stared. Brandon paled even more; his eyes wide.

'It was *you?*'

He ducked when Tori hurled her clipboard at him.

'Why weren't you tasting Hannah's starter when the oven burnt like you were supposed to?' she shrieked, red-faced, with spittle flying from her lips. 'Why were you early for your latte? My god, you can't even eat poisoned sweets properly!'

Tori suddenly lunged across the table, her clawed hands slashing at Brandon. Officers sprang forward and caught her. She screamed and thrashed but they held fast and finally wrestled her into handcuffs.

'Victoria Gregory, I'm arresting you,' the constable's voice and Tori's raging faded as she was marched away leaving only stunned silence in her wake.

Two days later, Hannah was announced winner of, *Britain's Best Homemade Menu.*

'Poor Dave and Tristan,' Jones commiserated as we drove to our next case.

'Not really,' I said. 'Hannah told me she's marrying Dave and they're investing in Tristan's restaurant.'

'That's great news!' Jones' face fell. 'Teresa's announced she's retiring from *HM*.'

'So I heard. But she's found someone to help with her sensory problem, so maybe she'll be back.'

'I hope so. I can't imagine *HM* without Teresa Cavendish.'

'Do you know what I can't imagine?'

'What's that, Boss?'

'Why, after we'd solved everything, I didn't get to try any of the saké salmon, macadamia chicken or chocolate mousse cake. So, do you fancy joining me tonight at *Brandon's Brassiere* for seafood pie, Jones? I promise nothing but your taste buds will explode.'

Tapestry
by Nic Whittam

=A: 1962=

My father was beaten to death in 1913 by the housemaid whilst my mother was in her room feeding me. I was six months old. I don't know if it's possible to miss someone you never knew, but I'd always felt that there was someone absent from my life. I thought it was him.

In contrast, my mother's death was very peaceful. She died with round the clock nursing care, her pain carefully managed. She serenely fell asleep, shaded from the glorious sunshine, one beautiful summer's afternoon, and never woke up. Hers was a good death, if it's possible to think of it that way, she died exactly as she had planned to.

Whilst I was going through her papers some days later, I found a letter. I say found, but it wasn't really hidden. The finding was a function of sorting rather than searching. I was not a particularly inquisitive person, but I'm becoming more so.

The letter I'd found was dated a month after my first birthday, written on behalf of a Miss Yolanda Pierce. I remember my heart pounding in my chest reading that name, a name I was so familiar with, someone whom I'd never met, but who had profoundly changed my life. My hatred of her was visceral, and barely controllable. Yolanda Pierce was the woman who had murdered my father.

The letter was not written by Miss Pierce it had been dictated to her legal representative in the brief period after sentencing and just before incarceration. The individual doing the writing, Mr. Edwards, clearly felt it was important to ensure this was known.

The letter itself was seemingly important to my mother. She had kept it for nearly fifty years, isolated from other papers, in a lined desk drawer. It's thumbed-smooth appearance and well creased folds suggested it had been regularly read. As I read it, I found the contents to be alarmingly at odds with what I knew of Yolanda Pierce. She was wicked, despised men, and was apt to fly into unprovoked violently jealous rages. But here, in this carefully spoken letter, she sought to reassure my mother. She mentions the anxiety that my mother must have shared of being a lonely parent, encouraging her to find a loving husband. Shockingly she suggests that my mother 'find a kind man too, so's he can be a good father for A, that'd be lovely for both of you.' My world started to spin, and I began to feel very unwell.

There is a brief allusion to my father's 'passing', and an odd comment about having made it through the court proceedings 'like we said'. The last paragraph is a request that the photograph from her room be forwarded, with an addendum from Mr. Edwards that this can be facilitated should my mother be willing to bring the item to his offices. What the letter doesn't do is offer any explanation or ask for forgiveness. In fact, there is nothing to indicate that the letter's author has just been sentenced to life imprisonment for the brutal murder of the husband of the woman to whom it is written.

Whilst I was reeling from this discovery and deciding what, if anything, I should do about it, I received a letter from the legal representative for the estate of Yolanda Pierce, forwarded by my mother's solicitor's office. It said:

'We regret to inform you that Miss Yolanda Pierce died in her sleep in the secure unit of a private nursing home. The home is licenced by the Home Office to care for prisoners suffering from age related dementia who cannot be released from the prison service. Miss Yolanda Pierce has bequeathed all her worldly goods to Mrs. Jeremy

Boothburgh. Please complete the enclosed claims notice and return in the envelope provided for such use. On receipt of confirmation of action, the box containing these items will either be dispatched directly from the nursing home to the delivery address or disposed of as deemed appropriate by said nursing home.'

Mrs. Jeremy Boothburgh was my mother.

My mother had kept safe a letter from her husband's murderer for fifty years, and the murderer had now bequeathed everything she owned to my mother. I was dazed and very confused. Wrapped in a fog of grief, I managed to reply appropriately and three days later a box was duly delivered to our home, now just my home. I couldn't look at it to begin with, I didn't want to give this woman any of my time, she didn't deserve it. I very nearly burned the box without opening it, a pyre to the loss this woman had inflicted upon me, but I didn't have the energy. In retrospect I'm very glad I didn't.

I tried to put the letter to my mother out of my mind. That didn't work. So, then I tried very hard to explain, justify, or somehow account for it, and for why (oh why) my mother had kept it. I went round and round in circles in my mind. I was just so utterly confused by it, by everything it didn't say. Eventually, possessed by a need to understand, I cautiously opened the box of worldly goods and gingerly picked through the contents.

It was a remarkably small box for a life that had generated so many inches of copy in the newspapers. It contained the client notes from the nursing home (name redacted), some of the legal correspondence from her trial and time in prison. There were copies of the annual prison reports sent 'to whom it may concern' at the Home Office, a journal, a blouse, some needlework of a Vermeer painting (I think), and a framed photograph. My breath caught in my chest as my world stopped. I recognised the photograph; it was an image of my mother holding a swaddled infant me. My mother had had the same photograph in the same frame on her bedside drawers.

=Y: 1928=

Everyone in here says they're innocent. Either that or they've given up being angry and they don't say much at all. I don't bother with any of that. It makes no difference to me what anyone thinks. Stuff happened. Some of it were me, some of it weren't, but that doesn't matter. I were found guilty by a jury of my 'peers'. Which is an odd thing because I'm not a beardy grey fella, but here I am. My solicitor says likely as not I'll die here, so best just to get on with it.

I've been here a while now, got my routine, I know what I'm doing. Mrs. Mallory (the Lady visitor) says I need to practice my writing in a diary. I don't know what she thinks I'm writing in a diary. It's not like we have surprise visits from the Queen or trips to the zoo to write about. Then I thought I might see about writing some of what I've done. I don't know how much, but maybe some.

When I were new here, Mrs. Mallory wouldn't stop going on at me about doing something wholesome with my time. She said I had three options. No way were I joining the choir, and the reading group were a non-starter (I couldn't read back then, and I were ashamed), which left the sewing club. Best of a bum lot to be honest, and a bad match to boot. I'd never sewn anything before in my life. I had to start with the basics, sewing buttons and patches to mend stuff. I thought I was doing alright, but then I saw some of what Judith had mended and my jaw dropped. She mended my blouse that got ripped when I were convicted. The copper were really rough, he almost ripped my arm off. Judith sewed the sleeve back together. She mended it better than it were when it were new. I never thought I'd have anything that was so lovely put together. Her work took my breath away. It looks so well, her having worked on it, you'd never guess it had been ripped. And you'd never guess to look at her that she were so good at mending things. But there it is. You can't always know things by looking at them can you.

Having said that nowt happens in here, something did. The sewing club got a present.

The local haberdashers donated some stuff to the prison, and it came to us. Turns out they'd agreed to take some new products from the yarn merchant, but the products didn't shift, so they gave them to the prison to get them out the stock room. They're called 'Craft Kits'. You get a bit of calico with a famous painting printed on it and coloured yarns (Judith said they're called 'silks') to match the colours on the picture. Then you do little stitches all over the picture matching the stitch colour and picture colour till you can't see the calico. It's a new-fangled thing for people who don't know what to do with their time and can't come up with ideas for themselves. Like I said, they didn't sell. I don't think much of it, but beggars can't be choosers can they.

Anyways, some of the paintings they sent these calico pictures of are really famous. I don't know paintings, so I don't recognise any of them. Some of the other women got very excited about this one, it's got a building on it, a windmill. I've never seen one, not a real one, outside in the world. Judith didn't believe me, so I said about the mills I did know. I think I lived near a watermill when I were a babe. I have a memory of a big wheel and grinding and splashing noises. And then when I lived by my wits I were in a cotton mill for a little bit, on the looms, to earn food. But I got out of there soonest I could. Too many of the other children had bits missing, what the loom had ripped from them. I didn't fancy my chances of staying whole. But I never seen a windmill. Judith asked if I'd seen one in books or at the picture house. I told her I never went to school, there weren't no one to make me go, I think I were on the streets when I were abouts five. I did sometimes go in the library and sneak in the picture houses, but not to watch the pictures or do learning, that's when I were really desperate to be inside. They were bad places, other folks preying on cold children, we knew that, but beggars don't have much choice. Judith looked at me all sad for longer than I were comfortable with, which were odd for Judith, because she's usually very polite. And then she said I must have had a very eventful childhood. I said that I'd not thought about it that way before but that I reckon I did.

I wasn't bothered about what picture I got so I ducked the bunfight and waited for whatever were left. The picture I got is called 'the housemaid', or 'the milkmaid', or something like that. Judith says it depends how depraved you think the woman in the picture is. Judith had to tell me what depraved meant because I didn't know, I don't know a lot of words. But I like that one, it's a good one, it reminded me of what people said about me. The lass in the painting, she doesn't look depraved to me, she looks like she's busy with her job, but it doesn't take much for folks to talk does it. Sometimes folk look at you and they decide they know better about who you are than you do. And then they talk about stuff you didn't do, but they think you could have, so in their minds you already have. And then all that's left for you to do is decide whether you may as well, or not bother. I gave up arguing a long time ago.

Well, I started my sewing, and it weren't going so good. So, I took it to Judith who said that I should do some practice on an off-cut. I looked at her feeling a bit slow, my mother called it my blank look. Anyway, Judith looks back at me with her own blank look.

'I haven't got an ov-cut.' I said.

Judith breathes out slowly and smiles with her eyes, you know, a proper smile.

'I'm sorry Yolly,' she said, 'an off-cut is what I call the left-over cloth in the cloth bin. Some of the other women say scraps.'

'Ah,' I said, feeling even more daft than before for not knowing something so simple.

I wandered over to the cloth bin and Judith follows. She helps me find a pretty bit of cloth, and some decent lengths of silks that nearly match so I can have a proper practice.

I've sewn some extra flowers on my bit of cloth. It looks right nice. It reminded me of the garden at Long Hall House. Then I got maudlin. I'll not keep it. I'm gonna edge it so I could put it in the patches bin.

It'll get used to mend something. It'll be nice to see it turn up on a pinny or a shirt or something like that and think 'I did that', but quiet like, just in my head.

Nowt much else has happened. Mrs. Mallory says my writing's coming on, but my spelling and my grammar need more practice, and it wouldn't go amiss if I could speak a bit more proper because then my writing would be more proper.

I just nodded when she said that.

I don't think I need to show my book to Mrs. Mallory anymore.

=A: 1962=

The Prison Service's initial letter to the nursing home's managers asks them not to inform staff of Yolanda's status as a convicted murderer, as this 'is likely to taint the quality of the relationships she may build during her time with you'. A dizzy sickening feeling started to rise up inside me. She didn't deserve to 'form relationships' she stole my relationship with my father, she murdered him.

The nursing home notes say that, towards the end of her life, Yolanda was increasingly unresponsive to verbal instruction but was able to understand simple gestures and picture cards to guide her through the daily routine. Yolanda would spend much of her time at her window quietly humming. She was neither aggressive nor obstructive. The way that the notes are written-up, the words that the nursing staff use, suggests that many of them harboured soft-spots for this 'whimsical old lady'. I was beginning to feel physically sick. This wasn't an old lady; this was a violent killer.

Yolanda had been resident for almost two uneventful years when she received a letter from my mother's solicitor. The letter advised of the 'passing' of the wife of her victim and the surprise request that a rose be sent to Yolanda to mark this event. The nursing home responded that they were able to receive a rose as per the request. Thus, a rose was delivered to Yolanda on the day of my mother's funeral. At the time, I knew nothing of this arrangement.

Yolanda's response was documented in the nursing home's notes:

> 10.00: Placed rose on windowsill in Y's room (it smells glorious and is the biggest one I've ever seen). She stopped humming and looked directly at it then at me. I told her it was from a lady she used to know who had just passed and wanted her to have it to remember her by. Y looked at the rose again, then out of the window and started humming, I don't think she understood but she was happy enough.
>
> 11.30: Went to check in on Y before lunch and she was holding the rose to her chest and silently crying. I pointed to the rose and then the vase on the windowsill, but Y clearly wanted to keep hold of the rose (there aren't any thorns, I checked earlier).
>
> * Advise all staff notice (B3) added to client door:—'Allow Y to hold rose until it deteriorates'.
>
> * Will have to think about what to do when the rose dies.

They didn't need to decide what to do about a dead rose. Two days later Yolanda Pierce died in her bed with the rose from my mother clasped to her chest. Whilst the timing of her death was unexpected, it was not a surprise. There was no requirement to investigate the cause of death and whilst it was not treated as a secret it was very quietly recorded. None of the publications that had whipped up mobs to bay for the noose at her trial, were interested any more.

Reading all these documents I had a growing sense of disquiet. The woman writing this journal did not seem to be wicked. In her annual prison reports the officers repeatedly call her compliant and helpful. I scoured her notes, and there is no record of her ever 'flying into a fit of rage', and she was tested by other inmates on more than one occasion. She was known to the infirmary staff by name, being a regular customer in the first decade of her imprisonment due to beatings inflicted by fellow prisoners. She never retaliated or pressed charges.

Once I had read the nursing home notes I was spurred into action. I needed to search the house, my house now, for any of my mother's writing, anything. Letters, notes, shopping lists even, I was desperate. Anything. Whatever I could find that might shed light on what had happened to my father all those years ago. Because I wasn't convinced that Yolanda Pierce was the vile killer she'd been convicted of being.

I searched the house from top to bottom. I found all sorts of things that I had been ignorant of. Though as I reflect, I'm not sure if it was wilful ignorance on my part or secrecy on my mothers. There was a growing chasm in my knowledge of this woman who I dearly missed. Between bouts of sobbing, achingly desperate to see her again and be hugged, I tore through our home, her belongings, to find her past.

I found some of it, hidden under the floor in her dressing room.

=X: 1914=

I've been feeling very low since. . . Jeremy is gone and now Yolly is gone. Neither will be coming back. Amelia and I have only each other.

Yesterday I went to see a psychiatrist recommended by Dr. Montgomery.

'This fellow, Mr. Hartly, he's building quite a reputation don't you know. His methods are proving very effective.'

Mr. Hartly, MD, offered to admit me to a psychiatric hospital there and then. I quailed at the suggestion and demurred politely. I said I would really rather not but thanked him for the kindness of the offer. I attempted to clarify that I was seeking advice to help me recover myself at home. Unfortunately, nothing new of any substance was offered during the lecture that followed on the anatomy of grief and how the female psyche is particularly vulnerable. When he eventually ran out of hot air, I nonetheless thanked him for his words of wisdom and withdrew politely (despite the rage in my heart at his useless pontifications). I left his practice rooms, much lighter in purse if not in spirits.

However, it was not an entirely wasted day. For, on the return journey to Long Hall, I came across a ladies magazine that had been left in the train carriage. I became so drawn into the stories within it that I very nearly missed disembarking at Long Hall station. Thus, I have had an epiphany. What if I were to write down the events of the last year? My thoughts on the matter are somewhat in turmoil, but might it be possible to lift my spirits by writing?

Clearly, I must be careful. Any documentation must be cautiously stored and, most likely, burned upon completion. This is not a story to share in a magazine. But, to tell it to myself, would that cleanse my mind and free my soul from this burden?

I have pondered the matter further; in truth, I have thought of little else. I believe I will attempt this course of action. Within this notebook I will try to make sense of my life. I shall also reflect upon my demeanour as I write. My dearest hope is that this endeavour will give me sufficient optimism to carry on. I fear my future will be very brief if I cannot find a way out of this darkness, and I do not wish to leave Amelia just yet.

I have traced the start of my unravelling to my father's pronouncement, almost ten years ago now, that I was betrothed to Jeremy Boothburgh. It was announced lightly and with great enthusiasm. I was a little unsteadied by this as I had had no yearning for such a thing before it was decreed. However, I married a man I did not know and knew little of because my father had jollily told me to do so.

Jeremy Boothburgh was eighteen years my senior, from a very well to do family, and travelled to work in the City of London. The date of our wedding had been agreed, as had the location, and the list of invited guests, without my knowing a thing about it. This was curious to me at the time, but not alarming.

I would marry Jeremy, and my small collection of belongings would be moved into Long Hall House before the ink was dry on the marriage certificate. I would wear my mother's dress (after minor alterations), with flowers from the village meadow, and Jeremy would give me his mother's wedding ring. On the intervening Sundays I would travel to Long Hall parish church to be present for the banns being read. After the wedding I was not to return home until I was able to confirm that I was with child. This latter instruction led me to fits of giggles and rampant blushing, but my father was absolute on this point and would not be quieted until I agreed. Which I dutifully did with only a lightly furrowed brow.

With regards to a commonality of childhood: both my and Jeremy's mothers had died in childbirth. Mine had managed to deliver two healthy children to my father before very inconveniently leaving him to raise us alone. Sadly, Jeremy's mother managed only one child. Making him the sole heir to the family fortune, for which he was very grateful.

All the details for my wedding were negotiated without my knowledge. I had not needed to be party to this discussion as my assent was unnecessary. The very naïve young woman, no, child that I was, had no independent thoughts and no thoughts of independence. I was extraordinarily well trained in the art of silent subservience. I was proud to be the perfect attentive daughter. It did not, for one moment, enter my thoughts that my father may not have my best interests at heart.

I became captivated by the whirlwind of excitement that precedes such a celebration of impending matrimony. I revelled in this sudden and unexpected change of fortune. I had never been so doted on, so admired, nor so obviously loved. I was to become a beautiful wife and what girl is not excited by such an outcome. I was ignorant of the fact that the true centre of the excitement was miles away across the sea, I only learned of that later.

If I might pause for a breath. I am astonished by how liberating this is. Truly. Just to commit to paper how my journey to hell began is enormously uplifting. I shall most certainly continue.

My ignorance of the world also extended to that of my position within it. Once wed, Jeremy gloated regarding his luck capturing 'the prize' of the season. It took a few moments of frivolity before I realised that he was referring to me. It was most disconcerting being compared to a ribboned heifer at the county show and disquietingly close to the truth.

I had never expected, nor wished to be a debutant, but as Jeremy continued it transpired that that was the field in which I had unknowingly competed. I hung on his every word as he enlightened me as to the manner in which I had become Mrs. Jeremy Boothburgh. How he had seen a portrait of me and fallen in love. I have never sat for a portrait.

When he heard, from a friend of a friend, of whispers that the Prince of Wales and, more alarmingly, Mr. Roose (the dashing football player) were interested to meet the beautiful woman in the frame, he had to have me as his wife. His certainty cemented when he overheard a life-long antagonist discuss his own intention to make a proposal of marriage to the famed woman one evening at his club. This emboldened Jeremy, and the very next day he made a proposal to my father that was impossible to refuse.

His tale was not as incredible as one might have hoped and went some way to explain why I had been excluded from this endeavour until my participation was unavoidable. I could never have been party to such deception, the Prince of Wales indeed! I held my tongue, whilst quietly reeling from the details of the subterfuge and 'deal' that my husband and father had agreed. Regardless of the disturbing nature of our becoming married, I was committed to being a perfect, dutiful, blushing bride.

A year later, I made the anticipated journey to my ancestral home, excited to inform my father that he was to become a grandfather. I had sent a letter ahead to inform of my arrival but followed too close on its heels to receive a response. Expecting a joyful reception, I was somewhat surprised to be greeted by complete strangers. I was further discombobulated to be told that the house had been legally purchased not twelve months earlier. After a halting exchange, due in no small part to my utter bewilderment, the new occupants explained what they knew regarding the circumstances of the sale. A short while later they waved me off, no doubt relieved, having provided me with the forwarding address of the previous owner. The address was that of my father's solicitor, Mr. Kimble, who gave me a letter that my father had left in his possession and the key to a small safety deposit box at the bank.

With recognisable brevity the letter confirmed my abandonment, as I came to think of it, and advised of a small sum of money left for the child he anticipated I would be carrying. There was no information as to where in the world he had gone, or how to make any further contact. Mr. Kimble told me what he could, and I was able to piece together a few more details from others who had been unwittingly involved.

My brother's gambling habit had finally paid off and a West Indies plantation had been won at a high stakes table. The entire household would be moving, lock, stock, and barrel, to this new home across the ocean. Ah, but not quite the entire household – I would not be going with them. My father and brother had decided that my youthful fragility would be too much of a liability, I would attract too much unwanted attention. I needed to be 'shifted' quickly and left behind. Ordinarily one might expect the necessity of a quick sale to reduce the price of a commodity. However, my father was rather savvier than I would ever have appreciated. He was adept at marketing his goods and chattels, and his knowledge of who would be coming out that season was far greater than I could ever have imagined. He set his stall, then closed the deal, perfectly.

On deciding that I must be married off, my brother was smartly dispatched to tour the grand houses. In the guise of a stocking's seller, he appraised his sister's competition. On returning, he reported that I was by far and away the most visually symmetrical, therefore appealing, and chaste of all the innocents that would be on offer. He then went about subtly, quietly, marketing me to potentially interested, and financially vetted, parties. He built quite a chittering campaign in my favour. Just before the interest burst into the tabloids my father deftly stepped in and sold his daughter to the highest, would-be bidder. It was elegantly done, but with little regard for what might become of me. As far as I could ascertain, there were no enquiries as to temperament or aspiration of any would-be suitor. For my father, it was a purely financial transaction.

Needless to say, I was exceedingly distressed at this cold turn of events and due to my great sadness, the pregnancy progressed only a few weeks further. Had I known even a fraction of my father's duplicity, I would never have journeyed to share my joyful news.

Here I must pause to weep afresh for a loss long past, but no less for that. It is just as tender and raw as when I held it newborn. I wish it were not, but wishing is a childish attempt to change the world and is very rarely successful. I fear I have come too far in this journey to stop, and in truth, I do not wish to. My endeavour has proved itself useful to me. The solace I have derived from it is worth more than a hundred visits to useless doctors. Yet, I am upon the part where my tremors grow stronger. I am unsure of my own mind, and those around me, as to the truth of what happened in the years that followed the loss of our first child.

I was incarcerated into an unholy institution for a year and a half. Though the nurses wore cowls, none of them were decently Christian to those in their care. Further pain was inflicted at home, for whilst I was away my husband gave in to the basest of his instincts, drowning in a swill of his own despair and alcohol. When I returned it was to find that no female staff were resident in the house. Only the cook remained, she was a daily and, at that time, awful.

I must continue but I will rest for a while to calm my thoughts regarding the events still to come.

=A: 1962=

I had taken the notebook to the nursery, a place of warmth and childhood sanctuary. As I sat back on my heels against the hearth, I contemplated what I'd just read.

I had no idea that I was not my mother's first and only pregnancy. I became wracked with guilt for my ignorance. My mother had never spoken of this, and I had never asked. Oh, if only I had known this whilst she was still alive. Though, I don't know what solace I could have offered. The despair and sadness in these few pages has made me heavy with grief anew. So, as she stopped writing, I stopped reading. When I returned a few hours later, to pick up the tale, I discovered that the remaining pages in the notebook were blank. If she had picked up her pen to write again it was not in this book.

I had found the first notebook under a loose floorboard in my mother's dressing room. After further inspection I discovered that quite a few of the boards were loose, and it was more luck than judgement that the first one I'd checked hid the first of my mother's notebooks. Had I been even a modicum more methodical about it and started with the boards at one side of the room and worked to the opposite, the book I found would have been in the middle of the stack. I have lifted (and carefully replaced) every loose board and found a further four books. I had the first, next I needed put the rest in the right order.

I think I have it straight, I could be wrong, but I don't think I am. A few more of the entries from Yolanda's journal seem to corroborate the sequence of events.

=Y: 1928=

I saw my mistress in the lobby of a swanky hotel. I knew it were posh and I had no business being there, but a girl has to keep warm somehow. And if I kept myself quiet and made myself small only the meanest of the bellboys would shoo me out.

She were at the front desk and I overheard her talking about needing help around the house, and did they have any extra staff who they could give references for but that maybe they didn't need. And the desk man said if she were to come back tomorrow, he would have a list. I didn't even think, I just ran outside after her and gave a shout to get her to stop. And she did.

'I don't have no learning,' I said, 'and I can't read or write or do sums and that, but I can work hard, and I can scrub and I can clean, and I make a good potato soup if I've got a potato, and a pan, and a stove.'

And she stares at me, and I stares back. And then she asks how old I am.

'Old enough to be on the streets miss, by myself, and I do the best I can miss, to keep myself clean and that.'

And so then she looks me up and down, and she makes me turn round. She looks in my mouth (she says to check my teeth) and asks me if me head is itchy. And I says,

'Not today.'

And then she takes a deep breath and closes her eyes, and then she opens them.

'Alright then,' she said, 'we'll give this a go. What's your name?'

'Yolanda Pierce, miss.'

'Very nice to meet you Yolanda Pierce, I'm Mrs. Boothburgh. I shall pay you a pound each month, along with bed and board. You may have every other Wednesday afternoon off, and every Sunday morning for church. If there are no breakages or damages, I will give you an extra penny on your afternoon off. Does this sound agreeable?'

'Yes miss, can I start now miss?'

And she eye's me up and down again.

'Yes, I think that would be wise.'

That's how I came to be housemaid at Long Hall House. It were a nice place. The gardens were lovely in the spring, and even in the autumn too, there were loads of flowers. The gardener were a gentle man. I liked watching him with the pots of seedlings. He said he were 'pricking them out', but he weren't. He was moving them between the pots so tenderly, like they were as precious as newborn babes. Sometimes he'd let me help. And it were warm in his shed.

The mistress were nice, it were hard work, don't get me wrong, but she were fair and did her best. She wasn't that old really, not much different to me. But she looked well for her age, and I was short for mine. The master wasn't there to begin with. The mistress said he were in London. I think he were at his club or something, he was doing business.

I settled into life at Long Hall House quickly, like a duck to water. It were nice and calm. I landed on my feet and no mistake. But there were dark rumblings in the village about the master and for me to keep a sharp look out.

After a few weeks the master came home. The mistress made me move into a room next to hers. It had been her dressing room, but she said it were mine now. She said there had been some trouble in the past and she wasn't having any more of it. Ha! I knew what that meant, I'd heard stories. I might be cabbage looking but I'm not that green. Well, I were, but I knew to listen to the other women in my pew at church. They told me the lay of the land. Women that work in other people's houses listen to what's going on, and they talk to each other too. They look out for each other.

The master had fallen apart when his babe died. The mistress were bad too, but she were sent away to recover her senses. And when she comes back all the girls who'd worked in the house had upped sticks. Gone back to their families or been taken on by other houses. The master had attacked the scullery maid while she was sleeping, and she'd screamed enough to fetch the devil. After that none of the local girls would go near the place, apart from cook – but she kept a skewer and a cleaver in her pinny just in case. And she went home to her house every day too. But she were scary, she were. I don't think there was ever a man brave enough to get within an arm's reach of her. She was sweet on the gardener though. He always got the sticky end bit of the date cake, that's how we all knew. Apart from the gardener, he didn't know. Anyways, that's why the mistress were looking for a new housemaid in town, she couldn't get a local girl. I didn't mind being there, I were just happy to have a roof over my head an food in my belly. The mistress had picked me up off the street and was keeping me safe. I was fine.

The master were coming and going every few weeks. He mostly kept away from everyone. But he was an odd one. He started off not speaking to anyone, not even cook, and that were asking for trouble, and then he'd be chatty and jolly. And then he'd be in a temper fit for a fight and hit the walls as he walked past, then he'd be sat in a chair for hours with a book on his lap just looking out of the window, not reading it or anything. He was proper up and down and all over the place. But after a bit, we all got used to him, and that was just how he was.

I were there nigh on three years when the mistress fell pregnant. I knew there'd been a child that was lost. That was the start of the troubles in the house, and I'd seen a tiny headstone tucked away in the garden, but I'd never asked about it.

The babe arrived perfect. The master wasn't at home, I think he were hoping to miss it. Me and cook helped the mistress, and she did well. And when the doctor come to check them both over on the next day he said we all did a good job for untrained folk. I looked after her, well, both of them really. Mistress was a bit up and down, she'd had trouble before, but I was holding her together. Making sure she didn't have any worries on her mind. I would sing them both to sleep. And hold them both close.

The master were back to his usual coming and going when it happened. The babe was nearly a year old and we were planning a party. I was setting the grate and refilling the log store in his room and then he were there behind me. I wasn't expecting him. I had a big heavy log in my hand as he grabbed my skirt and spun me round. He wasn't expecting that.

=X: 1914=

It transpired that Jeremy's father was acutely aware of his son's weaknesses. Upon our marriage he intervened to ensure that property that had been mine remained so. Whilst the law states that a woman's property no longer passes to her husband upon marriage, I know of few wives who could afford to instruct representation to enforce it. The law would not have protected me should Jeremy have chosen to take everything that was mine, but he would never cross his father. Each of us was independently afforded a monthly allowance. My purse was safely mine. At the same time Long Hall House was placed in trust for his father's heirs and their issue and thus it was unavailable for use as collateral or to sell. Not that Jeremy was above testing this, pointing to the lack of issue when he was at his most pitifully aggrieved. Upon the death of his father, he tried, and failed, to sway the family lawyer, Mr. Edwards, to apply to revise the terms.

I pride myself that I am an excellent judge of character, a skill that, to my loss, was not inherited from my father, and quickly came to trust Mr. Edwards' counsel. Jeremy's father had been candid with the lawyer, and he was privy to the flaws my husband tried to supress and hide. He kept a benevolent eye on my interests and would support or advise when necessary. I had tried to be wife enough for my husband, the Lord knows how much and how hard I tried. But I had to face the fact that I was not enough. I'm not certain that anything or anyone could have been truly enough. He had demons, worse than anything in my nightmares, but I loved him as only a wife can, and I tried to protect him.

After the incident we found it increasingly difficult to recruit staff from the village, the surrounding villages, and some of the towns too. Searching for a clean slate I went to the city with the innocent optimism to recruit from one of the hotels. I expected to pay handsomely for their assistance, and for the help we recruited to be truculent and poorly performing. However, I was resigned to this being a necessary step in the rehabilitation of our reputation as reliable employers running a respectable household.

In the end I visited only one hotel for, as I left the premises, an urchin accosted me in the street. I do believe she had been skulking in the corner of the lobby whilst I spoke with the concierge and had listened to the whole conversation. I was quite taken aback that from such blatant eavesdropping she now hoped to profit. She was filthy and lice infested with the affront to offer herself as a potential housemaid. Her absolute conviction that she deserved to exist, and ask for what she wanted, staggered me. I was face to face with female confidence, I had never encountered anyone quite like her and being in her presence was intoxicating. After a moment to regain my composure, feigning consideration, I acquiesced.

Yolanda Pierce was everything we needed, that I needed, at Long Hall House. She was keen, strong, and quick to learn. She blew away the darkness that had fallen upon us as the fresh air of spring will the winter cobwebs. She was a gift. We became a popular stop when at home due to Yolly's outspoken nature towards our guests. Her observations were often rather more accurate than some were ready to admit, even to themselves. This tendency was helpful to some, but not always welcomed. Regardless, her insights could not be challenged as untruths. She was brutally honest.

Despite my albeit feigned discomfort, she refused to be quieted.

'God put that thought in me head for it to come out me mouth.'

Or to whisper only to me.

'Whisperin's summat for the devil to hear.'

Many were the times that I was rebuked by more worthy visitors for keeping such a 'goatherd' amongst my staff, but they were all well aware of the trouble we had had and the dearth of alternative candidates. Not that I would have traded Yolly, not for anything in the world. Yolly aided and assisted me during the day, she was the best housemaid I've ever had. After she moved rooms, we would spend the evenings chattering like the March sisters, and she loved listening to me read aloud. Neither of us had had a friend before and we quickly became inseparable. She became the best friend I'd ever had. She was a little older than me, but not by as much as she looked. She was twice as strong though. Where I was quick to react, her countenance was more considered and thoughtful. We were as close as could be, which, as I reflect on our conjoined pasts, may well have been what drove Jeremy to attack her.

At Christmas, in 1912, Jeremy came home to me his best self, bright and glittering, filling the house. He joyfully placed himself in the centre of my world, charming and doting. I fell in love with him again. Unfortunately, this mood did not endure. On his return to the City of London some calamity befell his office. He slumped to the lowest point I had ever seen him fall. It was shortly after this that I was able to tell him, with some trepidation, that he was to be a father. I hoped it would fill his heart with joy, as it had before. He was neither pleased nor displeased, but just nodded and bade me close the door on my exit. I was shocked but vowed to keep my head and spirits high to keep the baby safe.

Yolly was everything to me through that winter into spring. I was extraordinarily ill. Vomiting twice or three times daily. She held me and made me sip water, or whatever concoction cook had made to keep me strong. I had come to value cook's unflappable wisdom, and her skill had improved beyond measure my having taught her to read the recipe books.

By the summer I was blooming and enjoying the freedoms afforded to conspicuously successful wives – the delivery of progeny being of the utmost importance in high society. Jeremy spent more and more time away from Long Hall House, which we, the household, took for granted as a sign that we could continue as we were. I do not believe that I will ever be so happy again. I try to find solace in the conjecture that it is 'better to have loved and lost than never to have loved at all', but I wonder if these deep, dark feelings of loss might be lessened if I had never felt completely connected to another person as I had with Yolly.

I find that I am increasingly fearful of the coming entries. I have been avoiding it, I know now. I have spent too much time re-reading older entries, considering them, and editing my thoughts according to current mores. This is neither helpful, nor does it further the enterprise of lifting the weights of the past from my thoughts and heart. I believe I must promise myself to burn this notebook to be fortified to continue.

I have been in contemplation of the cleansing power of fire alongside an innate instinct to protect truths. The act of burning may not be the appropriate conclusion to these activities. Whilst I believe it can be cleansing, I am forced to consider whether creating a hidden repository of truth might be the right thing to do. I will cling to this thought, as a life vest, as I face the barren emptiness of the home I wander through now.

=A: 1962=

There are no more words in the notebook in my hands, but as with the previous ones, I optimistically flick through the pages to check. Repeatedly. As an ex-lover observed I have never been one to move onto a new opportunity without having first drained all the joy out of the current one. It was a very painful end to a brief, intense, relationship, where my thoroughness was under appreciated.

I bring myself back to the present and gaze around the room, my safe space, before allowing my eyes to fall onto the fifth and final notebook. I share my mother's hesitations as I look at it. This unopened tiny tome. It is the slightest of the offerings hidden for me to find and as I look at it, I acknowledge a growing sense of expectation and fear. I am scared to read its contents. Her despondency is catching, but 'barren emptiness'? I think she is about to share the events surrounding my father's murder, but this is also my early infancy. Did my mother suffer from depression? Given all that happened it would be understandable. I realise again how little I really knew about my mother.

I want to hide under my blankets and ignore the world. I want to go back in time and not open the drawer, tell the nursing home I have no desire to received anything from them. But then I hear an echo, from ages past, of a teacher's voice:

'You learn most about yourself by facing the things you fear.'

How much do I want to learn about myself? If ignorance is bliss, then I'd rather be blissful than tormented by knowledge. My imagination may well be running away with me, however. I would not describe myself as an inquisitive person, but I have always had a vivid imagination. I need to consider everything I have learned, or think I know, as I'm not sure how much of this to believe. Here in these notebooks my mother says she was abandoned by her family and sold to my father. I had known that my parent's marriage had been arranged. But I am shocked that it was sprung upon her as a *fait accompli.* I also know that whilst divorce existed as a legitimate legal option during her marriage, there was significant social stigma surrounding divorced mothers and their children, as there still is. She would not have chosen that for either of us had there been any way to avoid it.

At school, thirty-eight or so years ago, I remember writing an essay over the summer holiday. The topic was selected from a list provided by the English masters, and I picked slavery in the West Indies. When mother revealed that my grandfather and uncle had left to run a plantation there, I had excitedly pressed her hard for information. I gave up when it became evident that she knew nothing of the details. I had always promised myself that I would try to locate where they had gone, but as yet had not found the time. I don't know for certain that they really did leave, and I have no-one to ask, but it seems an odd thing to fabricate.

I had no idea that she had miscarried her first child. I also didn't know that she had been admitted to a psychiatric institution shortly after. At that time treatments for mental illness were often barbaric. From my sparse knowledge of institutional care, she must also have been astonishingly strong to have managed to leave the institution and return home. To then discover that whilst she was away, enduring who-knows-what treatments, my father had assaulted one of their employees must have been a deep betrayal! I wonder if she considered it better or worse that she had been absent, and more importantly that he wasn't held accountable. They were both made to face the only sanction that the community had – they were ostracised. But mother's tenacity circumvented this punishment. As a result, she brought her husband's killer into their home. If he had been brought before a court to answer for his actions, would he have survived?

With all that said, the Yolanda Pierce that I've read about doesn't match the description of her in the court papers. My mother called her Yolly, an affectionate nickname, and seemed to like and greatly admire her. Mother kept a letter from her for almost fifty years and shared a cherished photograph. The story isn't adding up.

I look again at the final book, this little thing. Surely something so slight cannot be filled with too much horror. I look out of the window. It's very dark. I consider whether this is the right time of day to be reading revelations. I really ought to wait until it's a socially acceptable time of day, just in case. Nobody likes an unexpected, unarranged call between the witching hour and the alarm clock.

=X: 1914=

This endeavour has been illuminating and calming. I am much lighter in spirit for having detailed what I have of my life thus far, and I anticipate feeling even more so once this next chapter is concluded. I have come to realise that I have experienced very few opportunities in which to make a choice. I will use this day to finish this work. I have sufficient sustenance to hand. I will not read it once it is done, and I will immediately bury it within the house. I have identified a suitable location, and already placed my previous notebooks within it. Then, as I close up the room, so I will close up my thoughts.

Jeremy never really recovered from the humiliation of his depravity toward Sarah, the scullery maid. I would like to think that he repented before he died, but I expect he thought he would have more time to make his peace with God. Our child was born on Thursday, twenty sixth of September 1912. A beautiful baby girl. I do not wish to repeat that experience. It made me realise the true nature of what we women do. The fine line we walk between life and death.

The household welcomed Amelia Mary with jubilation and that year the harvest festival was a particularly buoyant affair. If it were possible, Jeremy sank even lower into his fugue and turned again to drink. He was usually a very sleepy drunk, but he was starting to become frustrated and even angry. The infant was making excellent progress, and I was managing to feed her by myself, which given her size and voracious appetite was more than I had hoped to achieve. As preparations were afoot to celebrate her first year, Jeremy died.

In an angry drunken stupor, he decided he would have at Yolly whilst she was laying the grate in his room. He tore her skirts, but she managed to fight him off. In so doing, he fell hard against the mantle in his room, hit his head, and collapsed to the floor. She thought him dead and came running to find me. I immediately went to Jeremy in his room, splayed on the floor with a stain spreading about his head from a gash above his eye. I fell to my knees and gently cradled his head in my lap, Yolly took his hand, both of us hoping desperately to rouse him. He opened his eyes, and I was about to shout joyfully for more help, to get him into bed, and retrieve a cold compress, I don't know what else, but he looked at me so fiercely, the yell stuck in my throat. Such hate filled blasphemy fell from his lips that I shrank back from him, shocked by the venom in his spewing. He tried to stand, and Yolly and I staggered backwards away from the verbal assault.

I tripped over a large log on the floor. I looked down and saw that there was a small snag of fabric stuck in the splinters of it. My attention flew back to Jeremy and his continuing vile outpouring, then I saw a hole in his jacket matching the snag on the log. He reached for Yolly but she recoiled. He continued to hurl abuse at us, with threats of violence were he to catch hold of either of us, as he clasped the bed frame to stand. At that, a rage I did not know I possessed, boiled up within me, for him, my father, my brother, his father, at the world and all the injustice in it. I remember calmly lifting the log above my head. I heard screaming, I think from all three of our voices in demonic chorus, and repeated thundering crashes, then silence. Yolly said I fainted, and she was left alone in the mess of what I had done.

I awoke in bed, clean, and in a fresh nightdress with the baby sound asleep beside me. I left my room and wandered the house trying to piece together what had happened. I found Yolly washing my clothes in the scullery. She had sent everyone else away. We talked, we cried, we argued, we held onto each other tightly. Yolly told me what had happened, but there was no sense to her description and my memory was dull then. She went to see the local constable the next day and I instructed Mr. Edwards to act on Yolly's behalf. We had talked through the court proceedings, but they progressed far more quickly than we had anticipated. Her full confession meant that none were called to the stand in prosecution or defence. Mr. Edwards was at least able to call the scullery maid, Sarah, to the stand and her brave testimony saved Yolly from the hangman's noose. He could not, however, protect any of us from the hatred and lies in the press. They were despicable. Whilst none of my meagre household spoke out, other households, and visitors we had hosted in the past, told stories about us all. Small shreds of truth were so stretched and embellished as to be grossly unrecognisable were it not for the attributed names.

Mr. Edwards took messages from me to Yolly, and I received a dictated letter in return. I have kept it dear and will do until the end of my days. I will not marry, as she entreated, but I hope to find close friends, in time, to help me to raise Amelia. If I were to be taken into custody, charged, and executed Amelia would be left orphaned. Yolly saw her own past being repeated. She was insistent that Amelia needed her mother, that I was not a danger to anyone having removed the person who was a danger to us all. Whilst the size of the inheritance pot would attract self-serving relations, Yolly would be unable to protect our child from them. Yolanda Pierce sacrificed herself so that I might raise my daughter. Yolanda Pierce was the kindest and bravest person I have ever known. I did not deserve her friendship, and she deserved far better than mine.

=A: 1962=

This note fell from the final notebook whilst I was reading it:

May 1960

Dearest Am,

These notebooks are for you. I do believe that you will find them. Once your sense of curiosity is awoken, you are ceaseless. I wish I were able to tell you directly, but I have left it too long, and I do not have the energy to face your relentless questioning nor your judgement. I will be judged, soon and I have made my peace with that, but not by you. I hope I have presented enough for you to understand. Please, forgive me. Know that I am so very proud of you, everything you are, and everything you will become.

I love you.

Mother

The Bureau of Impossible Crimes

by Jonathan Ruffle

Episode 1: The Case of the Vanishing Spitfire

FADE IN

PRE-TITLE SEQUENCE

EXT. ENGLISH COUNTRY ROAD - DAWN

Caption : **19th May 1935**

A crisp spring morning. A middle-aged but youthful man powers his Brough Superior motorbike along a deserted road.

T.E. LAWRENCE, 47, his fair hair whipping above his goggles, is looking thoughtfully ahead. He grins.

INT. BENTLEY CAR - DAWN

Lawrence on his bike is framed in the Bentley's rear-view mirror. The driver pulls over to let him pass.

DRIVER
It's Lawrence. He lives up the road.

PASSENGER
Lawrence who?

DRIVER
You know. Lawrence of Arabia.

PASSENGER
Good lord. Here?

DRIVER
Want a race, do you, you blighter?

Lawrence beeps his horn. The car and bike accelerate away.

EXT. COUNTRY ROAD - DAY

The beeping horn is in the distance. Two boys in tweed cycling outfits take it as a signal to peddle their pushbikes into the road.

BOY 1
Ready?

They flex their muscles, bounce on the saddles, check their brakes.

EXT. COUNTRY ROAD - DAY

Powering downhill, Lawrence looks in his mirror. The car drops out of view far behind. His nerves provoke a devilish laugh.

He takes the next bend, sees the boys on the other side of the road. He has a clear path past them. But he yanks the steering over and ploughs off the road into the bushes. The boys athletically tumble off their bikes.

BOY 1

Looked good to me.

EXT. BUSHES - DAY

Lawrence nimbly jumps from his speeding bike into a net strung between the bushes in a clearing. The Brough Superior careens riderless into a tree. A muffled WUMPF - the bike begins to burn. Goggles hang from a branch.

Another man - MALLORY, 49 - quickly disentangles Lawrence from the net.

MALLORY

As quick as you can!

EXT. COUNTRY ROAD - DAY

The Bentley men have stopped to help the two boys, sprawled on the road. One clutches his knee.

BOY 1

My knee, sir. I've bust it!

DRIVER

Where's Lawrence?

BOY 2

The bloke went in the bushes, sir.

EXT. BUSHES - DAY

The net folded and unhooked, Mallory and Lawrence make a hasty exit into the trees as the Bentley men reach the clearing. The bike is on fire, and near it is a twisted body with an appallingly injured face.

PASSENGER

Oh no!

DRIVER
He's dead. Lawrence of Arabia is dead.

BOY 2
Crikey, sir! It's not possible, sir!

But as the men crane forward to look closer at the corpse, one boy catches the other's eye. They grin and exchange 'thumbs up'.

TITLE SEQUENCE

EXT. 'THE BLIND BEGGAR', EAST END PUB - EVENING

Caption: **Six Months later**

A wet winter's evening. Boyish but priggish BOB, 34, carefully puts his bicycle clips into his new suit pocket.

INT. 'THE BLIND BEGGAR', EAST END PUB - EVENING

The publican has his pint all ready.

PUBLICAN
There you go. Tuppence.

BOB
Chin-chin.

He's aware of a devastating beauty in a sheath dress on the barstool next to him. It's ALMA RAT-TENBURY, 38, but he doesn't know that.

BOB
And give me a scotch to go with it.

ALMA
Celebrating?

BOB

Do I know you, miss?

ALMA

I'm Constance. Win on the horses?

BOB

You should know, miss, that I am a detective inspector in the Criminal Investigations Department, but I can still run you in for any hanky-panky.

ALMA

I was just making conversation.

He's interested. And not just professionally.

BOB

Alright. I'm Bob.

ALMA

Why don't we go out and find a party, Bob?

BOB

Miss, I thought I said-

She opens her clutch-bag. Looks into it to avoid his eye.

ALMA

(*Quietly*) What would you do in my position? Lonely. Widowed. A man comes into a public house - happy. Wouldn't you make a beeline for him?

INT. SERGIO'S NIGHTCLUB - 3 A.M.

It's an East End club. There's a small band playing. People dance closely together. Alma looks glassily into Bob's eyes.

ALMA

Take me home with you?

INT. BOB'S HOUSE. BEDROOM - 4 A.M.

Bob's face is tense, expectant. Alma peels off the sheath dress. Underneath she's naked. He's ecstatic as he pulls her to him.

INT. BOB'S HOUSE. BEDROOM - 5 A.M.

She's in the crook of his arm.

ALMA

Do you love me - a little bit?

BOB

You're the prettiest girl I've ever seen.

ALMA

Who are you - really?

BOB

I'm a copper. A newly-promoted copper.

ALMA

What?

BOB

'Nuff said.

ALMA

No. Tell me all about it, Mr. Copper.

BOB

It's a secret job. (*Mock 'under-interrogation'*) That's all you'll get from me.

ALMA

Are you sure?

She slides down the bed, under the covers. He gasps.

EXT. BOB'S HOUSE. BEDROOM - 6 A.M.

She lets herself out onto the landing. Very silently - she's expert at it.

EXT. EUSTON ROAD, LONDON - MORNING

Bob is neat and tidy, but a bit red in the eyes as he steps off a tram. Peers at his police notebook. It reads 'The Bureau, 40, Marylebone Road.' But number 40 is *Madame Tussauds*. He frowns.

INT. MADAME TUSSAUDS - DAY

Bob crossly clambers a twisty staircase to find a door marked 'Roof Only - No Exit'. He purses his lips in anger, turns to go, but there's a faint noise. The door behind him is LOCKED.

INT. BUREAU H.Q. - DAY

Bob realises he's in a small glass hallway. Lights come on and he sees it is a cube in a vast space, with a huge arching glass roof, crammed with files, machines, disguises and equipment reaching right up to the ceiling.

Suddenly chutes release rivers of sand that half-fill the small space instantly. Bob is trapped up to his chest. Mallory calls from above.

MALLORY

Who are you?

BOB

I can't move!

MALLORY

I'll ask you just once more. Who are you?

BOB

I'm D.I. Fabian, C.I.D.

MALLORY

Warrant card?

BOB

Under this lot.

Mallory climbs down from the gallery, not using the stairs. It's a creepy sight, a man able to scurry so vertically down a wall. He hits a switch that vents the sand through the floor.

MALLORY

It brushes out.

Bob hands over his warrant card.

MALLORY

Sit down. We've been expecting you. I forgot to disable our welcome mat.

BOB

Very effective. And who might you be, sir?

MALLORY

My name is George Mallory. Mean anything to you?

BOB

Spelt like the mountaineer? The one lost on Everest in '24? The 'because it's there' chap? The Human - (*It's dawning.*) - Fly?

Bob sits down involuntarily.

MALLORY

And this is Mr. T.E. Lawrence. Been with us for six months now.

Lawrence was sitting there all along, but so immobile it was possible to miss him completely.

BOB

(*Stunned*) Lawrence of Arabia? Sir. Hello.

Lawrence doesn't move.

MALLORY

It's some sort of Arab thing. Can be like that for hours. The others are next door.

INT. BUREAU H.Q. DINING ROOM - CONTINUOUS

STAN, 28 and only 4'10" tall, laughs at the sight of Bob.

STAN

Surprise, surprise, Mr. Fabian.

BOB

Christ!

STAN

(*As to a little boy*) Language - Bob.

Bob stares at the third dead man he's met that morning.

MALLORY

I think you've met Mr. Hobday professionally? We recruited him after he was hanged in '33 in Winson Green prison.

BOB

I've collared him four times, sir.

STAN

Honest, Mr. Fabian, I didn't kill the old geezer. I just put my dabs on everything for that berk Fred Cherrill to find.

BOB

Chief Inspector Cherrill to you, sonny. And I want to talk to you about-

STAN

They've washed my slate, guv. They wanted a peterman, drummer, penman - all sorts. You lucky people!

MALLORY

It is a good thing you're here, Mr. Fabian. Now we'll have someone to act as interpreter for Stan's arcane criminal vocabulary.

BOB

It's crooked nonsense, whatever way you look at it, sir.

Suddenly, Alma - Constance, to Bob - is in the room. With an amused look.

MALLORY

And this is Mrs. Alma Rattenbury. But, of course, you've already met.

Constance is Alma? Bob is stunned.

ALMA

Hello, Bob.

Bob limply takes her proffered hand.

BOB

Miss.

MALLORY

Mrs. Rattenbury committed suicide at the end of the most glamorous *crime passionnelle* old England could bear.

She's not who she said she was, *and* she's the fourth dead person Bob's met in as many minutes.

BOB

Ah - yes - ah-

ALMA

How very nice to meet you. Again.

Bob gulps in embarrassment. Mallory notices.

MALLORY

Oh yes. I'm pleased you said nothing about this job last night - even under considerable pressure.

BOB

Oh. Right, sir.

STAN

But neither did I, guv, even when -

MALLORY

Thank you, Mr. Hobday. Tea, Mr. Fabian?

Bob's head is in a whirl. Mallory busies himself with the tea things.

BOB

(*Quietly*) Do you vet all applicants in - that way?

ALMA

(*Loudly*) Oh, yes. All part of my job. Though Mr. Lawrence resisted all my efforts.

Lawrence smiles serenely.

BOB

Well. He's more of a gentleman than me, I suppose.

ALMA

Yes.

Mallory hands Bob his tea.

MALLORY

I shouldn't imagine you've been told very much about this new job of yours.

BOB

No, sir.

MALLORY

You're said to be a rising star in the Met. The newspapers seem to think you're pretty hot stuff, too. Well, you're working with us from now on. No glory, just very hard work.

BOB

Sir.

MALLORY

Your chief - our chief - remains Sir Philip Game, Metropolitan Police commissioner at Scotland Yard. But our work, our unique lack of identity, means we can operate outside the law. But ultimately we work for the government.

BOB

What sort of work, sir?

MALLORY

Last year we managed to apprehend those responsible for making 10 Downing Street disappear.

BOB

Good grief!

MALLORY

Before that we worked out how the British Fascist leader Mr. Oswald Mosley, could have been meeting a recently deceased Hindenburg in Munich - at the same time he was addressing a rally in Leeds.

BOB

Sir!

MALLORY

Do you detect the work of a foreign power in either of these?

BOB

I do, sir.

MALLORY

There are even moves to influence Edward, the Prince of Wales - our future King - in the merits of that cause.

BOB

Good grief, sir.

MALLORY

We will be at war in a few years, Mr. Fabian. But our opponents have started a little earlier than the published kick-off time. Thwarting them, and winning this secret war, is a job outside the bounds of legality. So it's our pigeon.

Bob is looking more amazed by the moment.

MALLORY

Mr. Hobday is able to use his nefarious skills to help us. Mr. Lawrence has the finest mind in England.

Lawrence mock-bows.

MALLORY

Mrs. Rattenbury is able to find out information no-one would dream of revealing. You, Mr. Fabian, are a policeman. Useful in itself. But no more actual police work as such for you for the time being. Your first duty is to help us - the ghosts who cannot operate in the open - to get what we need, wherever we may need it. Work hard and you've nothing to fear from me. It's a dangerous job. Your predecessor was killed in the line of duty.

BOB

Sir.

MALLORY

Please step into my office.

INT. BUREAU H.Q. MALLORY'S OFFICE - CONTINUOUS

BOB
I suppose we have lots of special equipment, sir.

Mallory waves at his bookshelf.

MALLORY
Good lord, yes. We have the new Encyclopaedia Britannica. 1936 edition, well before publication. And please don't call me sir.

BOB
But that trap at the door, sir, Mr. Mall -

MALLORY
Mr. Lawrence was working at an experimental sea-plane base just before he died. Still, sand remains a recurrent theme in his inventions.

BOB
Is he one hundred percent alright?

MALLORY
He's been a man of destiny - a god. Now he's striving to be a mere man. There's a mind working tirelessly on our behalf there. Often at great cost to itself.

BOB
Do we have any new weapons, Mr. Mallory?

MALLORY
I found in the trenches that it's men that matter.

Bob, like all men too young to have served, is chastened. Seeing this, Mallory remembers his more humane side.

MALLORY

And men armed with machine guns are the ones who matter most of all. Don't worry, Mr. Fabian: we're not too badly off for kit.

Bob looks reassured.

MALLORY

But now we need to restock our supplies. I'm sure Mrs. Rattenbury and Mr. Hobday will be able to steer you in the right direction.

INT. BUREAU H.Q. KITCHEN - DAY

Stan has put on a police constable's uniform.

STAN

Cut a dash, don't I, Bob?

BOB

Who did you pinch that uniform off?

STAN

You're laying it on a bit thick, aintcha? Best disguise for an ex-lag.

BOB

I'd have you on report for those boots. I need to restock, so make me a list, smartish.

Bob gets out his police notebook.

STAN

Make your own bloody list.

He stomps out with a bad limp.

BOB

Mrs. Rattenbury?

ALMA

Call me Alma. Can't have you behaving like George Mallory all the time.

BOB

Alma. Could you help me-

ALMA

Sadly, I have to go and check a minor sultan's *bona fides*.

And she's gone. Bob sighs. Turns to the cupboards. Nearly jumps out of his skin. Lawrence is sitting cross-legged on the table in a yoga position.

BOB

Sir? You don't know if-

But Lawrence isn't present, not in any real sense, anyway.

BOB

Is Mrs. Rattenbury-

Bob waves his hand in front of Lawrence's face. Doesn't even blink. Bob opens his notebook. Thinks twice about it, puts it in his pocket. 'Fabian of the Yard', Britain's brightest young detective, picks up an old paper bag and writes -

BOB

(*Writing*) Milk. Eggs. Bread...

INT. 'THE BLIND BEGGAR', EAST END PUB - evening

Pint of bitter ready as Bob drags himself in.

BOB

I've had a bloody terrible day.
I'll buy you one.

PUBLICAN

Very kind, Mr. Fabian! A bottle of
Bass. Sixpence in all, sir.

BOB

That's odd. Where's all my change
got to?

The publican's seen this a million times.

PUBLICAN

(*Bonhomie gone*) Oh.

BOB

(*Blurts*) Stan Bloody Hobday!

PUBLICAN

More master criminals, Mr. Fabian?

BOB

No. Just thinking of someone.

He checks his pockets. His wallet's still there.

PUBLICAN

You'll have your picture in the
News Chronicle again, I shouldn't
wonder.

BOB

Hm.

And there's a pound note in the wallet.

PUBLICAN

(*Perking up*) I'll make it a scotch, then, if you don't mind.

BOB

Err, no.

PUBLICAN

One and fourpence. What would I give to be a few years younger?

BOB

Yes.

PUBLICAN

Did I ever tell you about when we was in the Third Royal Welsh?

Here comes another half-hour of reminiscences by the wartime hero generation.

PUBLICAN

We was at the Somme. Norman Blake - old Blakey - and me was going out on a night patrol...

Bob sighs and tries to look interested.

EXT. DIGBY, LINCOLNSHIRE - DAWN

Beautiful clear strong sunlight falls on horse and cart with milk churns on the back.

EXT. R.A.F. DIGBY AIRFIELD. RUNWAY - DAWN

There's a dusting of snow over the aerodrome. The only things flying are the skylarks. All is peace.

EXT. R.A.F. DIGBY AIRFIELD HANGARS - DAWN

An RAF Police flight sergeant stands guard. A small fuel lorry is driven up.

SERGEANT

What time do you call this?

LORRY DRIVER

Sorry, flight.

They start to unlock the hangar.

SERGEANT

This is an RAF aerodrome, not a bloody holiday camp.

LORRY DRIVER

Yes, flight.

SERGEANT

Oh-six-hundred, d'you hear me? Not oh-six-hundred and one!

LORRY DRIVER

Yes, flight.

The doors are pushed back. The ground crew stand amazed. There is nothing there. The hangar is empty.

SERGEANT

Christ. The thingummyjig's been pinched!

LORRY DRIVER

We're all going to catch it now.

The sergeant blows his whistle.

SERGEANT

Call out the guard! Call out the guard!

Men run from all directions.

INT. BUREAU H.Q. - MORNING

Bob arrives in the middle of a meeting. There's some sort of flap on.

MALLORY
Be seated, Mr. Fabian. News. Mr. Hobday, you took the telephone call. Brief us, please.

STAN
A top secret prototype aircraft. They locked it up overnight. Opened up the hangar in the morning. And there it was. Gone.

MALLORY
Sounds impossible.

STAN
Certainly is, guv.

MALLORY
What do we know about the aircraft?

STAN
The geezer said we might as well not bother to show up for the war if we haven't got it.

MALLORY
What is it called?

STAN
Dunno. Spigot? Spittle? Spittoon? Something like that?

Bob has his notebook out.

BOB

Perhaps you should have used one of these.

MALLORY

Can you at least remember where it was?

STAN

RAF Digby, guv. In Lincolnshire somewhere.

MALLORY

Six miles north of Sleaford. Get both incident bags. We'd better all be armed.

STAN

(*Smirking*) There was something else. Bob's to report to the Commissioner. Immediately.

Bob tries to spin this insulting order from the old lag.

BOB

I'll tell the Commissioner we're on our way, Mr. Mallory?

MALLORY

Do that, will you?

All disperse. Mallory and Alma are left, alone.

ALMA

How will we be travelling?

MALLORY

In the two cars.

ALMA

May I be in your car?

MALLORY

Yes. Why?

ALMA

Stan's driving. It's really quite appalling.

Mallory sorts kit on his desk, mind on other things. Alma sashays out, very happy.

INT. SIR PHILIP GAME'S OFFICE, SCOTLAND YARD - DAY

SIR PHILIP, 59, is a big man behind a big desk used to making big decisions.

SIR PHILIP

Trickier than you can imagine, actually, Fabian. The aeroplane was completely under wraps at Number 2 Flying School RAF Digby. Which is also the secret home to every new wheeze the boffins can come up with. Something fantastical every day.

BOB

I see. Flying School's the perfect cover, sir.

SIR PHILIP

But your problem is that we've since found out that the man is charge is Trafford Leigh-Mallory. Mallory's brother.

BOB

Ah.

SIR PHILIP

Now there's every chance he's going to be meeting his own brother face to face. Mallory hasn't seen his family - except from a great distance - for eleven years.

BOB
Does Mr. Mallory know, sir?

SIR PHILIP
No. We're having radios fitted to the Bureau's cars - next month.

BOB
So he could blunder right into the wrong situation.

SIR PHILIP
Precisely. So get your skates on.

BOB
Can't you call and post the brother away, sir?

SIR PHILIP
No. Runs the place, vital witness. Mallory's normally excellent at disguise.

BOB
I can try to conduct the investigation with his brother myself.

SIR PHILIP
Do that if you can. I can come down in twenty four hours-

BOB
No sir, I can manage.

Sir Philip regards him steadily.

SIR PHILIP
Get weaving. They've got a head start on you. Remember, Fabian. The Bureau's security is paramount.

A pause.

BOB

Sir.

EXT. SCOTLAND YARD - DAY

Bob runs into the street.

BOB

Taxi!

But it's taken, and it trundles past leaving a nearly empty street.

Bob clenches his fists in frustration.

BOB

Bloody typical.

EXT. DIGBY, LINCOLNSHIRE - DAWN

Two Bureau Bentleys cruise along the country lane.

EXT. LIVERPOOL STREET STATION - DAY.

Bob swings down from the back of a coal truck. Runs into the station.

COALMAN

Oi! What about my pound note!?

BOB

(*Over his shoulder*) You've done your country a great service.

EXT. R.A.F. DIGBY AIRFIELD GATE - DAY

The Bentleys sweep up through the meagre snow to the main gate. Their papers are checked. The Bureau are all dressed as police officers. Mallory is in a full beard.

GUARD

The Wing Commander will see you at the hangars.

He hops onto the running board to escort them.

EXT. RAF DIGBY AIRFIELD HANGARS - DAY

A hangar in a long row of hangars. Bemedalled Wing Commander Trafford Leigh-Mallory, 43, salutes his four arriving guests.

He's visibly unfriendly. Mallory can't believe his eyes. The conqueror of Everest is thrown into a near panic.

TRAFFORD

Good morning. Gentlemen, lady. Inspector Wainwright?

MALLORY

(*Choked*) Wing Commander-

TRAFFORD

Leigh-Mallory.

He shakes his brother's hand. After eleven years.

TRAFFORD

I'd have thought RAF police would have handled this.

Mallory's not with it at all.

MALLORY

(*Mumbling*) We have a suspect who may be connected with this incident.

TRAFFORD

Who?

MALLORY
I can't name him.

TRAFFORD
I don't expect you to name him. But he exists?

MALLORY
I'm afraid I can't reveal any more.

TRAFFORD
Alright. But you are telling me that you do know of someone who is capable of disappearing a Spitfire into thin air?

Mallory is regaining his composure.

MALLORY
Something like that, Wing Commander.

TRAFFORD
Good. Soon have this sorted out then. Over there is the Flying School, my formal command: I'll happily discuss that with you till the cows come home. But this side of the aerodrome is the more secret work. And this - as you cloak and dagger types would say - is the scene of the crime.

Stan smiles at this. Mallory frowns. So his brother is still a pompous windbag. Trafford shows them through a pre-fabricated hangar door.

TRAFFORD
This is where the Government's top secret new aeroplane - the Spitfire - was shut down and secured last night.

He picks up two chocks.

FLASHBACK SEQUENCE

INT. RAF DIGBY AIRFIELD HANGARS - NIGHT - FLASH-BACK

Two ground crew are putting the same chocks under the aeroplane's wheels, and the action follows on as...

TRAFFORD (V.O.)
These chocks were placed under the wheels. The RAF police then locked the door and placed a guard at each corner of the building.

The guards put their collars up as it starts to snow.

MALLORY (V.O.)
The door was locked?

TRAFFORD (V.O.)
With a padlock. Not tampered with in any way.

EXT. RAF DIGBY AIRFIELD HANGARS - DAWN - FLASHBACK

TRAFFORD (V.O.)
Following morning: petrol lorry arrives to do the first duty of the day - fill up the aircraft.

The guards greet the lorry driver.

TRAFFORD (V.O.)
Doors pushed open: no Spitfire.

One of the ground crew actually walks into the middle of the hangar. Nothing is there.

FLASHBACK SEQUENCE ENDS

EXT. RAF DIGBY AIRFIELD HANGARS - DAY

TRAFFORD

I had the station sealed off the moment I knew.

MALLORY

What time?

TRAFFORD

Oh-seven-hundred. They rang me. My family and I live in the village.

MALLORY

Then what did you do?

TRAFFORD

All the other hangars were immediately sealed shut - and guards put on them - as per the standing orders I agreed with the technical staff.

Stan smiles again.

MALLORY

And the guards on sentry-go saw nothing?

TRAFFORD

Nothing, Inspector Wainwright.

Alma smiles, winningly.

ALMA

How many times was the guard changed?

TRAFFORD

Three, madam.

ALMA

Miss.

TRAFFORD

Miss. What we call four hour stags.

ALMA

Stag?

TRAFFORD

That's a turn of sentry duty, miss. But the guards replaced each other on their points at each corner of the hangar. There were no gaps in the watch: those were my own standing orders on the matter - in excess of the RAF minimum.

MALLORY

And there were no disturbances in the snow?

TRAFFORD

You can see for yourself. Apart from the tracks left by the guards, nothing.

MALLORY

Unless they could get it to this perimeter track -

ALMA

- which is wet through constant traffic.

TRAFFORD

There would be tire marks stretching from here to there. And the only ones here are from the petrol lorry.

It is still there, rather forlorn.

MALLORY
And that's just where they left it?

TRAFFORD
Yes. So, how would your suspect have done it, then? Done this kind of thing before, has he?

Stan - examining the padlock - quickly butts in to save Mallory.

STAN
This is rubbish, this is.

TRAFFORD
Indeed, constable?

Stan opens it with a pick in an instant.

STAN
See? Rubbish. Sir.

MALLORY
Someone was always by the padlock. The sergeant in command, correct?

TRAFFORD
Flight Sergeant. A good man.

EXT. COUNTRY LANE - DAY

Bob's taxi is gingerly negotiating a ford.

CAB DRIVER
I'm going as fast as I can, sir.

INT. RAF DIGBY OFFICER'S MESS - DAY

Trafford's still a bit taken aback at this constable with no sense of hierarchy.

STAN

They didn't carve the whole plane up, did they?

TRAFFORD

No shavings were found, and there's no hole to pass it through. And everyone was out of the hangar when it was locked.

STAN

A bloody big magnet, then, someone on the roof-

TRAFFORD

I'm a keen fisherman myself, but I think we can discount it being hooked up through the ceiling.

Mallory is neatly caught between supporting Stan and his stuffy brother.

MALLORY

It's still a question we must address, Wing Comm-

TRAFFORD

Have it your own way - the snow is undisturbed on the roof. It fell from 1800 to 1900. No-one's been up there.

ALMA

That's between six and seven at night, correct?

TRAFFORD

Precisely, miss.

The door bursts open. A flustered Bob is shown in.

BOB

I'm sorry I'm late, sir. The London and North Eastern railway, sir. Useless.

MALLORY

Ah. This is the famous Mr. Fabian, 'Fabian of the Yard.'

TRAFFORD

Good afternoon.

Bob looks from face to face. Have the Mallory brothers twigged anything yet?

BOB

Good afternoon, sir.

MALLORY

Did anyone see the aircraft leave the field in any shape or form?

TRAFFORD

No, they did not.

Mallory looks at his brother. He can tell when he's lying.

MALLORY

I very much hope you are giving us the full story, Wing Commander.

TRAFFORD

As full a one as you are giving me.

Now Bob looks really worried.

MALLORY

Let me ask you again. Did anyone see the aircraft leave the

aerodrome by any means at all? The truth. Please.

Wing Commander Leigh-Mallory puffs out his chest. His medals jingle.

TRAFFORD

Nothing, but nothing, left the aerodrome by land or air. Of that I can assure you.

MALLORY

(*Quoting*) 'For secrets are edged tools, and must be kept be kept from children - and from fools.'

Trafford is stunned.

TRAFFORD

Extraordinary! That's just what my mother used to say.

Mallory's lost for words. Bob looks sick. Everyone freezes. Completely out of the blue, Lawrence finally speaks.

LAWRENCE

It wasn't your mother, it was Dryden. *Sir Martin Mar-All.* Act two, scene two - I think.

Everyone relaxes.

TRAFFORD

So it was. If you have any further questions, I'll be with my adjutant. I can take it you'll arrest this chap, p.d.q?

He's gone. Stan spills the contents of a wallet on the table.

STAN

Let's see what he's got.

BOB

You lifted that off the Wing Commander?

STAN

Course!

MALLORY

What does he have, Mr. Hobday?

Stan holds up a card.

STAN

Nuffink. Unless the local golf club is a prohibited organisation.

Bob is outraged.

BOB

You give that back this instant.

MALLORY

Please remember, Mr. Fabian, that the Bureau may gently break the law when necessary. (*He permits himself a wintry smile*) Otherwise, being dead could be judged a waste of time. Please assist Mr. Hobday in this matter, if you can - I want to look at the tracks again.

Mallory leaves.

BOB

God, what did he do when he saw it was his brother?

ALMA

Handled it magnificently.

She sweeps out in pursuit.

LAWRENCE

(*Amused*) Don't worry, Mr. Fabian, I'd have dealt with the situation had he looked like blowing our cover.

A curved Arab knife magically appears in his hand.

BOB

Oh. Right you are, sir.

Lawrence uses the knife to clean the bowl of his pipe.

LAWRENCE

These days, though, I tend to trust in the will of God and not rush too precipitously into things.

BOB

God, sir?

LAWRENCE

Always remember, Mr. Fabian, it doesn't really matter who you think God is. So long as you remember that it isn't you.

He swans off.

STAN

I nearly understood that one. But most of the things he says are proper corkers.

Stan puts the wallet into his pocket.

BOB

He had six pounds in there. I counted them.

STAN

(*Grinning*) And I'll let him have his change back, and all.

Bob ponders hitting him.

BOB

I've got my eye on you, Stanley Hobday.

STAN

Shouldn't I be getting it back to him before he misses it? Or am I being detained for further questioning?

BOB

Very clever. You may have fooled Mallory but not me, see? Now hop it.

STAN

Yes. (Doesn't mean it) Sir.

INT. RAF DIGBY AIRFIELD technical site - day

Reginald MITCHELL, a bespectacled, thin man, 40, greets Mallory as an engine is started on a test bed.

MITCHELL

I'm Reginald Mitchell. I designed the Spitfire. Any clues?

MALLORY

Not yet, sir, I'm afraid.

They go into a quieter office.

MITCHELL

Please. Sit down. I'd sit down too but I can't. This thing.

He taps a canvas case on his thigh. Mitchell's cancer has meant he is fitted with a colostomy bag.

MITCHELL

Most people would try to conceal it, I suppose. But it's an amazing piece of engineering, don't you think?

MALLORY

Yes.

MITCHELL

I'd hate it if I came up with something as useful as this and a lot of prudes tried to cover it up. Tea?

MALLORY

Please.

Mitchell leans forward. Drops his voice conspiratorially.

MITCHELL

Confidentially, I never let it see it's got me worried. What do you want to know?

MALLORY

Any theories yourself? Something that can dissolve metal, make it invisible, something like that? I feel a bit of a fool asking-

MITCHELL

Not at all. How would we ever think of anything if we didn't start with the 'impossible'? They could have got it down to its individual atoms and whizzed them out somehow.

MALLORY

Good lord. That's possible?

MITCHELL

Not in your or my lifetimes. And if they'd managed to do that, then they'd have to have a way of reconstructing it again. And we'd have to ask our grandchildren about that.

Mallory smiles.

MALLORY

Your Spitfire. Why do they want it so badly?

Mitchell looks into his pipe modestly.

MITCHELL

Oh, it's good. Even Willi Messerschmidt will have his hands full with this one.

MALLORY

Why?

MITCHELL

The elliptical wing. Beautiful - always a good start. Pilots'll tell you that if a plane looks right, it'll fly right. That wing makes her fast - the fastest. And it makes her balanced and streamlined and manoeuvrable. Test pilots say you just have to think where you want her to go - and she's there.

MALLORY

Flown her yourself much?

MITCHELL

Good lord, no. I've got my pilot's licence - learnt when I found the cancer had really settled in. But I couldn't fly a Spitfire. Be like getting onto a racehorse when you've only been on a donkey at the seaside.

MALLORY

Will it win the war for us?

MITCHELL

(*Simply*) Yes.

They laugh together. There's nothing boastful about his statement. Mitchell looks into the distance and the future.

MITCHELL

I won't be here to see her do it, though. Shame, really.

INT. RAF DIGBY OFFICER'S MESS - LATER

Alma and Bob interview the guard sergeant.

SERGEANT

We was ordered to be early at the third 'angar from the end at 1800.

ALMA

Six in the evening?

SERGEANT

Yes, ma'am. Knowing that to be the case, I therefore marched the piquet up at 1750. Being ten minutes early. (*Helpfully*) Ten to six, ma'am.

ALMA

Please. Not so stiff. Stand at ease.

He does. Still stiff, though.

ALMA

Stand easy.

He does.

ALMA

Relax. Talk to me as if I was a human being. I really am, you know.

SERGEANT

Yes, ma'am.

ALMA

Miss.

SERGEANT

Err, miss. Yes, miss.

ALMA

(*Purring*) Now I'm sure you didn't get those stripes just for your good looks, Sergeant. Did you observe anything unusual?

SERGEANT

I'm not sure I'm quite following you, miss.

ALMA

(*Admiringly now*) Well. A big responsible job like locking the hangar. Had you ever done it before?

SERGEANT

(*Flustered*) No, miss. I mean, yes. Locked up many times. But not one of the new hangars.

BOB

New hangars?

SERGEANT

Oh yes. New. Made of prefabricated Duro-alumino-tin. Strong as the Bank of England.

She sits on the desk.

SERGEANT

Perfect for a place like this. It's a building site here. Everyone coming and going.

She's intent on his every word.

SERGEANT

We haven't a clue what's in 'alf of them. There's always something new.

ALMA

And there's no way, thinking back, that your men could have been outwitted?

SERGEANT

No miss. I locked up that 'angar and posted a man stood at all four corners. Nothing went in, out or on that 'angar till the morning.

BOB

Thank you. That'll be all.

ALMA

And Sergeant?

SERGEANT

Yes, miss?

ALMA

Thank you.

SERGEANT

Thank you, miss.

The sergeant flusters out.

ALMA

What a dear little man.

BOB

You're quite something.

ALMA

It's good to be appreciated.

BOB

To think I hadn't met you this time yesterday.

As quickly as she has flirted, she withdraws.

ALMA

That was yesterday.

BOB

How can you be so cold?

ALMA

Don't be boring, Bob. Let's find the others.

INT. R.A.F. DIGBY AIRFIELD HANGARS - DAY

Stan and Lawrence. Stan jumps on the ground as best his limp will let him.

STAN

Hard packed earth. All the way to Australia.

LAWRENCE

Actually, Mr. Hobday, through to a patch of sea southeast of Dunedin, in New Zealand.

STAN

Blimey.

LAWRENCE

What does the lack of any tracks in the snow tell us, I wonder?

STAN

It tells me I'm bloody freezing.

Lawrence looks mildly irritated. It's as cross as he gets.

LAWRENCE

I think I'll ponder this on my own. (*Quoting*) 'Down to Gehenna, or up to the throne, he travels fastest who travels alone.'

He strides away.

STAN

(*To himself*) Bloody Sheik of Araby...

INT. RAF DIGBY MALLORY'S QUARTERS - DAY

Mallory climbs among the rafters for relaxation as he thinks. Finds toe-holds and perches beyond any normal man.

EXT. THE FOX PUBLIC HOUSE, DIGBY - EVENING

Bob's switching from pints to scotches. Looks mistily at Alma.

ALMA

Don't you think you drink rather a lot?

BOB

Lawrence doesn't drink at all. Like one of his camels.

ALMA

Perhaps you should cut down a bit.

BOB

(*Thickly*) Don't you think you're rather superior?

ALMA

Nasty boy. I'll be going.

BOB

Don't.

ALMA

Why should I stay?

BOB

Just - don't. I - love you.

ALMA

I don't love you. Couldn't love you.

BOB

Why not?

ALMA

I only met you yesterday.

BOB

Don't you believe in love at first sight?

ALMA

I love someone else.

BOB

Who?

ALMA

George Mallory. You won't tell him, will you?

Bob snorts into his drink.

BOB

Don't talk wet. How many snitches d'you think I've dealt with? 'Don't tell'. Hah! 'Do tell', you mean. How big a fool do you take me for?

She purses her lips and goes. He calls after her.

BOB

Pretty bloody big one, I'd say. (*To anyone*) Another drink?

INT. RAF DIGBY OFFICER'S MESS - NEXT MORNING

The breakfast table. Mess waiters hover in white gloves. Alma toys with half a grapefruit. Lawrence has a glass of hot water with lemon. Bob has a mug of tea. Stan eats toast as he eats eggs and bacon as he stirs sugar into his tea, all at horrendous speed. All watch amazed.

LAWRENCE

Your body, Mr. Hobday, is a temple.

STAN

You what?

LAWRENCE

Merely a suggestion, but the rate at which you eat. Surely your-

STAN

Goes to show you ain't done stir.

ALMA

Stir?

STAN

Prison. Done porridge, like. You lucky people.

LAWRENCE

I was a guest of the Turks for five days.

STAN

Oh yeah. I done some jobs for them.

LAWRENCE

I beg your pardon?

STAN

Abdul the Turk. Bethnal Green. Lead off church roofs, mainly. His real name was Henry Fry. Probably wasn't Turkish at all.

Lawrence laughs. Pleased he's made a joke - however unintentional - Stan laughs too.

LAWRENCE

No, he probably wasn't.

Bob wants to be the centre of attention.

BOB

If we can think this through, please. We know it didn't leave the hangar. It didn't even leave the ground, and it didn't go out the gate. And it was short of petrol. And it left no tracks in the freshly fallen snow between the hangar door and the tarmacked perimeter road. So it can't have got far.

STAN

(*Mouth full*) Wheelbarrows!

BOB

I beg your pardon?

STAN

A job I done once. Garden tool factory.

BOB

A real job? I don't believe it.

STAN

Every day I went out the gate to the other yard. Bit of sack on my wheelbarrow.

BOB

Oh yes?

STAN

Every day the gaffer looked under the sack. Always - nuffink there. Never found what I was nicking.

ALMA

And what were you - nicking?

STAN

Wheelbarrows.

BOB

(*Seething*) I suppose you think that's very clever.

STAN

Yes. Mr. Fabian. Bob. I do.

LAWRENCE

Is this getting us any clo-

SUDDENLY, the windows SHATTER and the red-raw flame of an explosion splashes into the room.

LAWRENCE
(*Finishing his sentence*) -ser to solving the problem?

EXT. RAF DIGBY AIRFIELD EXPLOSION SITE - LATER

The team and Trafford stand before a small anonymous brick building blown into a shell. Lawrence and Stan pick among the smoking ruins. The equipment may be smashed, but they were obviously radar screens.

MALLORY
You didn't mention this establishment to us, Wing Commander?

TRAFFORD
My secret command here is based on the tightest security of any RAF field in the country. Only I, for example, know what is in each of the hangars.

MALLORY
What was in this building?

Trafford cracks a little.

TRAFFORD
(*Sighing*) About the most secret thing we have. We called it our Radio Direction Finder.

ALMA
A rather cumbersome name.

TRAFFORD
The name is deliberately misleading, miss. But what it can do is

incredible. It can actually see aircraft, hundreds of miles away and up in the sky, moving around on these screens.

ALMA

Radi-find.

TRAFFORD

I beg your pardon?

ALMA

Or Radi-screen. Nice new names for it.

TRAFFORD

RDF suits us very nicely for the moment, miss.

MALLORY

(*Angry*) We should have been told about this.

TRAFFORD

It was, of course, the reason I knew the Spitfire hadn't taken off in the night. No trace of anything moving was recorded that night.

MALLORY

What else do you have on this site we should know about?

TRAFFORD

All sorts of things.

He gestures at a huge line of hangars containing god-knows-what.

TRAFFORD

There's a chap called Barnes Wallis, working on a special bomb. Some eggheads giving a German coding gadget the once-over. Look, I'd really rather write you a list I can copy to my superiors.

MALLORY

Covering your backside as usual.

TRAFFORD

What do you mean, as usual?

MALLORY

(*Busking quickly*) You RAF types are all the same. I suggest you disperse all these state secrets before there's another mysterious incident.

TRAFFORD

Well, I'm the senior officer present, and I shall be referring this upwards. Goodbye.

He storms off. Mallory sighs at his brother's intransigence. Lawrence sidles up to Stan.

LAWRENCE

Could you possibly lend me a hand with something?

EXT. RAF DIGBY OFFICER'S MESS - DAY

Alma interviews scientist Norman Harding, 28. Fair-haired, very good-looking, knows he's in her league.

ALMA

But why not steal the plans for the aeroplane?

HARDING

The blueprints?

Alma is able to flatter Harding instantly.

ALMA

Blueprints. Of course. Silly me. Why not steal them? Lighter, easier to copy - you could roll them up into a tube and that would be it.

HARDING

Miss Bishop - Constance -

She simpers. He acts on the approval.

- Constance, blueprints are three feet by four. And there are over four thousand of them. (*Laughs*) A Spitfire probably weighs less.

ALMA

I see.

HARDING

And there's another thing.

ALMA

What's that?

He leans forward.

HARDING

Four things, actually. If you have the Spitfire itself, you have every last component, as well as the way it connects to every other component. The Rolls Royce Merlin engine, for example.

ALMA

So stealing the aeroplane means you don't have to steal the blueprints from the Rolls Royce factory as well.

HARDING

Exactly. And you also get every last modification, some of which may have been done on the test bench for this prototype, and may not have been detailed on a blueprint. Boffins are human, after all.

ALMA

They are.

HARDING

So you not only get a Spitfire, but you get a Spitfire that works. That flies. And then there's the third thing.

ALMA

What?

Harding plays his emotional side perfectly.

HARDING

Everyone on this project likes - admires - loves - Reginald Mitchell. Every bit of that admiration and affection will have informed every rivet and every panel on this plane. All that finely tuned expertise, that desire to get it right - that's not going to be found in any blueprint.

ALMA

Do you admire him?

HARDING

There's no Englishman that wouldn't.

ALMA

And the fourth thing?

He leans forward. A lock of her hair has tumbled down. He gently tucks it back up.

HARDING

How about tea? Or something stronger?

ALMA

Tea. Will do. For now.

EXT. RAF DIGBY AIRFIELD EXPLOSION SITE - DAY

Lawrence and Stan are on their own deep in the rubble. Shattered radar screens surround them.

LAWRENCE

Ah-ha. Found this earlier. Tucked it away.

He picks up a crushed tangle of metal.

STAN

Why?

LAWRENCE

Because I wanted your professional opinion. Before I made a fool of myself in front of the others.

Stan goes to mock - but doesn't.

STAN

(*Uncertainly*) What do you want to know, then?

LAWRENCE

Do you know what it is?

STAN

It's an alarm clock. Very old-fashioned. For a timer.

LAWRENCE

Hm, so it is. Stanley Eric Hobday, play a guessing game with me. Let's say we're two geezers - (*Aware he's slipping into 'Stan-ese'*) - out to do this job. If we were going to blow this electrical gubbins up, what would we use?

STAN

We'd use gelignite. A few sticks and - ker-boom tinkle tinkle.

LAWRENCE

Why?

STAN

It's all delicate electrical stuff. Lots of glass valves and stuff. Shatter it all.

LAWRENCE

And where would we blag the gelignite?

Stan looks at him. Is Lawrence mocking his way of speaking, or making overtures of friendship?

STAN

The Paddies always have some.

LAWRENCE

Right. Easy. Satchel charge, bung it through the door. Off we go on our motorbike, maybe.

Stan is suddenly struck by what Lawrence is driving at.

STAN

But we didn't do that, did we?

LAWRENCE

Oh, Mr. Hobday, I do believe you are onto something there.

Stan and Lawrence regard each other.

STAN

Alright. So the question we have before us is as follows. (*Shows he's aware he's slipping into 'Lawrence-ese'*) Why did we blow this place up using dynamite, properly placed in the foundations, relying on the collapse of the building to bugg– do the dirty work?

LAWRENCE

Exactly.

INT. RAF DIGBY AIRFIELD - TRAFFORD'S OFFICE - CONTINUOUS

Mallory and his brother. Sagging a bit. Trafford folds a bit of paper.

TRAFFORD

On the highest authority. I'm to do whatever you tell me.

MALLORY

It'll be for the best.

TRAFFORD

This command was going so well. After this, a foreign posting, then, who knows - a Group, maybe.

MALLORY

We're working hard for you.

TRAFFORD

If this isn't solved I'll get a foreign posting alright. We've an aerodrome in Iraq. At Habbaniyah. Generally agreed to be the backside of the world.

MALLORY

Ah.

TRAFFORD

So that'll be me. Sent sideways and only ever remembered as bloody George Mallory's brother.

Mallory nearly chokes.

MALLORY

If you'll excuse me.

EXT. RAF DIGBY AIRFIELD runway - continuous

Lawrence and Stan pause to let a Gloster Gladiator biplane waggle in to land.

STAN

(*Taking it step by step*) We'd only blow the building rather than the technical equipment if we had to hide the bomb for a few hours or days or whatever.

LAWRENCE

But! But! (*He waves his arm theatrically at the other side of the airfield.*) There's a huge hue and cry across the aerodrome! A Spitfire's been pinched!

STAN

We'd have to hide it well enough so anyone taking a butchers wouldn't find the bomb.

LAWRENCE

Hence we put dynamite deep in the foundations. But there's a problem with that-

STAN

Why don't we blow the gubbins the moment we've got the Spitfire away?

LAWRENCE

Exactly. Unless we wanted to create the impression that this was the next attack, and that attacks would keep on coming.

STAN

Even though we've flown off with the Spitfire.

LAWRENCE

So this is a way to get Leigh-Mallory to disperse all the secret projects-

STAN

-and make them easier to pinch in the future.

LAWRENCE

And it looks as if we, or us, I should say - have just played into their hands.

STAN

Bugger.

LAWRENCE

Quite.

EXT. RAF DIGBY AIRFIELD HANGARS - CONTINUOUS

They join Bob and Alma and Mallory at the third hangar from the end.

LAWRENCE
It was a bomb on a timer.

ALMA
To make us think they were still here?

Lawrence and Stan exchange winces. They hadn't thought of that one. Lawrence makes himself scarce.

MALLORY
Mr. Hobday. Remind me to tell Wing Commander Leigh-Mallory not to take the seals and guards off just yet.

STAN
Will do, guv.

MALLORY
Hm. But why not steal the electrical equipment? It's top secret.

BOB
Yes. They'd got away with a Spitfire. Those technical boxes were lighter and easier than a Merlin engine weighing two tons in a solid block.

ALMA
But it's equipment. Lighter and easier than blueprints. You know how it connects to every other component. Every last modification. You even get the sweat and ingenuity of the men who made it.

STAN
(Admiringly) Bloody hell.

She looks to Mallory for similar praise.

MALLORY

Hm. So why didn't they blow up the Spitfire and steal the secret equipment? Both are equally valuable.

She sags.

EXT. R.A.F. DIGBY AIRFIELD RUNWAY - DAY

Two airmen at a run.

AIRMAN 1

Sir! Sir!

AIRMAN 2

Sir! You can't sit there.

In the middle of the snowy runway, cross-legged, is Lawrence.

LAWRENCE

Is there nowhere here anyone can get any peace?

As he stands and walks towards them a Gladiator takes off just yards behind him.

AIRMAN 2

We mostly go and sit on the karzi and have a fag, sir.

LAWRENCE

Do you indeed?

EXT. RAF DIGBY OFFICER'S MESS - LATER

Bob and Alma.

BOB

(*Enthusing*) I can see you're a natural police officer. C.I.D. even. Except there are no women in the C.I.D.

ALMA
Really? You make a tempting offer.

BOB
Gosh, you're brainy, you're beautiful, you're - well, blokes like me don't get to - to sleep with ladies like you.

ALMA
(*Cold*) Bob, I slept with you as a security matter.

BOB
Please don't say that. Look, I'm sorry about last night.

ALMA
Hangover giving you gyp, is it?

BOB
That thing you said about Mr. Mallory.

ALMA
Which you were very hurtful about-

BOB
Well, I've been a copper for many years. Human nature - that's sort of my speciality.

He kicks a stone like a schoolboy. It plops into a water reservoir.

ALMA
There is a point to this?

BOB
Alma. Look. Ladies who go after married men. Impossible men. They don't often want to get what they

are after. They choose married men cos that makes certain that they'll never be happy.

ALMA

Riddle-me-ree.

BOB

It isn't. You think you don't deserve love - so you put yourself in situations where it can't work.

Alma looks straight at him.

ALMA

Shut up.

BOB

Being in love with a dead married man. Sort of doomed to failure, wouldn't you say?

ALMA

Shut up.

BOB

Alma. What if I've fallen in love with you?

ALMA

You can't have.

BOB

I could have. What then?

ALMA

Men don't fall in love with me, let me tell you. Not real love, anyway.

BOB

But I'm no ordinary man. Please? A cup of tea, a sandwich? Anything?

Alma turns and waves.

ALMA

Norman!

Harding is driving towards them in his two-seater Singer sports car.

BOB

(*Pleadingly*) Alma - Constance!

ALMA

I have to go. (*Quickly to Bob*) Men only say they love me in bed.

She breaks away. Harding pulls up.

ALMA

Where are we going?

HARDING

A little pub I know.

They roar off. Bob picks up a stone and hurls it across the pond. A boffin, carrying boxes and files out of his shed, sees it skip and jump across the pond. Starts making copious notes.

INT. RAF DIGBY AIRFIELD SERGEANT'S MESS - NIGHT

Stan's dealing cards to a table of groaning airmen.

STAN

Just another hand. So you can win it all back, eh?

Lawrence looks on, amused.

INT. RAF DIGBY AIRFIELD MESS - MORNING

The breakfast table. Bob stares at a cold teacup. Alma bustles in.

ALMA

(*To the waiter*) One of your lovely cups of coffee, please.

BOB

You didn't come back last night.

ALMA

Didn't I?

BOB

Were you with - him?

ALMA

My darling, you sound like a story by Ouida. Too, too melodramatic.

Bob turns away in disgust and despair.

ALMA

You poor thing. You seem to be tak-ing this like a foreigner.

BOB

And I suppose Harding took it like an Englishman.

INT. THE FOX PUBLIC HOUSE, DIGBY - MORNING

Harding is nervously on the phone. Pushes coins into the box.

HARDING

Hello? Hello? You've got to come and rescue me. I can't hold out for much longer. It's too dangerous!

INT. RAF DIGBY OFFICER'S MESS - DAY

The Bureau and the Sergeant.

SERGEANT

No, sir.

MALLORY

Are you absolutely certain?

SERGEANT

The boff - the gentleman who helped me lock the hangar did not report this morning, as what is detailed in standing orders for gentlemen at RAF Digby, sir.

BOB

That's a little different to what you told us yesterday, sergeant.

SERGEANT

Indeed, sir?

BOB

Yes. It is.

FLASHBACK SEQUENCE

INT. RAF DIGBY AIRFIELD HANGARS - NIGHT - FLASHBACK

BOB (V.O.)

You told us the RAF police locked up.

The guard arrives in the gathering dark. The sergeant is greeting Harding at the door.

SERGEANT (V.O.)

We did, sir.

BOB (V.O.)

You didn't mention Mr. Harding.

SERGEANT (V.O.)

Did I not, sir? He was the gentleman I was hexpecting, sir. He was

the last man by the third 'angar
from the hend, sir.

FLASHBACK SEQUENCE ENDS

BOB

Harding directing you what to do
makes all the difference.

SERGEANT

It does, sir?

MALLORY

Thank you. Dismissed.

SERGEANT

Sah!

He marches out.

BOB

I'm sure it's important, but I
can't see why.

MALLORY

We must now think of Mr. Harding as
a compromised individual. Mrs. Rat-
tenbury. How have your investiga-
tions been proceeding?

ALMA

We spent the evening at the 'Fox'
public house.

Bob tenses.

MALLORY

And?

ALMA

Harding's had an impressive career,
most recently at Cambridge with some

chap called Rutherford. He's been security vetted here.

MALLORY

Doesn't count for much.

ALMA

He also resisted my deeper investigations.

MALLORY

(*Nearly joking*) Really, Mrs. Rattenbury? Are we dealing with some sort of superman?

LAWRENCE

Not necessarily.

MALLORY

What do you mean?

They all look at Lawrence uncomprehendingly.

LAWRENCE

It doesn't matter.

ALMA

I never even got as far as Harding's bedroom.

Bob perks up.

ALMA

But I've got to check his *bona fides* in London. I'll go there today. Who'll drive me?

She looks hopefully at Mallory.

BOB

I will.

MALLORY

No, I want your forensic frame of mind here, Mr. Fabian.

Bob turns grumpy.

ALMA

Then, you, Mr. Mallory-

LAWRENCE

I'll go.

STAN

And I want to see 'Beesley & Sons,' the hangar blokes.

EXT. A1 GREAT NORTH ROAD - DAY

Alma, Stan and Lawrence at speed in one of the Bentleys.

ALMA

But what I don't understand is: let's say he's working for a foreign power - how does that help him completely disappear a Spitfire out of a locked hangar? A Spitfire that was very low on fuel, remember. That's still impossible, isn't it?

LAWRENCE

Wasn't it the White Queen who had trouble believing six impossible things before breakfast?

STAN

Drop me at the next crossroads. The hangar people are round here somewhere.

ALMA

Are you sure? This looks just like green fields to me.

EXT. A1 GREAT NORTH ROAD - DAY

Birds sing. Sun's out. An old sign, half hidden behind the brambles: BRENT CROSS. Stan, in his policeman's uniform, climbs over a five bar gate towards a couple of rustic sheds.

INT. HANGAR FACTORY BRENT CROSS - CONTINUOUS

In the accounts office.

BEESLEY

No, officer. No hangars supplied to be erected by us last week.

STAN

Not a single shed to RAF Digby over the last seven days?

BEESLEY

(*Emphasis*) Hangar.

STAN

Shed? Hangar? Who cares?

BEESLEY

Sorry, officer. (*Blurting*) Look, if it's about Mabel, she led me on.

Stan quickly realises coppers lead interesting lives.

STAN

Did she now? We suspected as much. Why don't you tell me all about it?

EXT. RAF DIGBY AIRFIELD RUNWAY - DAY

Trafford, Bob and Mallory watch a stream of Gladiator aircraft take to the air.

BOB
What search radius have you set, sir?

TRAFFORD
We think the Spitfire had a maximum of twenty miles worth of fuel in its tanks, so I set it at thirty.

BOB
Will they search hard enough, sir?

TRAFFORD
Brotherhood of the skies. I told them a fellow pilot had come down on a night flying test. The problem will be getting them to come back.

BOB
Can you trust them not to talk, sir?

TRAFFORD
What they don't know is that they're being sent on a two day exercise the moment they land. They'll be able to tell a few rabbits, but that's all.

MALLORY
I think we are nearly done here. We have to hope the Spitfire has been taken by those who merely wish to sell it on. And we can attempt to foil that process. We'll be gone by lunchtime tomorrow. Keep the hangars sealed, mind.

TRAFFORD
Good. And double guards?

MALLORY
Until you hear from us.

TRAFFORD
Fine. Back to the normal routine. Nearly.

MALLORY
Quite.

TRAFFORD
Tomorrow's a big family day for me, actually. Whole brood visiting. My family, my brother's family. (*Laughs*) There's more organisation than a Hendon air day.

Mallory goes pale.

MALLORY
(*Whisper*) I'll have to be gone by then.

INT. HANGAR FACTORY BRENT CROSS - DAY

Stan is hearing the last of Beesley's confession.

BEESLEY
...to South America by banana boat. And that's everything, constable.

STAN
Hm. Well, as long as you pay me the spot fine for dodging the parish newsletter sub I'm sure we can overlook the adultery. Ten pounds?

BEESLEY
Oh thank you, thank you, officer. Will cash do?

STAN

Nicely. Now, how many sheds have you built over the last six months?

BEESLEY

A good twenty. The RAF are buying these for all their new aerodromes.

STAN

So who else has been buying them? Any new customers?

Mr. Beesley picks up another ledger.

BEESLEY

This'll tell us. Old. Old. Old. Hang on a tick. Harding and Co. Just the one hangar. That's odd.

INT. RAF DIGBY OFFICER'S MESS - EVENING THE SAME DAY

Stan and Bob sit. Mallory paces.

STAN

Six days ago. But all the RAF Digby paperwork looked kosher to me guv.

BOB

I could get the force scouring the country for her, sir.

MALLORY

Absolutely not. We skate on thin ice as it is. Getting every policeman in the land looking for her face is going to blow Mrs. Rattenbury's cover. And do no good for the rest of us, I shouldn't wonder.

BOB

But surely this is an exceptional case, sir.

MALLORY
Mr. Fabian. I have made my decision.

Trafford enters, sifting a file.

MALLORY
Their paperwork? Any good?

TRAFFORD
Just as normal.

MALLORY
It's big, then.

BOB
Very big.

TRAFFORD
This is awful. What do you mean?

MALLORY
The fake company orders the hangar, all well and good. But they would need Harding on the inside to wangle the permissions to get them onto the station.

STAN
And someone to fake these letterheads and forms. You can't tell the old ones from the new. They're perfect. And I should know.

BOB
Harding probably stole some examples this end, and I shouldn't imagine the hangar company would have taken long to burgle.

STAN
Christ, no, guv. I could have been in and out in-

Mallory coughs, indicating Trafford.

MALLORY

And, in a way, that's the easy part.

TRAFFORD

The easy part?

BOB

Yes, sir. We're dealing with an organisation big enough and well organised enough to tap your telephones and intercept your post.

TRAFFORD

Impossible!

MALLORY

No. Just highly efficient. Think about it. They only need one extra letter from some fussy clerk to verify what is going on, or just one telephone call checking a detail, and their mission collapses.

BOB

But they had a prize that justified the cost.

STAN

I'll get down to the Smoke to warn her ladyship.

BOB

I'll go, sir.

STAN

I've got the keys, lover boy.

He's off at a run, trying not to let his limp impede him.

BOB

She doesn't know what trouble she could be in. Please let me put the Force onto it, sir.

MALLORY

No. Consider the matter closed. One thing is for certain. Whatever the secret of the disappearing Spitfire is, it is in that shed.

INT. RAF DIGBY AIRFIELD HANGAR - LATER

Trafford, Bob and Mallory are checking every inch.

TRAFFORD

They are made of Duro-alumino-tin. Goes up in a jiffy, the makers say. Whatever a jiffy may be.

BOB

But why get one and - we suppose - put it up here?

MALLORY

Quite.

Mallory goes to climb the girders.

BOB

(*Indicating Trafford*) Let me do that, sir.

Bob starts to climb.

MALLORY

When did the workmen, posing as the hangar company and carrying the fake permits, come onto the station?

TRAFFORD

The guardroom log has disappeared.

BOB

That Harding. He's good.

Mallory turns on his brother.

MALLORY

This is the most secret place in Britain, you bloody fool. What have you been playing at?

TRAFFORD

Yes. I'm sorry.

He sits down.

TRAFFORD

I shall have to resign my commission, of course. That's it.

Suddenly he looks every one of his 43 years.

MALLORY

We'll see. You're supposed to be the brainy one - tell me why Harding went to all the trouble of putting up this hangar? It's identical to all the others.

Bob calls from the rafters.

BOB

I'm stuck up here, I'm afraid.

INT. BUREAU H.Q. - NIGHT

The window in the Bureau's glass ceiling is silently opening. A figure skilfully climbs down. Searches about. The silhouette catches the sound of breathing. Heads for the side room. As he gets across the doorway - he's firmly grasped by the throat. A LIGHT snaps on. Lawrence releases him.

STAN
Christ, guv, you gave me a turn.

LAWRENCE
Hm. An honest mistake.

He pockets his Arab knife.

STAN
Don't you ever sleep?

LAWRENCE
Are you normally quite so noisy?

STAN
I never. I was coming in like any normal geezer who thought there might be enemy agents all over the shop.

LAWRENCE
What?

STAN
Harding. Bent as a nine bob note.

LAWRENCE
Ah.

STAN
Where's Alma?

LAWRENCE
She did not share her domestic arrangements with me. But she said she had a lead on where he was staying.

STAN
She's one for not telling, ain't she, guv? And she don't show up for rendezvouses - it's her way.

LAWRENCE
She could be anywhere.

STAN
We've got to find her. And catch him.

INT. BAYSWATER HOTEL BEDROOM - NIGHT

Alma is awake, looking at the sleeping Harding next to her. Goes to put her arms round him. In his sleep, he shrugs her off. Her eyes fill with tears.

INT. THE FOX PUBLIC HOUSE, DIGBY - NIGHT

Bob sits drinking on his own. Looks off into space, occasionally glancing at the telephone on the wall.

PUBLICAN
That's it, last orders was hours ago.

Bob gets shakily to his feet.

EXT. STAPLEFORD TAWNEY FLYING CLUB, ESSEX - DAWN

Harding's checking the rudder on his tiny Avro Tutor two-seat trainer biplane. Open to the elements, it's very basic. Alma is apprehensive.

ALMA
Taking me up to heaven twice in twelve hours?

HARDING
I'll do my best. Flown before?

ALMA
Only to Le Touquet. I was petrified.

HARDING
Nothing to be scared of. This is a training plane. Stable old bus.

Pupil in the front, instructor in the back. Hop in.

Alma looks really frightened now.

ALMA

If you're sure.

INT. RAF DIGBY AIRFIELD ACCOMODATION BLOCK - MORNING

Bob's jumps in his sleep. He's fully clothed on the bed. Gets to his feet. Looks at the whisky lying in the bottom of the glass. Goes to toss it down his throat. But chucks it down the sink.

INT. BUREAU H.Q. - MORNING

Stan and Lawrence.

STAN

I feel bloody useless sitting here.

LAWRENCE

We've telephoned Mr. Mallory. We wait here for her telephone call. From wherever she is.

He adopts the lotus position.

STAN

You're a cold-blooded one, and no error.

LAWRENCE

On the contrary. But as I have no alternative, the best I can do is reserve my energies for when they are needed. Not dissipate them through useless fretting.

STAN

You're a loony, you are.

LAWRENCE

Please. Go and pace about, or do what you will. I am sure Mrs. Rattenbury can take care of herself.

EXT. MID-AIR OVER ESSEX - MORNING

Alma is white with fear as Harding revs the plane low out over the Thames estuary. She huddles in the front cockpit. He steers from the back one. They can communicate by shouting through a speaking tube.

ALMA

This really is rather frightening.

HARDING

Nonsense.

ALMA

Wonderful view.

HARDING

Yes.

ALMA

Please take me home.

HARDING

I going to take you to my home instead.

ALMA

Where's that?

HARDING

Oh, I think you know, Constance.

ALMA

What do you mean? It's freezing, by the way.

HARDING

It is where you're going.

ALMA

I beg your pardon?

HARDING

The cellars on Prinz-Albrecht-Strasse.

ALMA

Geheimstatspolizei headquarters?

HARDING

Gestapo H.Q., yes.

ALMA

Hold on a tick.

Transformed from a shivering victim, Alma now stands serenely in the shaking airframe. Calmly leans into the back cockpit.

HARDING

Sit down!

She pulls the split pin from the startled Harding's harness. The straps flap in the slipstream. He struggles to control the aircraft and get the pin back from her.

HARDING

Give that back! We haven't got parachutes!

Sitting down, she secures her own harness. Smoothly takes the controls.

ALMA

Don't worry. I've got her. Don't do anything silly.

He does. He reaches inside his jacket for the glint of a gun.

ALMA

Whoops-a-daisy!

She as neatly inverts the biplane as a stunt pilot would. Harding falls out. He actually fires at her - and misses - as he falls.

ALMA

What a nasty man you are-

He plunges, parachuteless, towards the grey waters.

ALMA

- you were.

She rights the aircraft in her trained pilot's hands and puts on full power.

EXT. RAF DIGBY AIRFIELD EXPLOSION SITE - DAY

Mallory picks among the rubble. Bob approaches cautiously.

BOB

Mr. Mallory - it's one o'clock. The Wing Commander's been asking for you all day.

MALLORY

Have you heard anything about Rattenbury?

BOB

Not yet, sir.

MALLORY

Hm.

BOB

What do you want me to say? To the Wing Commander? He knows you are on the station.

MALLORY

Hm.

In the distance, a small knot of visitors. Mallory's family, reduced to dots, like they always are.

BOB

Let me give you a hand-

Mallory slips down the dusty heap of rubble. Bob naturally starts to help him brush it off. And slows more and more as he does so-

Hang on a minute. The rafters. In the 'new' hangar. They were covered in dust. It's been there for ages. That's not a 'new' hangar at all.

They look across the field. The hangar which had the Spitfire in is, as always, the third from the end.

MALLORY

So, which one is?

BOB

They've all got the same amount of snow on them, except-that one.

The first hangar at the other end of the row is showing a much clearer roof.

BOB

(*More to himself*) Why would that one have escaped the snow that fell between six and seven?

Mallory picks up his binoculars.

MALLORY

I've got to get Ruth and the children away from there.

EXT. R.A.F. DIGBY AIRFIELD - THE FIRST HANGAR

Mallory and Bob hare round the corner. The Mallory family dog runs towards them.

TRAFFORD

Mr. Wainwright! Whatever is-

MALLORY

Pay attention, everybody. These hangars must be immediately placed out of bounds.

BOB

Absolutely.

Ruth Mallory is looking straight at her dead husband. Three children, Frances, Beridge and John look on. Mallory dare not look back at them.

MALLORY

(*Angrily*) Everyone must go. Immediately.

The children's dog, an ancient white-muzzled old thing, licks Mallory.

BOB

Yes, madam. You must.

MALLORY

Immediately!

Ruth Mallory's just six feet from him.

MALLORY

(*Furious*) Go! Now!

TRAFFORD

Come, my dear. Children.

He gathers them together. The dog is barking in aged enthusiasm.

FRANCES MALLORY

Come on, Sherpa.

JOHN MALLORY

Heel, Sherpa.

Mallory is nearly choking.

MALLORY

Go, Sherpa. Go!

RUTH

What a disgrace! What a rude man!

A taxying Avro Tutor biplane halts nearby. Alma spills out. Runs to Mallory. Puts her arms around him, sobbing.

ALMA

Harding's gone. It was over the Thames.

Mallory has to put his arms around her. Over Alma's shoulder he can see his wife and children being taken away.

(*Whispers*) I've been waiting for this moment.

MALLORY

Oh, for heaven's sake. Not again.

Mallory gazes at his departing wife as she occasionally glances back, disgusted, at this man. Sherpa follows, bemused in his doggy way.

EXT. R.A.F. DIGBY AIRFIELD HANGARS - DAY

Bob crouches in the mud by hangar one. The Bureau join him.

BOB

I've found the missing hangar.

MALLORY

Yes?

BOB

It was here. Not for very long, but it was here.

He's in a patch of scuffed up snow and wet grass. No hangar.

BOB

Can't you see how they did it now?

FLASHBACK SEQUENCE

EXT. RAF DIGBY AIRFIELD HANGARS - NIGHT - FLASHBACK

The boffins are inspecting the Spitfire, straightening things as they leave. Harding is by the door.

BOB (V.O.)

Harding stands by the door long enough to be certain that the others are on their way back to quarters...

They are.

BOB (V.O.)

...he locks the Spitfire hangar...

He clicks the padlock shut.

BOB (V.O.)

...before going quickly to the next hangar along...what we would call the fourth hangar along...

ALMA

The fourth?

He goes to the door of the next hangar along to await the guard, who are marching up as usual in the gloom...

BOB (V.O.)

The guard were looking for a boffin at the third hangar from the end.

STAN (V.O.)

There were no numbers, so-

BOB (V.O.)

Thank you. Exactly.

The guard surrounds the hangar as before.

BOB (V.O.)

Meanwhile...

A team of hangar constructors starts to deconstruct the hangar at the end. It is coming down in a jiffy.

BOB (V.O.)

...the last hangar in the row is being removed.

FLASHBACK SEQUENCE ENDS

EXT. RAF DIGBY AIRFIELD Hangars - AFTERNOON

STAN

Blimey! It's been in the hangar next door all the time.

BOB

Because Harding had told the guard that he'd meet him at the third hangar from the end. It's a dark winter's evening. The guard meets Harding - what he's expecting - and doesn't count the hangars. Why should he?

LAWRENCE

And they re-erect the hangar up at the other end.

BOB

A lorry with a lot of metalwork on the back isn't going to attract any attention on a research station like this.

ALMA

Everyone counts the hangars in the morning. It really is the third from the end. And there's the right number of hangars overall. Very ingenious.

BOB

It's not a formal camp. Everything is experimental, always changing. So who's to notice?

LAWRENCE

And it starts snowing after the aeroplane was locked in. So no tracks anywhere.

BOB

And guess who insisted on sealing every hangar?

MALLORY

Trafford himself.

BOB

As per previous orders devised with the help of his scientific staff-

STAN

Including Harding.

BOB

Yes.

Mallory smiles.

MALLORY

Excellent work, Mr. Fabian.

LAWRENCE

A relief for you.

MALLORY

Absolutely. In that hangar lies Britain's salvation.

LAWRENCE

I meant that your own brother isn't a traitor.

Mallory purses his lips.

MALLORY

Thank you, Mr. Lawrence. It had crossed my mind.

ALMA

I was with Harding every second since I surprised him at his love nest in London. He hasn't been able to warn them he's been rumbled.

LAWRENCE

Will they come without a signal from him?

ALMA

Can they risk not coming?

LAWRENCE

I have a suggestion on trapping our German friends.

MALLORY

Indeed?

LAWRENCE

But I may be jeopardising more than just our mission.

EXT. RAF DIGBY AIRFIELD HANGARS - DAWN

Guards stand at the four corners of the hangar, their breath hanging in the air. An extra guard patrols round and round. It is Mallory. The other four are the members of the Bureau. There's a distant noise.

ALMA

As we thought-

MALLORY

- an attack by air!

ALMA

Which is why they knocked out the R. D.-radi-thingy.

MALLORY

You were absolutely right. They know they can fly in undetected. Right. No shooting till they do!

EXT. RAF DIGBY AIRFIELD RUNWAY - DAWN

A Ju-52 German troop-carrying aircraft comes into land. Troops tumble from it, gathered around a running civilian.

GERMANS

To the hangar!

They swarm forwards towards the hangar door, bolt cutters to the fore.

GERMANS

Fan out! Attack position!

But they run straight into the Bureau.

STAN

You want some, do you?

Stan likes to kick his opponents in the balls with his good leg.

ALMA

Always a pleasure, never a chore.

Alma has neat karate moves.

BOB

Are you sure we shouldn't have told the RAF?

Bob lays about himself with his truncheon.

MALLORY

No, we can cope with these interlopers.

Mallory is more of a straight puncher. With a cry of -

LAWRENCE

No prisoners!

- Lawrence, madness in his eyes, draws a vast scimitar and chops his enemies to the ground.

GERMANS

Help! Help!

They start shooting.

MALLORY

(*Exasperated*) Get him down, someone!

The Bureau takes cover, except for Lawrence, who crumples as the first shots are exchanged.

STAN

Guvnor!

MALLORY

Stay where you are! Down everybody!

The Germans are into the hangar. Bullets whine everywhere. The civilian - the test pilot - starts up the Spitfire.

TEST PILOT

There's not much fuel!

GERMANS

Get on with it!

Now the Bureau start to fire in earnest. Alma is a ruthless dead shot, leisurely picking her targets. The Spitfire coughs into action, starts rolling immediately.

MALLORY

Shoot at the Spitfire!

The Germans retreat to the Ju-52, running aboard the moving plane. They are dragging Lawrence's flopping body with them.

GERMANS

Leave him - he's dead!

The two planes roar off into the breaking dawn. Bob checks and handcuffs the German bodies. The others gather round Lawrence's body. Alma kneels down and feels for a pulse.

ALMA

Absolutely nothing.

She stands. Stan kneels too. Tears in his eyes.

STAN

Oh no, guvnor. You can't be.

ALMA

Feel his pulse for yourself.

Lawrence opens one eye.

ALMA

How is that done then?

LAWRENCE

Practice. Spitfire alright?

STAN

You bastard. You're all bastards.

Alma pretends to be shocked.

STAN

Yes, even you, miss. How couldn't you tell me?

BOB

Need to know, Stanley. Your alarm would convince our German friends.

Mallory is at the next hangar along.

MALLORY

Not even scratched. Are you al-right, Mr. Lawrence?

LAWRENCE

Rising from the dead seems to be becoming a hobby for me.

MALLORY

Probably best kept to a minimum.

LAWRENCE

Probably, yes.

They smile.

INT. RAF DIGBY OFFICER'S MESS - DAY

Trafford and the Bureau are celebrating.

MITCHELL

They'll probably waste six months trying to work out some of those modifications.

BOB

And we'll soon have the fake hangar boys under arrest.

MALLORY

And you are sure the old model Spitfire is no use to them?

MITCHELL

Old engine. Old technology. All the mistakes crammed onto one airframe. Surprised it took off at all.

TRAFFORD

Rebuilding the extra hangar put them off the scent. Trust them to go to the third hangar along.

MALLORY

To Teutonic efficiency!

ALL

Cheers!

INT. BUREAU H.Q. - NIGHT

Mallory, in his office, alone. Stan knocks softly on the door.

MALLORY
Mr. Hobday. What can I do for you?

STAN
(*Nervously*) Sir. It's a bit tricky, see.

MALLORY
What on earth is it?

STAN
Well sir, I don't know if I've done a right thing or a wrong thing. You know, I sometimes wonder what St. Peter's going to say about all this thieving.

MALLORY
Yes?

STAN
I'm really grateful for this second chance. This chance to do the right thing at last.

Mallory just looks at him.

STAN
Well, it's something I done when your - your wife was about, sir.

Mallory stiffens.

STAN
(*Gabbling*) You see, I just acted on the spur of the moment, sir, and I pinched this for you, sir.

It is a small woman's handkerchief. It has 'RM' embroidered on it.

STAN

I thought you might like it.

MALLORY

Thank you.

He picks it up. Can smell her perfume.

STAN

Well, I'll be off, then, sir.

Mallory is left alone, holding the scrap of cloth.

EXT. EUSTON ROAD - DAY

Alma and Bob. He's trying to get her to see the error of her ways with his most 'reasonable' tone of voice.

BOB

So was that completely wise? Sleeping with that chap? I mean, you'd had all the information you wanted out of him.

She nods in agreement.

Afterwards, he was perfectly happy to hand you over to the Gestapo. So, in point of fact, you had accomplished your task to the complete satisfaction of the Bureau before you slept with him.

She furrows her brow, finally seeing the correctness of his argument.

ALMA

D'you know what, Bob? You're right.

She's got him right where she wants him.

BOB
I knew you'd see it my way.

He brightens.

ALMA
Next time, I'll take your advice.

BOB
Good.

ALMA
Sex first. Nasty revelations second.

He sags. She turns so he can't see her triumphant cat-like smile.

TITLES OVER

EXT. HOUSE OF COMMONS - NIGHT

Caption: **24th November 1935**

Big Ben is chiming 11 p.m. Trams and trolley-buses rattle around Parliament Square.

INT. HOUSE OF COMMONS CORRIDOR - NIGHT

A Sergeant-in-Arms, a man in tights, patrols the long corridors. SUDDENLY - hears a SCREAM for HELP!

SERGEANT-AT-ARMS
Hey - Fogle! Bennett! Give a hand here!

He tries a door. It's locked. The two others run up. The cries for HELP continue.

SERGEANT-AT-ARMS

I can see the key. It's in the lock on the inside.

FOGLE

Bust the door down?

SERGEANT-AT-ARMS

What else can we do?

The three men shoulder-barge the door. It splinters open.

INT. HOUSE OF COMMONS OFFICE - NIGHT

They spill into the room. One trips over, then kneels by, a body absolutely covered in blood.

BENNETT

It's Mr. Richmond. Better call Old Bill.

His companions don't react. He feels for a pulse.

BENNETT

Gimme a blanket or something.

He glances up. The other two are like statues.

BENNETT

Come on, the poor sod's-

He sees what they are seeing. On the other side of the empty room, half-lit by the window, is a figure clutching a knife. With blood up to the elbows.

SERGEANT-AT-ARMS

Mr. Winston Churchill. Sir. Whatever's going on?

The familiar figure steps into the light, the red of all the blood standing out against the whiteness of his shirt.

WINSTON CHURCHILL

I don't know. Who on earth are you fellows?

SERGEANT-AT-ARMS

Oh, Mr. Churchill. What on earth have you done?

INT. BUREAU H.Q. - NIGHT

The phone rings. Mallory's hand picks it up as we...

CUT TO BLACK